In the
Shadow
of Trees

IN THE
SHADOW
OF TREES

ELENOR GILL

HarperCollins*Publishers*

Grateful thanks to the Poverty Bay Pen Pushers for their
support and encouragement.

A special thank you to Graeme Mudge, New Zealand artist and
sculptor, for invaluable technical advice.

National Library of New Zealand Cataloguing-in-Publication Data

Gill, Elenor, 1945-
In the shadow of trees / Elenor Gill.
ISBN-13: 978-1-86950-627-8
ISBN-10: 1-86950-627-8
I. Title.
NZ823.3—dc 22

First published 2005
First published in this format 2006

HarperCollins*Publishers (New Zealand) Limited*
P.O. Box 1, Auckland

Copyright © Elenor Gill 2005

Elenor Gill asserts the moral right to be identified as the author of this work.

ISBN-10: 1-86950-627-8
ISBN-13: 978-1-86950-627-8

Cover design by Nada Backovic

Cover images courtesy Photolibrary

Internal text design and typesetting by Springfield West

Printed by Griffin Press, Australia, on 50 gsm Bulky News

ONE

Wood never dies. Not really. Not completely.

A bolt of lightning, cleaving the heart, destroys but cannot kill. The fibrous flesh, like a torn peach, glows golden beneath the axe. Leave it to crack in the parching sun; let wind batter and bleach it to the grey-white of old bones. Still, it will live.

True, it sleeps the sleep of Lazarus, yet there is always a warmth, a whisper of life. I feel it pulsing, faint, so very faint. Sometimes, when I touch it, I know that I can bring it back.

As a surgeon, I am harsher than its cruellest tormentor. But the wood knows this to be the pain of genesis and it works with me. I cut and scrape and hack. The sinewy grain swirls beneath my fingers, struggling to find shape. A faltering pulse becomes a sob, a groan, a cry of triumph and the form emerges, reborn through my hands.

Yes, there are some things about wood that never die, and I think it would be better if they did.

MY arm rested on the open window of the truck to catch the sun. I knew I'd regret it later when my skin grew tight and red, but just then I needed to feel its hot sting, the coolness of air slipping through my fingers, the wind tumbling my hair.

I had been too long in the city. Although it was early summer and the heat made the road surface quiver, the sunglasses I wore were there to hide the redness of my eyes. They also allowed me to take surreptitious glances at the driver, tiny sips of honey.

Of course Jason knew I was looking at him. He turned and smiled. 'Not far now,' he said, 'the turn-off's just up ahead.'

I resisted the impulse to say something, to place my hand on his arm. I knew it would start all over again. So I turned away and tried to concentrate on the small hills slipping past the window. He watched the road.

This truck was mine, my latest toy, a Land Rover, all chrome bull bars and rows of superfluous spotlights. For tax purposes, or so my accountant said: a necessity for transporting my work. That's my excuse too.

I took another sip of honey. He was everything in the sunlight. The hairs on the backs of his hands were like the finest threads of spun toffee. I wanted to lick their sweetness. His face was tanned, the fringe bleached from leaning backwards over the sides of yachts. His eyes were too blue, the pupils dilated from something I didn't ask about. As of the previous evening, it was no longer my concern.

It's all wrong, you know, what they say about young men and older women. Jason had not restored my fading youth. I was only twenty-nine — less than a decade between us, and he made me feel ancient. On the way down he had begged me to stop for ice cream, then sulked until I let him drive. If this had gone on much longer, I thought, I would have turned into his mother.

We slid left onto a dirt track and started pulling uphill, weaving between rows of green baize mounds, each higher than the last and cut into sections by posts and wire. I looked back to find the road no longer existed, so there was no going back.

'When do we get to your father's place?' I asked.

'We are there. This is it. As far as you can see.'

'All this is yours?'

'Dad's, to be exact. Though I suppose it will be mine eventually. I can't imagine the old bugger ever selling. Family's been here for generations. Some of them are buried here. I'll show you.'

'Oh, great. I'll look forward to that!' I waved at some sheep, unmoved by our passing. They'd seen it all before. 'He doesn't look after all this by himself, does he? There doesn't seem to be anyone working.'

'"Look after" isn't exactly how I'd put it. Nah, he's usually got some men around the place. No one regular, just drifters. He drives about in one of those off-road things that farmers have. Moves a few sheep about and there's some cows that need attending to. Doesn't really need the money, you see. That's all taken care of. You know, family stuff.'

We reached the highest point and the world was suddenly full of sky before the truck tumbled over the brow and started to nose-dive through a forest of pine. The track was enclosed in a tunnel of indigo shadows through which we bumped and shook over submerged roots. It was like being in some carnival ride, a ghost train maybe. Abruptly Jason slowed the vehicle to a crawl, the trees broke up and the fairground was left behind.

And there was the sky come down to earth.

It was laid out before us, a watery palette of cerulean and white set between the green of the hills. The water's edge crimpled against swathes of long grass, its surface buckled by the wind. We drove on as the road wound around the lake's edge and under groves of hanging willow. Patches of vegetation scrambled over the banks and a flock of birds, startled by our passing, exploded from a reed bed and flapped for the safety of the branches.

'Jason, you didn't tell me. A lake!'

'I said you'd like it. You should trust me.'

'It's amazing.'

'Full of trout. I learned to fish there, and swim. Look, that's where you'll be staying. The cottage.' He nodded over his shoulder and I saw a dolls' house perched near the opposite

7

bank. 'The road goes right the way round. We'll stop at the house first.'

A distant volley of barking announced our arrival. I was still watching the cottage dwindle to the far edge of the lake when he stopped the truck and cut the engine.

'This is it.' Jason jumped down, slamming the door.

The house lived only in shadow. I had to blink and rub the sun from my eyes before it emerged from the murkiness of the trees. What I felt was disappointment. Everything else was perfect, and then this decaying carcass of a place.

'Your father lives here alone, you said?'

'Yeah, though he spends most of his time in the pub. Just comes to the house to eat and sleep. Come on, I could do with a beer.'

He bounded up onto the verandah and through the open door. I followed cautiously, the rotten steps groaning with each shift of my feet. The deck was speckled with flaking paint that had drifted down from the weatherboards, like confetti from some long-forgotten wedding. Once-rich curtaining formed cataracts over the windows and I entered unseen. The hallway, which ran through to the back of the house, was caked with neglect and the kitchen smelt of stale cigarettes and old fat.

'Struck gold!' The top half of Jason had been swallowed up by the fridge. He struggled free, arms loaded with bottles. 'Here. Can you manage the top?'

'You think I can't open my own beer?' I hadn't realised how thirsty I was. Between gulps I held the glass to the side of my face, then the insides of my wrists. 'I hope there's a shower at this cottage.'

'Of course. Look, you're going to love it, I promise. Have I ever lied to you?'

'Constantly.' No, I didn't want to start that all again. 'And you're leaving tonight, aren't you? You promised that too.'

'Sooner probably. Just say hello to the old man, get you unloaded, then I'm away.'

8

The back door banged open and suddenly the room was a whirlpool of black fur and wagging bodies and pounding tails. The Hound of the Baskervilles hurled itself at me. Beer slopped down my front.

'Badger! Bramble! Down, you hear me!' A man tried to drag the dog off me by its collar.

'Hi Dad,' Jason gasped. He was on the floor wrestling with another beast who was giving him a rough going over with its tongue.

'I said down, Bramble!' I guessed Bramble must be the one with its paws on my shoulders, helping to clean the beer off my shirt. Eventually the man won and Bramble, undeterred, waded into the assault on Jason.

'Sorry, they're not used to visitors.'

'I'm all right, really. Not sure about Jason though.'

'Yes, well, nothing he can't handle.' The man was tall and lean. He just stood there, hanging from his shoulders, and twisting the brim of his hat through his hands.

'OK guys, that's enough. I give in.' A grinning Jason surfaced from the doggy heap and scrambled to his feet.

'What sort of dogs are they?' I asked. 'They don't look like sheep dogs.'

Jason shook his head. 'The sheep would run rings round these two. No, they're German pointers. At least, that's what it said on the label.'

'Aren't they like Dobermans? They're guard dogs, aren't they? Are they supposed to be fierce?'

'They're good watchdogs. It said that on the label, too, only the dogs can't read. We think their ancestry got crossed somewhere. Anyway, intruders don't know that. Hey, let me introduce you to my father. Dad, this is Regan.' The man whipped round to stare at me.

'*This* is Regan? But I thought . . . you said one of your mates.'

'That's right. This is my mate, Regan. Oh, I see, you thought she was a man?'

The father stared hard at me again, then turned to Jason. He looked as if the ground had rocked beneath him. Of course he thought I was a man. That's what he was supposed to think. What the hell was Jason playing at?

'She can't stay here. You know that.'

'It's all agreed. Three months, you said—'

I felt the heat rising. I had to say something. 'Look, if it's not all right, I can make some other arrangement.'

'Like hell you will.' Jason's face darkened.

'All right Jason.' I stepped between them, knowing how quickly he could become angry. 'I'm sorry. There's obviously been some misunderstanding. I thought your son had explained all about my being here. Perhaps it's my fault. I should have contacted you myself, made everything clear.'

Jason's father wiped the palm of his hand down his face. The dogs, sensing something was wrong, sat panting, their tails gently drumming the wooden floor. The man looked . . . not angry. Concerned, maybe. And something else.

'Mr Sullivan. Is there some problem about my being a female?'

He gazed at me. His eyes were watery grey, his skin suddenly ashen beneath the tan. 'No, no. It's just . . . just . . . isolated. The cottage . . .'

'Look, Mr Sullivan, isolated is what I need right now. I want somewhere I can work. The cottage looks perfect.'

'Not right for a woman on her own.'

'But we're on private land. What can possibly happen to me?'

'Yes, tell her, Dad, what could possibly happen to a woman out here?' Jason swigged his beer. A smile flickered at the corner of his mouth.

Mr Sullivan looked from one of us to the other. I could feel the

10

undercurrents swirling between the two men, with me caught in the middle. This was one of Jason's games and I was being sucked in. I floundered, struggling to find the words.

'I just need to get away for a while. Somewhere on my own where I can work. I've come this far, brought all my stuff.' I stumbled on, though it seemed he was only half listening to me. 'I can look after myself. I'll keep right out of your way. I can work quietly — you won't know I'm there. Promise I won't scare the sheep.' Still no response. 'Couldn't we just try? If it doesn't work out I'll leave straight away.'

'I'm sorry, Miss Regan, it's not what I was expecting. I'll have to think about this.'

'It's Regan — that's my first name. I'm Regan Porter.' I held out my hand. He looked at it for a moment with no understanding. Then it was as if he shook himself out of a stupor and stepped toward me.

'Sullivan, just call me Sullivan.' His hand was rough, but surprisingly dry, his grip definite, not the sweaty paw shake I'd expected. The sleeves of his checked shirt rolled up to the elbows showed arms that were muscled and weather-worn. The hairs were fine like Jason's, but grey. They matched the stubble on his face. How old? Jason was only twenty but his father looked sixty at least. He had Jason's build, but where the son was smooth and svelte, Sullivan was gaunt, as if life had sucked the youth from his veins.

'You say you'll be on your own. The lad's not stopping then?'

'Yes. That's right, isn't it, Jason?' I looked around for confirmation.

He was leaning against the fridge, watching the exchange as if it were staged for his amusement. He raised one eyebrow in response. I could have hit him.

'He says he's got a motorbike here. He'll drive back later today.'

'It won't be easy, you know, being out here on your own. The

11

cottage is round the other side of the lake, a good few minutes away, even in a car. There're possums and rats.'

'I don't scare easy.'

'Yes, I can believe that. It's nothing fancy, you know.'

'That's OK.'

'Well, I suppose you could take a look.'

'What the fuck was all that about?' I slammed the truck door. Jason already had the engine running.

'What was what about?'

'You know bloody well. What's the game this time, Jason? Don't you realise you've put me in an awful position, embarrassed me, and your father.'

'You? Embarrassed? Never. Look, we just got our wires crossed, that's all. You should have heard yourself sweet-talk him down.'

'No bloody thanks to you.'

'Thought you didn't need my help any more. Anyway, everything's cool now. You two are going to get along fine.'

'What's he got against women, anyhow?'

Jason watched the road while I fumed and struggled with the seatbelt. Sullivan was a hundred yards ahead, driving a sort of mini-tractor. Badger and Bramble stood and barked in the back despite the violent rocking of the vehicle. They seemed incapable of being still.

The dirt road continued around the lake, leading to the little white building at the far end. Pine trees had given way to open meadow. Then smaller, native trees edged the water, building up to an area of standing bush that formed a backdrop to the cottage. Even at this distance it looked like a home, the afternoon sun dusting the corrugated roof and the windows burnished with gold.

I had gone into the wilderness to be alone with my art. This is what I took with me:

A suitcase of clothes, jeans, shirts, sweaters, the usual stuff.

Two spare pairs of boots (the only sort of footwear I possessed at the time) and a full-length raincoat.

My laptop (I can't function without it) and a new cellphone.

Travel bag of face creams and shampoos and bath foams (yes, I do all the girlie stuff too).

Portable radio/CD player and a stack of CDs (Mozart, John Coltrane, Black Sabbath, Mahler).

A stock of food, vegetables, pasta, rice (no animal stuff), a coffee grinder and beans.

Crate of red wine.

Drawing materials.

A pile of books (Pasternak, Duffy, Keri Hulme, Atwood, etc.).

Disassembled workbench, vices, clamps, etc., and a bag of smaller tools.

A tree trunk.

The trunk was planed and smoothed and cut into three sections. I had it lashed to the inside of the truck.

'You've brought your own firewood.' Sullivan turned to scan the pine-clad hilltops. Pyramids of stripped trees awaited the logging truck. There were fallen twigs and branches. Slices and chunks of manuka and red beech in random piles, the carnage of the chainsaw. And, although it was early summer, neat rows of logs were stashed under the decking. He looked across at Jason. 'She brought her own firewood?'

I covered my face with my hands and tried to suppress the bubbling volcano threatening to explode from my mouth. Jason was out of control, his body doubled over in a seizure of hysterical wailing. He clutched his stomach and pounded a knee with his fist. Poor Sullivan could only look on, bewildered. It was a while before either of us could speak. Eventually Jason wiped away his tears with the back of his hand and took a deep breath. He draped an arm over my shoulders.

'Let me introduce you again. Dad, this is Regan Porter, *the* Regan Porter. Sculptress, artist of the year, darling of the darling crowd. My father doesn't read the Sunday supplements, do you Dad? And those chunks of wood are her chosen children, selected for their perfection. If we're going to get them off the truck they have to be handled with the tenderness accorded a newborn infant.'

'Where can they go? I'll need somewhere to work that's dry. This place doesn't look big enough.'

'Look, what about the deck here?' Jason leapt up to pace it out. 'It's almost as big as the inside. The roofing's sound, so if we rig up a cover or something down the side it would make a sort of studio. What do you think?'

'Yes, I suppose so.' Actually it would be perfect. I'd be working almost in the open, the lake right in front of me. 'Is that possible, Mr Sullivan? Could we make some sort of shelter?'

He took off his hat and wiped his head with a grubby handkerchief. 'I'll see what I've got in the shed.'

Jason and I jumped up and down in a bear hug. Then I remembered why I was there, disentangled myself and went inside.

My treasures of the forest were safely tucked up under a tarpaulin on the deck along with the rest of my equipment; the other stuff was dumped in the kitchen area. Sullivan had driven back to the house with Jason on board and I was alone.

Well, almost alone. Bramble declined the lift back to the house. She was busy checking out my bags and boxes, her nose into every open opportunity. Her claws clicked on the wooden floor and the enthusiasm of her tail sent everything flying. Thank God

Sullivan didn't go in for china ornaments. I'd never had a dog, didn't really understand them. But her coat was like dusty velvet and her eyes could melt snow.

'It's OK dog, you can leave the unpacking till later. Let's see where I've landed up, shall we?'

This place felt good. There was a calmness about it. After Sullivan's house I had begun to have serious second thoughts, but no, this was clean and bright. One big room — at one end a huge overstuffed sofa set in front of a wood-burning stove, at the other end a kitchen with a cooker and fridge and a stripped wooden table. Thank God there was electricity. And running water, probably down from some buildings on the slope behind here. Shearing sheds, I thought Sullivan had said. Anyway, there was a huge water tank there and a generator in case the mains power failed. The walls and woodwork were freshly painted, the floors sanded and varnished. The couch was obviously ancient but the cushions and curtains were new. The rug in front of the fire looked homemade.

Bramble jumped on and off the sofa and tried to climb into the kitchen cupboards. Her ears were long and floppy and edged with a dusting of brown. They fell forward over her eyes, like a pair of silk handkerchiefs dipped in cinnamon.

'What's through here, girl?' I opened a door off the kitchen. Bramble led the way, her nose doing a sweep search of the floor. A tiny hallway with a washing machine and a cupboard with a hot-water tank and shelves stuffed with clean sheets and towels. Then another door.

'Wow, would you look at that!' The bathroom was huge, all new except for the bath that was ancient and could hold enough water to float a dinghy. And a shower, praise the Lord.

'I wonder if anyone thought of a bedroom?' Bramble snuffled her nose in my hand. 'Come on, let's look at the other end.' She set off on a mission, leading me back through the hall and across to where another door looked promising. I turned the knob and swung it open. Bramble bounded forward, then froze solid.

'What's the matter, girl? Just a bedroom, look.' Yes, that's all it was. Twin beds, separated by a small table with a bedside lamp, a wardrobe. There were two long windows, creamy muslin curtains tied back and a dressing table placed between them. Yes, just a bedroom. I went in first, waltzing over to the window, my arms spread wide to show how safe it all was.

'Come on in, girl, it's OK.' But Bramble stood rigid in the doorway, tail tucked down beneath her rear, making little whimpering sounds.

'Hey, what's wrong?' I went back to her, laying a hand on her head. I could feel her trembling. Suddenly she turned and ran, her claws skittering over the floor and across the deck.

'Well, nice meeting you, do call again.'

Like I said, I'd never had a dog. Didn't know much about them then. But I knew enough to recognise fear.

And she was terrified.

TWO

I⊤ had all happened so quickly. I looked at my pile of worldly goods and wondered how the hell I'd landed up there. Jason, of course. Still, I didn't have to stay, did I? I could just throw the whole lot back onto the truck and drive out. But then it wasn't just Jason. It was the whole scene, all the parties and press calls, the hangovers and the hangers-on. Oh yes, I'd encouraged it. So what's wrong with being the centre of attention?

I love it when heads turn as I enter a room, elbows nudge, the little whispers — it's her! I love seeing my face on the magazine stands. I always look surprised, which I suppose I am. The man from the *Listener* asked all sorts of questions about my motivational integrity and points of reference, or something like that. I got all nervous and just agreed with him. The resulting article was really impressive but I didn't understand a word of it. I knew better by the time *Cosmopolitan* came to me. I had prepared some pretty inspired quotes, only to find that all they were interested in was my sex life and if I wear a bra. They asked about my nose stud and I said it was about integrating my work by projecting my whole physical self as an art form. That's not strictly true. What happened was this. I promised Sally a navel ring for her birthday. We did lunch and drank lots and lots of red wine to build up her courage for the ordeal. Later that evening, after we'd sobered up, I found I had a rivet in my face. Fortunately, once the swelling went down, it didn't look too bad. So, I decided to keep it.

And then there was the money. I'd always said that money wasn't important to me. That was, of course, until I got some. All that crap about art being its own reward. That was fine while it was also its *only* reward. Then those big, fat cheques started arriving. Money is an affirmation of my worth. One of the best highs I know is people outbidding each other for my work. You know what I did with the money from my first exhibition sale? I got a tattoo, a little Celtic horse on my shoulder. It's my testimony. No matter what happens, I'll always have something to remind me that I made it to the top, if only once. But it wasn't only once. I just kept on climbing and the money kept rolling in.

The problem was, the better it got the less work I produced. I could never concentrate, my head never seemed to be clear. Being focused is the key, and to do that I have to be alone. I need the freedom to spend hours, days on end if necessary, working with a piece. It's a relationship between me and the wood. We have to get to know each other, allow a rapport to develop. The wood needs to tell me about itself and I have to be able to listen if we are going to grow together. That's how it happens.

At least that's how it was when I was with Andrew. He understood. He would write and I would carve and we would meet for supper and commiserate over our mutual failure. Three years we were together. Then I started to sell and didn't need consoling any more. He couldn't take it. I'm making it sound as if he resented my success and I think there was a little of that. But it was more about my not being there for him, being too busy to read his latest chapter. I had left him long before he left me.

In a way it was good being on my own for a while. It gave me a chance to find out who I was. I seemed to be the only one who didn't know. And then I met Jason. That was three months before and I hadn't worked since.

Oh, there were all sorts of excuses. Of course the exhibitions needed supervision. The galleries always demanded a presence, and the publicity was time well invested, they said. Then there was time out for the trip to Europe. Jason was right there with me and, I admit it, I was having a great time. But then that's what I worked for, to have my art acknowledged. Only, I didn't know fame was so . . . so . . . noisy. I needed space and quiet.

I walked out onto the cottage deck and watched the wind move through the treetops. A bird crossed the sky in frantic flight, heading for the lake. It swooped low, wings rigid as it came in to land, bracing paddled feet to gouge a track in the water's surface. Then it folded its wings and settled them to rest.

Yes, that's what I needed, a place to fold my wings.

A sound cut the air, an aggressive whine that shattered the afternoon and scattered the pieces. Then Jason broke through the tree line, a black leather knight on a black oily charger. He skidded the bike to a halt in front of me and revved the engine. I knew he was grinning under that stupid helmet, but I couldn't help laughing at him. He pulled off the helmet and shook out his golden hair. It was, as always, like seeing him for the first time, and I caught my breath. He had a way of being more alive than anyone else I knew.

He followed me inside and said, 'Well, what do you think. Neat, eh?'

'Yes, I have to admit you were right. It's perfect. Looks like it's just been renovated. What made your father do that?'

'Ah well, it was my idea. I love this place. Used to stay here quite often during summer nights, like other kids camp out in the garden. I couldn't bear to watch it go the same way as the house. So I persuaded the old man to do something with it. I reckoned it would be good for tourists, you know, backpackers, that sort of thing. Get some people through the place.'

'He got me instead. He was really put out.'

'He'll get over it. And you'll be alone, if that's what you really want. But you've got the phone. I can be here in a couple of hours.'

'No, Jason, I don't want you here. You promised.'

'I can't promise not to visit my father. This is my home. But I won't bother you. Not unless you want me to. You can have all the solitude you want.'

'Well, I nearly had a house guest.'

'Oh?'

'Yes, Bramble. She seemed to be planning on moving in. Then something spooked her and she ran off. I hope she's OK, she looked really scared.'

'That doesn't sound like her. What was it?'

'Something in the bedroom. I couldn't see anything, though.'

Jason walked through and surveyed the room, looking under the bed and behind the curtains.

'Didn't your father say something about rats?'

'No, dogs don't get scared by rats. Other way round. Bramble's a catcher.' He opened and closed the wardrobe. 'Nothing here. All safe and sound.' He flopped down on the bed, stretching full length, one hand behind his head, the other stroking the mattress. His voice dropped to a warm whisper: 'And very comfortable.' He stretched out his hand out to me. 'Come here, I'll show you.'

'No, Jason. That's not what this is about.' I stomped out of the room and back to the deck.

He followed a moment later, hands held up in surrender. 'OK, OK. It was worth a try.'

'I think it's time you left. '

'Yeah, you're probably right.' He picked up his helmet and remounted the bike. 'Come with me.'

'No, Jason, I—'

'No, I mean just up the hill. There's something I want to show you. You can walk back. Besides, you've never ridden with me, have you?'

The bike was panther black. Sunbeams spiked off the handlebars.

'Just a few yards? No tricks, mind.'

'I promise. Just a few yards. You still don't trust me, do you?'

'Did I ever?' But that was what drew me on — the angel eyes and the devil smile. I never knew which I was dealing with.

The machine roared deep in its throat and sprang forward. I was behind him, clinging tight to his back, my nose buried in the smell of leather. We scooted around the remainder of the lake road and back to where the forest trail started its upward climb through the dark pines. The bike bucked and stumbled, swinging from side to side on the path, Jason's feet scuffing the dirt. I yelled at the sweet terror of it. Of course he was making it worse for my benefit.

Then he suddenly veered to the right, following a barely discernible path through denser trees. Undergrowth tore at my clothes and caught in the spokes, threatening to pull us down. We screeched to a halt in a clearing and I fell off, rolling in dried grass and laughing with relief and exhilaration. He stood the bike up, reached into the saddle-box and fished out his camera, looping the strap round his neck. It had been strange seeing him without it on the journey.

'This is a special occasion — calls for a drink. I happen to have just the thing.' He reached into the box again, then stood over me, waving a bottle in each hand. 'Bit warm. But it'll do. Here.' He was right. Dust clogged my nose and throat and had laid a brown film over my arms.

'So, what's so special? You said you wanted to show me something.'

'That.'

21

He nodded at some rocks half hidden in the long grass. I wandered over, gratefully upending my bottle. No, they weren't rocks. As I moved nearer I could see that they were carved and inscribed.

I could hear the familiar click and whirr as he took shots of me. It had become a part of his presence, so familiar that it had moved to a different level of my awareness, like the ticking of a clock.

'Gravestones?'

'Meet the family. Regan, this is my grandmother, great-grandmother and, over there, my great-great-grandmother.'

'No. Really? I thought you were kidding. There really are people under there?'

'Sure are. Though I don't suppose there's much of them left.'

'Why? I mean why were they buried here? Why aren't they in a proper graveyard? I didn't know you were allowed to bury people like this.'

'I suppose they had to in those days. Too far to move the bodies. Families set up burial plots on their own land. Suppose it made the land more theirs. Generation to generation, that sort of thing.'

'Isn't a burial site supposed to be consecrated or something?'

'I guess it was consecrated at some time.'

I moved between the stones. Not proper monuments even, just flat slabs hewn roughly into shape. They all showed the passing of time, the edges worn and weather cracked. Moss and lichen clogged the chiselled lettering but I could make out the name Sullivan and 'beloved wife'. One of the stones bore the name Jane but the date was unreadable. I felt sad and very sober, as if a dark cloud had blotted out all the laughter of the afternoon.

'Why did you bring me here? To these graves, I mean.'

'I wanted you to see that I'm part of this.' He looked suddenly older; his eyes, for once, were serious. 'This land, this place. I came from these people and there were others before them.

I came out of this earth. This land *is* me.' This was a Jason I hadn't seen before and I didn't know what to say or how to be with him.

I put my hand gently over his. 'It's one of the most beautiful places I've ever seen. I envy you.'

'Sometimes I need to come back here. It reminds me of who I am.'

'And your mother, Jason, what happened to her? Is she buried here?'

'No. No, she's someplace else.' He pushed away from me, his arm swinging away. The bottle spun through the air and bounced across the grass. Then Jason was striding back to the bike and pushing the helmet over his head so that when he turned again I couldn't see his face.

'Right, I'm out of here. You can find your own way back, can't you? Just follow the path.'

He kicked the bike pedal and the engine exploded into life as machine and rider crashed through the trees, disappearing in a cloud of dust and fumes. I ran to the edge of the clearing but he was gone. I knew that was the last I would see of him. Well, for a while, anyway.

I gathered up the empty bottles and started back down to the cottage.

It was much cooler under the pines, and darker. Although I knew this forest to be a recent creation, a breeding farm for wood, I felt as if I had strayed into some ancient and forgotten place. The treetops stretched high above me. The branches dipped and swayed in unison, a congregation of giants all chanting in whispers. In their company I was reduced to insignificance. I felt that somehow they were aware of my presence. I could understand why pagans worshipped in such places, why they thought each rock and mountain spring was a living being.

23

Maybe that was why I was here. I had come to this place knowing I was ready to move into a new phase of my work. Over the past two years I had been exploring the presentation of the human body as a landscape in abstract form. Now, here, I was aware of consciousness in nature. I was beginning to understand why our ancestors believed in wood nymphs and satyrs. Perhaps I could create my own nature spirits.

The wood I carve has its own life energy within, a remnant of the elemental responsiveness of the parent forest from which it was taken. Perhaps, by being in the natural environment, by allowing myself to be a channel between the two, I could express something of the greater, primordial consciousness of its origins.

That was usually how it started. Assign a concept to the subconscious, leave it a day or so to ferment, then it would arrive, permeating my conscious mind in full force, demanding expression.

That's when the work would begin.

By the time I climbed the deck steps the sun was ready to dip behind the tree line. Now I really was alone. The house was visible across the lake with Sullivan somewhere inside it, maybe, although Jason claimed he spent little time there. I'd try to bother him as little as possible. He seemed a difficult man to be with: not hostile exactly, I could have coped with that, met it as a challenge. It was more like he was somehow absent. In any case, I'd feel more comfortable out of his way.

After all, it wasn't as if I were completely cut off. I had my cellphone and there were all sorts of friends I could call. The only one I really wanted to talk to was Sally. The other loss I regretted was Bramble. I had hoped that she would have returned during my absence, but I could hear her and Badger barking somewhere in the distance.

What was it about that bedroom? I wandered back in there. Nothing had changed. The covers were still crumpled where Jason had stretched out on the bed. I sat on the edge of the mattress and laid my hand where his head had dented the pillow. That's just how he had left me, empty and crumpled. A hollow part of me missed him already. I prodded at it, like when I'd had my tooth taken out and I couldn't leave the hole alone. But anything was better than a raging toothache.

Then my attention was caught by the reflection in the mirror and I looked at the woman who looked back at me. What a mess. Her hair, blonde and still spiky from the regrowth of an impulsive close shave, was prickled with bits of dried grass and leaves collected during the bike ride. Grey eyes, now red from lack of sleep and crying. Skin pale and streaked with dried mud. She never was good at keeping clean. Dust had even caked into the little lines at the corners of her mouth, making her suddenly older. Perhaps she needed another earring or two to even things up. There were two on one side, four on the other. Could that cause an imbalance? Sally would know about that sort of thing.

Then I noticed the dressing-table mirror, or rather the mirror and its frame. It was circular and set on hinges to swivel between carved posts. The glass had thickened slightly near the bottom edge, a sign of age as the semi-fluid succumbed to the forces of gravity. It had become tinged with yellow but the backing was still good, no trace of the quicksilver breaking down. The image was clear and without imperfection.

But it was the frame that made me draw breath — a circle of delicately carved oak in the form of tangled branches that twisted and twined around the glass. At least, it looked like oak, although that was hard to believe. Oak is excellent for most kinds of work, but it's nigh impossible to cut to that fine a detail. Even in the best wood the grain isn't hard and tight enough to produce such delicacy. But I was looking at swathes of leaves, each leaf perfect, each vein picked out in relief. Acorns coincided with spring buds,

25

minute creatures, birds, insects — all perfection. Perhaps I was deceived. Was it the real thing somehow dipped in a preservative? I bent closer, pulled the dressing table out from the wall so that the light from the window fell on it. No, this was definitely carved wood and it definitely was oak. I was sure of it.

There did not seem to be any join between the decorative edge and the backboard, as if they were carved all of one piece. Yet the mirror was sandwiched between them. Either the seam was so perfect as to be undetectable or . . . or what? What I was looking at appeared to be an impossibility.

Perhaps Sullivan would know about it. I'd have to find some excuse to talk to him. But I couldn't think about that then, I was too tired and hungry. I grabbed a loaf, some cheese and a bottle of wine and sat out on the deck to watch the sun setting over the lake. Through the dimness of the trees I could just make out the house where Jason grew up.

THREE

THERE was a flash of white light and Jason exploded into my life. I was so shocked that I screamed out loud and most of my drink splashed down my clothes. I could feel the wetness tacking my shirt to my skin, but I was blind to everything except the flare of a dozen flash bulbs searing the back of my eyes.

'What the hell do you think you're doing?'

'What I'm doing is my job.' It was a disembodied voice, as smooth and sweet as chocolate. The owner was still invisible so I swung out in that general direction with my clenched fist. It was either that or burst into tears. My hand made contact with a metal post, smashing it hard enough to nearly break my fingers.

'Well, fuck you and your job!'

'Yes, Ma'am. Certainly.' I swung out again. This time my wrist was caught in a vice. A face started to take form out of the darkness, the eyes first, like Alice's Cheshire cat, only these eyes were blue, far too blue to be believed. As the rest of the face emerged I realised he was laughing at me.

'Look what you've done. My shirt's ruined. How am I supposed to get through the evening looking like this?'

'I think you look just great.'

'Don't you dare patronise me. What are you doing in here anyway? The press isn't allowed in until seven o'clock. No one is.'

'So what are you doing here then?'

'It's my exhibition. I ask the questions. And let go of my arm!'

'Only if you promise not to take another swing at me.'

'I'm not promising anything except to have you thrown out of here.'

'In that case I'd better keep a tight hold. Come out here to the light so I can see the damage.'

Still clutching a glass in the other hand, I was dragged into the corridor.

'Oh dear. Red wine on a white shirt. Not good. Look, I'm sorry I startled you. Do you always react like that when someone takes your picture?'

'Not usually, no. Do you always break into private previews and scare the shit out of the artist just before their opening?'

'Not usually. Actually I'm here at the invitation of the gallery owner. Old Remborne invited me as his personal guest. Thought I'd get here a bit early and catch the star of the show before she got swallowed up by the rest of the crowd.'

'Chewed up and spat out, more like.'

'Do I detect a note of self-doubt?'

'No. Just terror. At least you've given me a good excuse to escape. I can't stay here looking like this so I suppose I should be grateful. It's OK, you can let go now.'

Instead he twisted me round, looking me up and down. 'I've got an idea.'

This time I was dragged into the ladies' room where the lights were blazing and the mirrors showed the full effect of the disaster on my outfit. He released my arm at last and started taking off his coat.

'Take your shirt off,' he said.

'What?'

'Take your shirt off. You can wear mine. It's a tad on the big side, but if you tuck it and button the sleeves tight so the arms drape loose it'll look good.'

'And what are you going to wear?'

'I'll just button up my jacket. It'll look cool. We'll both make a fashion statement.'

I didn't have much option. A few moments later we were standing side by side in front of the mirror. I barely came up to his shoulder. He was right, I did look good. The shirt I was wearing was a gentle silk and the same colour as his eyes. His hair was sun-bleached corn and his jacket lapels revealed a chest still too smooth to be a man's. The camera slung round his neck was all the explanation he needed.

'See? No problem.' He grinned at me from the mirror. 'You look great.'

'I wish I felt as good. I'm sorry I got so uptight earlier. I'm feeling a bit anxious.'

'Oh, really? I'd never have guessed. One piece of advice: when dealing with the press, always swing with the right arm. Oh, and never drink red wine when wearing a white shirt.'

I shot him what I hoped was a look of pure venom and headed for the door. As I went through I was stopped by his hand on my shoulder. He whispered so close I could feel his breath, warm on my neck. 'I've seen your work. I think it's wonderful. Don't be afraid. You'll be great. They'll love you.'

I was and they did. And that was the last I saw of him that evening.

Three days later he rang me. I asked where he got my phone number and he said it was a trade secret. Then he asked if he could have his shirt back. He was at the café around the corner and I could deliver it to him there. He said he would shout me a coffee if I promised not to spill it, as he was running out of clothes.

I thought, thank God I've washed the shirt. I'd felt I ought to just in case I saw him again. I'd actually ironed it, something I don't normally do with my own stuff. I dropped everything and ran all the way to the corner where I slammed on the brakes and strolled casually up to his table. He was seated under an umbrella on the pavement. In the light of day I saw how young he was and almost faltered. But, then, I was only returning his shirt.

I ordered a cappuccino with heaps of chocolate and three sugars, which he seemed to find amusing. Of course it spilled over into the saucer and then I dripped it all down my chinos. I explained that getting stuff spilled on me is a recurrent theme in my life. He said he had to have a record of this and clicked his camera before I could protest. We talked about the exhibition and he asked about my work, the sort of questions that showed he understood and led to further questions, which forced me to probe deeper. By the third coffee I had learnt a lot about my creativity and myself, things he seemed to have known all along.

As we talked he held up his camera and looked at me through the lens. He did this constantly as if he saw the world more clearly through that third eye. If something caught his attention he would click the shutter. He took several shots of me. At first I found this disconcerting, but after a while it became a part of his body language and I accepted it as naturally as if I were watching him blink. I was to learn that his camera was always with him, like an extension of his ego. He told me he worked freelance and, although I didn't recognise his name, I realised I was already familiar with his work from the pages of the more upmarket magazines.

Suddenly he said he had to go. I had somehow imagined we would stay talking forever and I could feel the disappointment running down my face but was powerless to control it. I frantically dredged around for something astounding to say that would keep him there. All that came out was, 'Oh — oh, OK.'

Then he said, 'You do like peppers, don't you?'

'Peppers?'

'Yes, I thought we'd have stuffed peppers for dinner tonight. I know you don't eat meat. Your place at seven. I'll bring the food and cook. You sort the wine.'

And then he was gone.

He turned up at seven-thirty, just late enough for me to think he wasn't coming. He was a good cook, much better than me. We drank a lot of wine, watched an old movie on TV and fell asleep on the sofa. I woke next morning to find him still there. And he was still there three months later.

I can remember the fairground that used to come to our town in the summer. Us girls, there were four or five of us, would hang around most evenings and giggle and squeal at the flashing lights and the raucous music in the hope of attracting the attention of the young men who worked the sideshows. But I think it was the rides that did it for me; the Loop-De-Loop that turned the Earth on its head and the Round-Up where only the scream jammed in your throat saved you from certain death. I got hooked on the head-sickening, blood-draining terror. All that addictive adrenaline pumping through my adolescent veins.

I suppose that's how it was with Jason. He would disappear for days on end. Then suddenly he was back and I was the centre of his universe as if what I thought, or felt, or did, was his whole life. His mood swings were infuriating. When he was cold and dismissive it was as if a cloud obliterated the sun. Then, just as inexplicably, the black moods would melt and he would be the blue-eyed little boy looking for friends to play with. Not my friends, of course. They lived in grungy bed-sits and shared one bicycle between three of them. The people he knew owned boats and private planes; they could party till three in the morning, and then get up at six to go water-skiing.

Sometimes he scared me. He could be so sweet and gentle, then the slightest thing would make him erupt with anger. I never knew what was happening and it was exhausting. Not that he was ever violent. No, that was me. He had me spitting and scratching like a wild cat while he calmly held me at arm's length. Then I'd dissolve in floods of tears and he'd be so sweet and gentle. He had a way of stroking my arms and shoulders that made every nerve in my body sing out loud.

Yet I don't know how I would have got through those three months without him. He even came to Europe with me. Two of the pieces that sold at the Remborne exhibition went to a French industrialist who gifted them to a new research centre near Paris. They offered to pay my fare and expenses if I would attend the presentation. Probably all a big tax write-off for them, but I wasn't going to say no, was I? Besides, the buyer did seem to know something about art and was talking about further commissions. While I was there I crossed over to London to visit the Barbican. Winston Remborne had arranged a small opening of my works there for the following year. But the thought of dealing with those high-flyers scared the hell out of me. Jason just dropped everything and came along. He fended off unwanted attention, gave orders to the hotel staff and renegotiated the new commissions in my favour. I wouldn't have survived without him.

So what went wrong?

Funny, that's what Sally asked the last time I saw her. Well, almost the last time. Sally and I had known each other since art school. Both away from home for the first time and trying desperately to appear cool and contemptuous while trembling in our boots, we gravitated towards each other, then clung together like tadpoles in a shark pool. At first we shared a room on campus, then moved into a grotty rental in town shared with three others, where we subsisted on endless pasta, overdue rent and a bottle of cheap plonk when anyone sold a painting. They were the best days.

Most of the students produced and sold work commercially to eke out their allowance. I, on the other hand, refused to compromise my art for the sake of a few extra bucks. As a result I was permanently broke and made up for it by doing most of the cooking and housework.

Sally painted, usually portraits. Commissions came easily, so it was usually Sally who supplied the wine. Even then she had an eye for people, or maybe it was more an intuitive knowledge of what goes on inside. Sally was our Wise Woman; she always knew what was hurting and how to heal it. As an artist she seemed to capture the essence of a person with just a few strokes of charcoal. Maybe that, too, was a kind of healing. And when she painted she did things with light that made your spine tingle.

After we all graduated Sally and I stayed together. She saw me through the first frustrating years of work and my tempestuous break-up with Andrew. Meanwhile she quietly established her own studio and built herself a name. Naturally she was my appointed guide and mentor on the merry-go-round with Jason so there was no surprise when I turned up on her doorstep, all red-eyed and puffy-faced and carrying bunches of soggy tissues.

'So, what went wrong?'

'Oh, nothing. Everything.'

'I've made us some green tea. Here, drink it and tell me what happened.'

'I'd rather have coffee.'

'You're getting tea. It'll calm you down. So what's he done this time?'

'Like — he asks people to stay without my knowing. I find strangers in my apartment, eating my food, and Jason's nowhere in sight.'

'And?'

'He has parties without telling me. I come home late, wanting to go to bed and the house is full of people. God, Sally, this tea is disgusting.'

'It's good for you. Drink it. So, what else?'

'And you know he does drugs. I'm not really into that.'

'Oh, come off it Regan, I've seen you stoned.'

'OK, I smoke a little weed occasionally, but that's all. Jason's into other stuff. I don't like it or what it does to him. And I don't like the friends that go with it.'

'Sounds to me like typical teenage behaviour.'

'Yes, well I'm sure he has stuff stashed somewhere in my flat. I can't afford that sort of publicity. The press already have me typecast as some kind of arty social rebel. Besides, he's not a teenager. In lots of ways he's more mature than I am. He knows the art world better than I do. I sort of rely on him.'

'Well, I know you don't like me saying this, but I still think he's using you.'

'To do what, for heaven's sake? He's got more money than I have. He's the one with all the influential friends. It's not as if he can't find work.'

'Yes, but you're flavour of the month, the name on everyone's "got to see" list. I've seen the way he parades you about. It's like he owns a champion racehorse.'

'No, that's not fair. He can be really kind and thoughtful—'

'And selfish and inconsiderate. But then I don't trust him, as you know. Drink your tea.'

'He understands my work and—'

'And you have great sex. Not that that would influence you.'

'OK, so we have great sex, that's not important.'

'Oh, really? That's not what you said last week.'

'No. Really. There's more to him than that.'

'Regan, you're so mixed up. Your whole world's been turned upside down these last few months. It's not surprising you can't see past him. Look, what do *you* want? I mean *really* want. Right at this moment.'

The answer leapt straight into my head, although I tried to cover it over with something easier. In the end I had to say it.

'I want to run away.'

A few days later I did run away. But I didn't know it would happen in the way it did.

I'd been to a reception, another presentation of one of my works. This time it was in the city and Jason was supposed to meet me there but he didn't turn up. I was jumpy all evening. He'd never let me down before — well, not like this. There had to be something very wrong. An accident? Jason didn't have accidents. For some reason I thought he'd been in a fight or had been arrested. I made some excuse to get away early and went home. Not that I expected to find him there, but I could make some phone calls. When I opened the door I found lights on, music playing. Of course it could have been anyone. I tried calling out. Hell, this was my home and I was acting like I was the interloper. Then I heard voices coming from the bedroom, whispers and muffled sounds. The door swung open and Jason walked out. I was so relieved that all I could see was him and nothing else.

'Thank God. Are you all right?' How stupid can you be? 'You missed the presentation. Where were you? I was worried sick.'

He leaned against the wall and said nothing. He'd been drinking but that was quite normal. Then I noticed he was wearing only jeans, the top button undone. His feet were bare. Something tightened inside me.

'What's going on?' Still he said nothing. 'Jason, talk to me.'

'I didn't think you'd be back this early,' he said. But it was the way his eyes turned toward the bedroom door. It was so obvious even I could see it.

'There's someone here, isn't there? You've got someone in there. I thought you were hurt or ill or . . . or . . . And you've just been screwing some bit you've picked up.'

'No, it's not like that.'

'What was it like then? Was she good? Was she worth it? My God, she's in my bed. You've got her in my bed.' I started towards the door but he grabbed my shoulders.

'Don't go in there. Regan, I'm warning you.'

'You're *warning* me? I want that bitch out of there. The two of you. Out!' I broke away from him and charged into the bedroom.

She was sitting up on the bed, sheets pulled tight around her as if they would hide what had happened. She stared straight at me, struggling to bring it all into focus with pupils that were wide and black as marble. But her face was filled with such sadness and despair that I knew she understood. In spite of the drink, in spite of whatever else he had fed her, she knew who I was and what he had done to us.

'Oh, Sally. Sally.' That was all I could say. As I stood there watching her, tears began to trace the line of her jaw and fall onto her shaking hands. I turned and walked out of the room.

I remember standing at the window watching the traffic lights at the corner change from red to green and back to red. I'm not sure I was thinking of anything. After what may have been a long or a little while, Jason was standing behind me.

'Sally's gone. I put her in a taxi. The driver will see she gets home OK.'

I nodded. The lights changed again.

'Don't blame Sally. It was all my fault. She came round to see you. We had a drink and then . . . Well, it all got out of hand. She didn't know what she was doing. She wouldn't hurt you.'

'I know that. Don't you think I *know* that?' I heard my voice rising to a scream. 'She was my friend!' I felt my fist beating at him and beating at him and this time he didn't hold me away but just stood there while I beat him and beat him until I couldn't any longer and my body sank to the floor.

He went down with me, folding me in his arms and I let him hold me because that's all I had left.

'She was my friend.'

'I know,' he whispered. 'I know.'

Jason left, but the night went on and on and the lights on the corner kept changing. When, finally, sunlight streamed through the window it hurt my eyes and made my head ache. All I wanted was Sally. I wanted to hear her voice. I wanted to apologise for what he'd done and make it right between us, but it never could be. Some things you can't mend.

The day threw itself away on endless cups of coffee. It was evening before Jason slid through the door, shoulders hunched in silence. He wouldn't look at me. All he managed was, 'Hi. You OK?'

There was no point in trying to answer so we sat on opposite sides of the table. He studied his hands and I looked out of the window. 'I don't suppose it's any good saying I'm sorry?'

'You want me to forgive you? You want me to make you feel better? Well fuck you, Jason. This isn't about you.'

'I know you're hurting now, but—'

'You don't get it, do you? It's over. I want you to take your stuff and get out of here.'

'What about you? What'll you do?'

'I don't know. I'll go away. I need to work and I can't do it here.'

'Yes, I know.' He took a deep breath. 'I've been doing a lot of thinking. I'm not the best thing that's happened in your life, I'm aware of that. Last night, well, I don't know what that was about. But worse than that, what I've done to you is get between you and your work.'

'You're probably right, as usual. I need to have my head straight and it just doesn't happen with you around. I'm going to get out of Auckland, go somewhere quiet. '

'So, where will you go?'

'I don't know. A place where there aren't any people.'

'Look, I might know somewhere. Let me go check a few things out.'

'Jason, I don't want you—'

'It's OK. I promise I won't try to change your mind. Let me do this one thing.'

Next morning he was back, saying everything was arranged. He was full of it, telling me how perfect it was and just what I needed and how I'd be able to work undisturbed. It was as if he'd found a new game to play and the day before had never happened. He behaved as if we were going on holiday, helping pack my bags and driving round to the studio to load up. I got swept along as I always did; it was easier than trying to think.

As the last of the day slipped away the lake's surface darkened to the purple lustre of ripe plums. It was good to breathe air that was cooler and untainted by yesterday's anger. The glass of wine was warm between my hands.

Had I forgiven him? Did my grandfather forgive his puppy when it chewed up a first edition Chekhov? Somehow, forgiving Jason seemed equally irrelevant. I didn't know what to do about him any more. I was only aware of a big, empty space inside me where Sally used to be.

FOUR

I am walking. Upwards, I think, and towards . . . somewhere . . .
somewhere I must go. It is night but I see my way clearly.
Moonlight drapes the forest, outlining the tips of leaves and pools
in white ruches between the trunks. I am walking through pine
trees, crunching on fallen needles, releasing their resinous odour,
pungent and sickly as it mingles with the smell of mildewed earth.
My feet are bare, yet I cannot feel the sting of needle tips in my
flesh. Nor do I feel tired, though it seems I have been walking
for hours. There is no urgency. Not yet. I have time to feel my
way over stones and twisted roots, time to hold back the branches
that would pull and tear at my bare skin. I am walking upwards,
going . . . where am I going . . . ?

There is no silence in this forest. Insects hum and crackle,
calling into the night, the drone and scrape of legs, the buzz of
rapid wings. Small things rustle and creep in the undergrowth,
their tiny eyes watching my progress. And something else watches
me, something that is waiting . . .

The ground is steeper now, my breath ragged from exertion
and anticipation. I can feel my heart. It kicks against my ribs
and throbs in my fingers. My feet slip and I snatch at handfuls
of twigs as if that could save me from a fall. And still I push on

and upward, pulse throbbing in my head. Or is it outside my head? Thumping and thumping and the ground beneath my feet shuddering with each beat. Trees shiver to the rhythm and insects join in the chant. Thump . . . thump . . . thump . . . I struggle against the tangle of branches that pull at my limbs and suddenly the ground slips away and I am falling into the rotting earth, crashing downwards into . . .

I wrestled to pull myself out of the corkscrewed sheet, gasping and running with sweat, my head still pounding. The walls were yellow with sunlight and, yes, I could smell pine resin and that early morning mustiness seeping through the window and saturating the cottage. The thumping was still there, even louder now, shaking the walls and floor. I fell out of the bed, still trying to remember where and who I was, angry and frustrated by this sudden awakening. I had been going somewhere and it had been important.

As my senses focused on the thumping it gained a harder edge and was now a definite, rhythmic banging, pausing after a few beats, only to start up again even stronger and louder. I could put the dream down to last night's wine, but not that noise. Oh, God, I thought, it's the Big Bad Wolf come to blow the house down — I knew this was too good to last. My feet got tangled up in my shirt, which was lying, crumpled, on the floor. Hopping about on one leg I snatched it up, dragged it over my arms and opened the bedroom door.

The noise was even louder in the main room. But there was my friend to meet me.

'Bramble, hello girl, how are you?' She barked with joy and her tail wagged all the way up to her ears. But she waited for me by the sofa, as if there were a line she could not cross. So I went to her and had to be licked and jumped over before I was allowed to go further.

'What the hell's going on out there, eh?'

40

We both headed for the deck where the morning air slapped me full in the face. But I'd found the source of the noise. It *was* the big bad wolf — a man, a strange, dark, hairy man, wielding a hammer. Still foggy-headed, at first I thought he was knocking the walls down, then saw that he was nailing up some wood. Badger sat beside a box of tools, his tail drumming the floor. He panted a greeting and shifted his paws as if he wanted to run to me, but he was on guard duty next to a jar of nails and obviously owed this weirdo some loyalty.

'Hello there.' I tried to sound friendly. Then '*Hello*', louder this time.

The hammer hovered in mid-swing and he turned to locate the source of the interruption. Sharp eyes pinned me down, then dismissed me. A quick nod of the head and the hammer continued its course.

'You woke me up.'

This time he didn't bother to stop.

'It's half past eight.' This was said with a degree of contempt for anyone in bed after the sun came up. He looked like your typical serial killer, steel grey eyes peering out from a wild tangle of black hair and beard, so thick that they had formed a single mask.

'What are you doing?'

This time he stopped but did not look at me.

'Sullivan told me to rig up some shelter round the deck. I found these.' He flicked his foot toward a pile of corrugated PVC sheeting. 'I'm putting up a batten to hold them in place.'

'Oh, I see. That's great.'

'Yes, well can I get on with it now?' There was a trace of something foreign in his voice.

'Sure. Would you like some coffee? I might as well make some now I'm up.'

'No thanks. I do have other work to get on with.'

And a good morning to you too, I thought, and went in search of the coffee grinder, dog at my heels. While the water boiled I went to the bedroom and pulled on a few more clothes. Bramble waited outside the door, tail down and whining. She looked relieved when I emerged in one piece. The aroma of fresh coffee permeated the cottage and drifted through the open door. I wondered if it had given Rasputin second thoughts and if I should repeat the offer. No, let him suffer. It tasted wonderful as morning coffee always does, and the first sip kick-started me back to life. Last night's wine bottle was on the table, most of it gone. Wine, fresh air and freedom — a heady concoction. No wonder I had had such strange dreams. My mouth felt like something furry had slept in it. A hot shower would have been wonderful, but it would have to wait until Jack the Ripper wasn't around.

The hammering was still going on, so I wandered back out to the deck holding my coffee mug. He'd already fixed wooden struts along one side and was working on the front, from the corner up to the central steps.

'Hey, this is great. I thought a tarpaulin would do but those sheets will let in all the light. A real studio. I need the light to work, you see. I'm a sculptor, you know, I carve things out of wood.'

'Yes, I do know what a sculptor does.' His voice was soft now, and patient, as if talking down to a precocious child. If I'd had my boots on I would have kicked him on the shins.

'You work for Sullivan, do you? You're not from round here, though. Is that an Irish accent?'

He froze. The muscles in his arm and shoulders tensed into iron. I could see the breath rise and fall in his chest. 'I'm employed to do a job. Perhaps you'd allow me to get on with it?'

'Yeah, right.' I didn't know what his problem was but I wasn't going to hang around to touch any more raw nerves. Especially when he had that hammer in his hand.

Downing the last of the coffee I collected pastels, drawing pad and various materials, tossing them into a bag along with a bottle of water and some cheese, bread and fruit. A quick search located my boots, one under the bed, the other in the bathroom, and I slipped out of the house. He had his back to me and didn't notice my leaving, or if he did he chose to ignore it even though Badger abandoned the nail jar and both the dogs came bounding after me. Well, serve him right, the miserable sod, he deserved to be left alone. As I walked off round the lake path the pounding of the hammer grew more distant and my anger eventually melted into the glory of the day.

The warmth of the morning sun laid its tender hands upon my face. This was what I needed; this was why I had come here. The heavy dew of the night was lifting in billowing clouds of steam, while birds called to each other, eager to pass on the good news of a new day. There were gentle rustlings in the bushes, which caused Badger and Bramble to go crashing off into the undergrowth, only to return a few yards further along the path, empty-handed but still smiling, their tongues flapping like pink dusters.

I followed the lake track for a way then branched off onto one of the numerous side paths that led upwards through the bush. This was the real forest. Was it ancient? It felt primitive, and yet the vegetation looked fresh and young. Unlike the pine groves, which were awash with indigo shadows, here the light was green and gold and told of open spaces up ahead. Just a few more steps, it said, and there will be a clearing, open to sunlight and azure skies. Only there wasn't any clearing, just that pale green-gold light to lead the wanderer further astray.

Here there were giants, the tallest of the trees, their roots stretched up on tiptoe to outreach their brothers in the race to the sky. I craned my neck back to follow the line of the trunks, straight and bare, shooting up to the tallest point where they exploded into masses of foliage. Below the canopy, scrawny youngsters strutted in their leafy finery, while the saplings, some barely the height of a man, shivered in awe of their elders. Ferns took up residence in every available space. Their fronds hung in graceful arches, as if forming an awning over pathways. But I think they lied. There were no pathways. It was all a deceit. But I had no fear of getting lost: the lake lay below and all downward routes would lead there. Besides, it all looked so familiar.

Suddenly I found myself in the shadow of a forest lord, a tree of such colossal stature that it humbled all around it. I stood back and stared, hardly daring to breathe. Time-raddled bark had twisted into matted cords, winding up and out of sight. The topmost branches must have reached way beyond the canopy. I felt compelled to walk around the base, to know its dimensions, running my hands over its surface as I paced it around. Roots like hawsers impeded my way. They drilled deep into the earth and held it in a grip of iron. This had to be painted.

A fallen trunk nearby offered a good seat and I rummaged in my bag for paper and pastels, starting to outline the demigod. The dogs soon grew bored with this and went off on some personal mission. After a while I could hear them barking away off by the lake, but I was lost in work. That's how it has always been with me: I become caught up with a project, and everything else, including time, ceases to exist.

The morning was gone before I put the page down, but the results were satisfying. There was something in the image about age and old knowledge. This tree embraced wisdom. It talked of things before and beyond man. Yes, this was where I was going.

A quick spray to set the colour and I was ready to eat. The water bottle was half emptied in one go. It was surprisingly hot and humid, even though the sun's rays were filtered. Cicadas were in full throttle and tui called to each other in secret codes like forest spies reporting on intruders. The fallen wood on which I sat had been honeycombed by termites. Other invisible life forms had tattered the lower leaves into lace. The place was seething with life. It felt electric, like the hum of energy around a generating station, only this was not in my ears but inside my head. It was time to move on. I dropped the remains of the bread on the forest floor — an offering to the tree gods. No doubt it would be seized upon by scavengers.

Still biting into an apple, I started walking, this time moving eastwards to follow a higher path around the lake. Soon bush gave way to patches of clear ground and then a rutted dirt track that marked the edge of the pine plantation. In there it was darker, cooler. Where broad leaves and fern fronds had filtered yellow-green rays to the bush floor, the pines closed out the sun as if it were not welcome. It was like being inside a huge building, somewhere cool and hollow, a place created for worship, but not for the gods of warmth and laughter. The pines took themselves too seriously, stretching tall and high but looking ever inward. It was as it was in the dream, only without the softening touch of moonlight. I tried to recreate more of the sensations of the dream walk by rubbing the leaves between my fingers to release their aromatic resin and crunching the dried needles under foot. On impulse I slipped my boots off to feel again the needles' roughness. But, unlike in the dream, this hurt like hell and, quickly abandoning the experiment, I had to sit down to pick the sharp spines out of the soles of my feet.

The path twisted upwards again and the trees broke their lines to give way to a sun-dappled clearing. There was something familiar . . . Yes, of course, this was where Jason had brought me the day before. Was it the day before? It seemed ages ago. Yes, there were the tracks the bike had scored in the earth. So, where were the graves?

I nearly stubbed my toe on one. The writing was barely legible, but I could just make out the date, 1836 to 1866. The rest was crusted with dried, brown lichen. I tried picking at it with my thumbnail, then rummaged in my art bag for a scraper. After a few minutes' work the epitaph was revealed:

Anne Sullivan
1836–1866
beloved wife of Michael and mother to David

What was it Jason had said? His grandmother, great-grandmother and great-great-grandmother? Eighteen thirty-six — this must be the great-great-grandmother. The other two were together, just a few metres away. I should not be doing this, interfering with graves. This was Sullivan's family, and Jason's. Perhaps they would be angry, and justifiably so. Perhaps I should just go away and leave it alone. But then I never could do that, so I went across to Jane Sullivan and Mary. I used the last of my water wiping the stones clean. There was a pattern here. I turned a page in my pad and scribbled down the names and dates.

Anne Sullivan
1836–1866
beloved wife of Michael and mother to David

Mary Sullivan
1876–1905
wife of David and mother to Thomas

Jane Sullivan
1912–1942
wife of Tom and mother to John

Successive generations. They all died so young. And why only the women? Where were the men?

I headed back out of the forest and found the track from the main road down to the lake. Occasionally a distant gunshot panicked water birds which rose in a scrambled formation, their flight reflected on the buckled surface of the water. This was too good to lose, so I found a sheltering tree beside the path and got out my paper and pastels once more. By the time the drawing was completed the shadows were growing long and there was a cold edge to the breeze.

The side path leading back to the cottage passed by the woolshed, a sprawling collection of buildings with rusty iron roofs and rotting walls. I could see Sullivan there, standing by his mini-tractor. I had promised him I would be no bother so I kept my distance. Besides, he was talking to the hammer-wielding maniac and I wasn't going to get involved. But I did wave to them and Sullivan touched his hat in response. He was carrying a gun and holding a bunch of rabbits. That's obviously what the dogs had been doing all afternoon. Bluebeard turned to stare at me but gave no sign of recognition. The dogs spotted me, though, and both came bounding over to tell me about their afternoon. They walked with me a little way along the road, before Badger turned and went back to check on the rabbits. Sullivan didn't seem to mind that Bramble stuck by my side.

I didn't realise how exhausted I was till I climbed onto the deck. I had a studio. One side and half the front were enclosed with the wavy panels, allowing the evening sun to flood the area. It was warm and sheltered and full of light. He had even swept the floor and stacked my equipment neatly against the wall. Perhaps the bearded wonder wasn't so dim after all. I should thank Sullivan, but that would have to wait till morning. I wasn't going to risk a run-in with the poor, dead bunnies. He might even offer me one.

A hot shower while pasta boiled — I was ravenous. I was aware of Bramble snuffling around the kitchen and occasionally putting her nose around the bathroom door. When I padded through to the bedroom she kept her distance, wandering out to the deck. She was still there when I joined her with my plate piled high.

'No bunnies I'm afraid, girl. You're welcome to a carrot.' An indignant sniff as she flopped down, leaning her head against my side. She smelt warm and dusty. I realised that this was the closest I had been to anyone all day. It came to me that this was the first time, for as long as I could remember, that I had spent a whole day on my own, completely immersed and happy in my own company, with no other human contact. This was the solitude I craved, just myself and the trees. Oh yes, there was the axe murderer, but I wasn't sure you could class him as human.

'And my dog, of course. Mustn't forget my dog.' She looked up at me with her chocolate eyes and nuzzled my arm and I knew I was falling in love.

Trees. Again the trees. This time I feel cold. Drops of dew cling to my arms and my bare feet are frozen. There are night sounds, the clicks and chirps of insects, leaves and twigs cracking beneath my feet. The wind is colder now and the broad fronds of ferns quiver around me. I must part them, like curtains, to force my way through. The path is not visible and yet I know that I am following a trail.

My progress is being observed, I feel the hairs at the nape of my neck rise and know someone is watching. It is like being in a crowded room when a stranger has you in their sights. Your fingers search out the place where their eyes touch your skin.

There is a sound, a very faint sound that should not be there. Music? A fiddle playing a long way off, the notes strewn on the night air. Could that be possible?

Upward, I must go towards . . . ? The ground pulls steeper and steeper. Now there are rocks to scramble over. I hold onto branches to pull myself along. Is there some urgency? I feel it and the night will soon be gone. I have to reach . . . to reach . . . ? There it is again, the fiddle music, something slow and sad. But it's all wrong. And there is someone through the trees. I can see a face in the shadows, it looks familiar somehow. I move towards her and she comes closer to me, so close that we could

touch. I reach out my hand as she does. We both reach out to
each other and I touch . . .

For a moment I couldn't understand where I was. But my hands moved to the edge of the mirror, fingers tracing the carved branches and leaves. It was me. The woman was me. I was at the dressing table, seeing my own reflection glowing dimly in the pre-dawn light. What was going on? I must have sleepwalked. My arms and legs were bare. No wonder I felt cold. And yet I could hear . . . Was that music? Or just the wind in the trees. No, there couldn't be music. Not here. Just the ragged remnant of a dream.

FIVE

It starts with the sharpening of the tools. It's a meditation that hones the mind ready for the task and prepares the body as a channel for communication with the wood, rather like a musician tuning up his instrument. That's how it always begins for me and that morning was no different.

I sat on the deck steps with my tool bag, unwrapping the leather rolls of gouges, chisels and knives, laying them in a straight row and greeting each one as an old and revered friend. The stones next, each lightly filmed with oil and stored in its own box since last use. I had performed this ritual so many times that my body knew the sequence of each movement, the exact pressure required to produce the perfect edge. Eyes and hands followed their tasks and conferred their own judgements, leaving the conscious and the subconscious minds to communicate without distraction.

My thoughts were still with the dream, the forest and the trees. And whatever it was that was watching me. I took each image in turn and focused on it until the edges were clean and sharp. Whatever was going on in my head, however shaken and distressed it had left me, the sensations it produced were also tools to be worked with. It was all a part of the process.

There was no chance of returning to sleep but a hot coffee and some warm clothes had made me feel more human. Even though I was still shaking inside I knew the best way to get my head together was to work. It was still early, no sun as yet, and the dampness of dewfall hung on the air. In the pre-dawn light the birds were creating that uproar poetically eulogised as the dawn chorus. Actually it is a territorial shout-off that puts me in mind of the racket set up by a rugby crowd the morning after a home win.

I claimed my working space by bolting the workbench together and adjusting the height. It's not really a bench, more like a square platform with a cradle in which I fix the wood to be worked upon. The pictures drawn the day before were taped to the wall, reference information about what I had seen and, more importantly, what I had felt.

Using the kitchen furniture as a prop, I levered the first piece of kauri onto the bench and looked at it from all sides. Moving around the block, I drew it from several angles. This is my usual approach since it gives me insight into the wood's true form. I always study the wood carefully, particularly the lie of the grain. If you ignore the grain, not only does it split, but also you find yourself at odds with what it's telling you. If it's not a straight grain then a circular movement is produced with spheres and hollow bowls. If the slab of wood has a flaw then the design generates around that, again working with the grain. The wood is the teacher. It carves itself if you're willing to follow its lead.

After making fresh coffee, warming my hands around the mug, I studied what I'd drawn. Now I was contemplating the wood in the light of the images that arose in my mind when walking through the bush and the pine plantation. Again I reached for paper and pastels. This time I drew blindly, trying to project onto the page what I had experienced while among the trees, both in waking life and in the dream world. Sunlight inched across the deck as I taped the new sketches to the wall.

The morning was well under way and the wildlife had settled into its routine. Bellbirds and tui conversed in a more civilised manner and cicadas revved their engines, promising another hot day. The sun rose higher as the wall started to fill with squares of paper. Eventually I stood back and observed what had been achieved. It was important not to force anything. I would have to leave it for a while to work on itself, like wine fermenting in a darkened cask. Very soon a concept of the form would emerge.

The aim was to produce six new pieces ready for the Paris exhibition. There would be time and, amid this richness of inspiration, I was convinced of my direction. The energy was flowing. I knew I had tuned into something powerful and would try to do it justice.

The sun had climbed high and I was suddenly hungry.

I was having breakfast on the deck when I heard the sound of an engine. It had to be Jason's motorbike. I jumped to my feet, tipping the bowl of cereal down my leg. Then, through the trees, I could see the bright red of Sullivan's mini-tractor, the dogs riding shotgun in the back. They found me first, bounding all over the deck. Sullivan followed at a slower pace, carrying something.

'Thought I'd better come over and make sure everything's OK. Brought you some eggs. Do you eat eggs? Jason was telling me you're on some sort of diet.'

'No, not a diet, just vegetarian.' I came down the steps to meet him, wiping wet bran flakes from my knees. Badger thought it was some kind of game and tried to join in. 'Yes, I do eat eggs. That's kind of you. I bet they're freshly laid.'

'Keep my own chooks.' He pulled his hat off. The old-fashioned courtesies. He still had that grey look about him, even in the sunlight. And a kind of vagueness.

'Look, I really need to thank you. About the deck I mean. This is absolutely perfect. It was good of you to go to so much trouble.'

'No trouble for me. I told Connors to rig something up and that's what he came up with.'

'Connors? That's the workman? The hairy one?'

Sullivan almost smiled. 'That's him. Good worker. Don't suppose he'll stay long. They never do.' He stepped up onto the deck and inspected the new walls. 'Made a good job of this. It makes a nice sundeck. Maybe Jason will keep it. He's put a lot into restoring the place.'

'Jason restored it?'

'Yes, well it's his cottage.'

My stomach did a flip. 'I must have misunderstood. I thought it was yours. Thought you'd done it up so you could run it as a backpackers' stopover.'

'Backpackers? What here? No, no,' Sullivan shook his head. 'What would I want with tourists running all over the place? No, this is Jason's. He used to spend time here when he was a kid. He won't stay at the house any more, not that I blame him. Said he wanted this place for a retreat. Did some of the work himself or paid the workmen to do it.'

'Oh, I see.' But I didn't see. 'Does he ever stay here?'

'Sometimes. Never know when to expect him. Just turns up out of the blue. He's always gone his own way, never easy to deal with.'

If Jason had said this was his place I would never have come. He knew that. So where did that leave me now? It was hard to know what Sullivan wanted. His voice told me nothing. His face was a mask, eyes always focused on some distant landscape.

'Perhaps it would be better if I left.'

'No, no. Don't do that. You're not the problem. It's the lad. Always been secretive. It's not having a mother around, I expect. Lonely sort of childhood for a boy.'

I wanted to ask about the graves. I wanted to ask about Jason's mother and how she had died and where they had buried her. But I also wanted to stay here and for once I knew when to keep my mouth shut.

'The dogs seem to like being here,' I said. 'Bramble's spending a lot of time with me. I hope that's all right?'

'Up to them. They have the run of the place. Yes, I can see she likes you. She'd be good company. It's a bit isolated here for a woman on her own. Good to have a dog around the place.'

'She doesn't seem to like the bedroom much. Won't go in there. I can't see anything wrong with it.'

'Dogs get notions in their heads. Any little thing can spook them.'

'Well, there's nothing unusual about it. At least, the dressing table is unusual. Quite beautiful. In fact I was hoping to ask you about it.'

'Dressing table? I wouldn't know. Don't know what the lad put in there. I know he got some new stuff.'

'No, this is old. Very old. A round mirror set in what looks like carved oak. A sort of wreath of branches and leaves and . . .'

As I spoke Sullivan's face remained motionless. But he seemed to grow paler and, for a moment, something flashed across his eyes that was more than concern.

'Would you mind if I took a look?'

'No, come on through.'

He stood in the middle of the room, twisting the brim of his hat through his hands. It was a long time before he spoke. 'Yes, it's hers. It's his mother's mirror. He's brought it down from her room. I didn't know he had it here.'

'Perhaps it should go back, then. It's beautiful piece. Must be very valuable.'

'No, no you keep it here. It's never used. I sleep in my study downstairs. Have done ever since . . . She'd made the room just how she wanted it and when she . . . Well, it didn't feel right to

54

change things. It's still as she left it. I don't know how he got in there. I always keep it locked.'

'Why is that?'

'It was Jason. When he was a kid, he kept wanting to go in there. Oh, I know he missed his mother and it was natural that he should want to be among her things. But it was more than that. He would just sit there for hours on end. Sometimes in the dark. Children are supposed to be afraid of the dark, aren't they? Didn't seem to bother him. It wasn't right for a child. The doctor said I should try to keep him out but he wouldn't have it. In the end I had to lock it up. Haven't been in there myself for years. That mirror, she used to sit in front of it, staring at herself. I'd make a joke of it, tease her about being too pretty for her own good. She'd say she was listening to the trees. I wonder how Jason managed to get it over here? No, we'll leave it here for now. As you say, it's a beautiful piece. It deserves to be seen. You would understand that.'

I walked with him back to his vehicle. About to drive off, he turned to me and said, 'You're very welcome here. Just be careful. If you need anything come up to the house. Or there's Connors. He's staying in the woolshed, over there — you can see it through the trees. He's a good man. The dogs like him, they can usually tell.'

'Thanks, Sullivan. But I'm sure I won't need him.' Too right. 'I'll be fine. By the way, I do need some milk and stuff. Where can I shop?'

'Along the main road, about two kilometres further on. Only a few houses, but there's a dairy and a good bar. Ask for Maggie.'

Then he left with Badger. Bramble stayed by my side. The man seemed so nebulous. It was as if he'd hardly been there at all. A grey man, with a grey soul. Perhaps he lived in the past. Maybe that was why there was so little of him here in the present.

I worked on the sketches until nearly noon, refining some and creating more with greater detail, until the wall was nearly covered. It had grown really hot and I was ready for a break.

Bramble tried to get into the Land Rover with me but I thought I had better not take her off the station without permission.

'Guard the homestead girl, I'll bring you something nice.' Then I keyed the engine and drove onto the lake track.

Driving over the pine-covered hill and down onto the highway I felt like a deep-sea diver resurfacing from the ocean bed. It made me realise how isolated the Sullivan place was, how removed from the real world. I noted the turn-off in case I couldn't find my way back, and then drove onward. The same road wound on as it had two days ago, as if I had never stopped. I drove through the same crumpled hills past sheep that had not moved. The sun pounded relentlessly on the car. Tar on the road had started to melt into jet-black slicks and a heat haze warped the surface into impossible waves. After a while some isolated houses appeared, their white painted weatherboards cracking in the noon heat.

Suddenly my foot slammed on the brake and I threw the gears into reverse, weaving the truck backwards till I could see over the hedge. White stones, marble, crosses — a graveyard.

I walked between the plots, along narrow strips of mown grass, neatly edged and weed-free. The church was a way off, over another hedge and through a garden, but close enough to belong to this land. Many of the graves bore vases of freshly cut flowers. There was even a mound of bare earth, piled with wilting wreaths. All was cared for and loved, laid to rest by a small community who still tended their dearly departed.

The names were all strangers to me, of course, but the dates were not all recent. Some of the stones looked old, very old, especially over the far side, under the trees. I navigated the square set paths to head in that direction. Here the graves bore signs of age and wear, no fresh flowers, but everything was neat and orderly. Of course the older stones were weather-marked and hard to read. But I saw 1945, and a little further on 1936. What had Jason said? The graveyard was too far away to take the Sullivan dead? This was barely two kilometres from the house, no distance, even by horse and cart. There was another marked 1925, another, 1931.

Then I found a name I knew:

David Sullivan

1865–1940

son of Michael and Anne Sullivan,

father of Thomas

Anne Sullivan. I had knelt by her gravestone yesterday, had washed her name clean and traced the letters with my fingers. Jason's great-great-grandmother. This was her son, who died seventy-four years later. She had died in 1866 when David Sullivan was just a year old.

It was darker in this corner of the cemetery and most of the gravestones were smaller and less ornate, some a simple wooden cross telling of hard times and poverty. But a tall monument dominated the farthest corner. No carved figures or ornamentation; just a plain, marble block, some two metres high, and on it:

Michael Sullivan

1832–1913

The dairy turned out to be the only shop in the area and large enough to be a small supermarket. It was crammed with all manner of stuff: food, tins of paint, towropes, batteries. I was still trying to juggle with the maths, who was born when and how long they managed to survive, as I took a wire trolley and filled it with milk, asparagus and melons, more wine (I was getting through quite a lot), fresh strawberries and some herb bread. In the pet section I picked up a packet of dog biscuits, then found an earthenware water bowl. You don't need a dog, I tried telling myself, and she's not your dog anyway. Even so, the bowl and the biscuits found their way to the checkout. On impulse I picked up a torch. There wasn't one at the cottage, I rationalised, and out there in the bush it was an essential item in case of emergencies; one good, practical purchase to offset the others. What was really on my mind was that music the night before. I know I was confused but I was sure it came from outside.

I hovered by the ice cream freezer and considered an orange ice block. No, a beer would be better.

The heat outside was becoming oppressive and the bar was a cool oasis. Ceiling fans skimmed cold air down onto my face and I received their blessing with gratitude. It took a few moments for my sun-blasted eyes to adjust. A few men were leaning on the counter at the other end of a long room and they tried to stare me down as I came in. I stared back and called down to them, 'G'day, gentlemen,' as I perched myself on a bar stool, plonked my boots on the ledge and ordered a Speights. The men continued to stare while the barmaid poured my drink. She then hovered at my end of the room, polishing a row of glasses.

'Take no notice of them, love,' she said. 'They've never heard of women's lib. Women have no business coming into pubs on their own. They think you should be home minding the kids.'

'Where does that leave you then?'

'Oh, I'm just a skirt. As long as I keep to my side of the bar there's no problem.' She looked about my age but more handy with the make-up and hair dye. Her mouth was full and soft and the corners of her eyes crinkled when she smiled, which was most of the time. She wore a tight pink T-shirt that clashed, gloriously, with her red curls. I knew I liked her straight away; you do with some people.

'Would you be Maggie?'

'Sure am. And you're new round here.'

'Sure am. My name's Regan. I'm staying at the Sullivan place.'

Maggie stopped the polishing, her face flooding with questions. 'He doesn't often have visitors,' she kept her voice on a tight rein. 'In fact, you're the first I've heard of.'

'I'm staying in the cottage. It's his son's place really. Do you know the family?'

'No more than anyone else. Old man Sullivan's here most days. Been coming for more years than I can remember. But I can't say I know him. Can't think of anyone who does.'

The beer was ice cold and worked miracles on my throat. It was also hitting an empty stomach and rushing to my head. 'You wouldn't have a sandwich would you?'

'Sure. Chicken? Ham?'

'How about cheese or salad?'

'I can do both.' She started work on the ingredients, which kept her down my end of the bar. As she cut and sliced she glanced at me from the corners of her eyes, her curiosity rising like bubbles in a beer glass. Eventually one of them popped.

'What's it like, the house?'

'Bit run down. No, very run down, what I saw of it. He seems to look after the rest of the place. Though there's not much to look after, now I think about it. I've only seen a few sheep and cows, not what you'd call a herd. But then, what do I know about that sort of stuff? There's the trees. I suppose he makes some money from them.'

'No need, they're sitting on a pile of money. The only thing he spends it on is beer. They say he let the house go since his wife . . . well, you know. Hasn't touched the place for years. Though nobody knows why. He's fanatical about the land, as you say, but he doesn't do anything with it. That's the story, anyhow. Not that any of the locals have been there to find out. Keeps himself to himself, as the saying goes. Here's your sandwich, cheese and salad. Mayonnaise?'

'That's great, thanks. He does seem rather vague. It's as if he's living somewhere else and has just bumbled into the real world by accident.'

'Yes, that's it,' she laughed. 'That's exactly what he's like. Another beer?'

'Yeah, why not. You from round here?'

'Yep. Tried getting away. I was living in Auckland. Then Mum got sick and Dad needed a hand around the place. It's just till she gets back on her feet, then I'll be off again.'

'I gather the Sullivan family's been here forever.'

'Since the early days. Michael Sullivan came over in the eighteen hundreds and bought up acres of land. An old family, from Ireland apparently. Very wealthy. Not that it's brought them much happiness.'

'Was that his monument in the graveyard? Big marble thing? Looks like the obelisk out of *Space Odyssey*?'

'That's him. The old man himself. He's quite a legend in these parts. Opened up a lot of this area for farming. There's quite a few Sullivans up there with him.'

'I gather a lot of the women died young.'

'Yes, well I suppose they did in those days. Though they do seem to have had more than their share of bad luck. But you don't want to believe everything — you know how people love to make a drama out of nothing. I suppose it was the way she died.'

'The way who died?'

'Anne Sullivan. That was his wife. He met her after he came here.'

'What happened to her?'

'One day she went out riding and never came back. Fell from

60

her horse apparently and struck her head. They say she bled to death. That's all I know really. It was up in those hills around the lake. They say that bush area still has a strange feel about it. Haven't been up there myself. But that land's never brought them any luck in all this time.'

'What, you mean it's haunted or something?'

'Not sure I believe in that sort of thing. Just a story hereabouts. I suppose every place has its ghosts and ghouls, you know, stories to frighten the kids. We were always told not to go near the Sullivan land or Anne would be after us. I guess it was just a way of stopping us young 'uns from trespassing. You never knew how Old Man Sullivan would react.'

'Really? Doesn't seem the sort to go scaring kids.'

'Oh, not him. I mean his father, Tom Sullivan. Died a few years back now. Grumpy old bugger he was, wouldn't let anyone near the place.'

There was a burst of laughter from the other end of the bar. Then singing, one of the men making a poor imitation of Rod Stewart.

'*Hey, wake up Maggie, I think I've got something to say to you . . .*'

'Don't you think that joke's wearing a bit thin, Jack?' Maggie called back.

'Don't let me keep the men from their beer,' I said, grabbing a handful of paper serviettes to wipe the mayonnaise off my sleeve.

'Right now I think they're more interested in you,' she whispered. 'Back in a mo.'

She moved away, swinging her hips and smiling dutifully. There was quite a bit of laughing and elbow nudging. Maggie pulled the beers and flirted and they rose to the bait, as those sort of men do. She was so good at it I almost felt sorry for them. I certainly felt sorry for anyone who dared put a hand out of place. They kept looking in my direction. I had finished my sandwich and started on the second beer when she came back.

'Idiots,' she smiled indulgently. 'I told them you were the new Avon lady and we were discussing the latest lip gloss. I think they actually believed me. I doubt they could raise a dozen brain cells between them. Now, what *were* we talking about?'

'You were telling me about the Sullivan family.'

'Not much to tell. There were just the three of them, old Tom, then his son John Sullivan and young Jason.'

'What about Jason's mother and the grandmother?'

'Who knows? There's always been rumours. But that's more to do with them being so isolated. You know what people are like. And you won't get much out of the Sullivan men.' She hesitated, picking up another glass. 'How is Jason, by the way? Haven't heard from him for a while.' It was the way she avoided looking at me that told it all.

'He was fine the last time I saw him. And,' I waited until she turned, then looked her straight in the eye, 'I expect it will be a while before I see him again.' With that out of the way we were free to be friends. 'So who should I talk to? If I want to find out about local history I mean.'

'I could always introduce you to some of the old boys round here. Not that lot,' Maggie nodded at the lunchtime beer crew who were now re-enacting the salient moves of last Saturday's rugby match. 'They're mostly hired workers, casuals. You won't see the landowners here lunchtime. After tea's when they drift in. Pity my mum's not ready for visitors yet — needs to rest after her op. She's lived here forever. Perhaps if you're still around in a few days, depends how long you'll be staying.'

'I'm not sure. No definite plans.'

'So what are you doing up there?'

'Time out. Time to work. I sculpt. The cottage is an ideal retreat. Sullivan got one of the men to fix up a studio space for me.'

'Ah, that would be Liam.'

'Could be. He didn't say who he was. I think Sullivan called him Connors. Big, hairy Irishman. Belligerent.'

'Yes, that's Liam Connors. There couldn't be two of them. Though he's not really as bad as he first seems. He's a bit suspicious of people. One eye looking over his shoulder, if you know what I mean.'

'Well, as long as he's not looking in my direction.' Noise rose from the men's corner. 'I think your fan club's trying to catch your attention. I'd better get back or the afternoon will be gone. Thanks for the sandwich. And the company.'

'Pleasure. See you again? I'm here most days.'

'Sure will.'

SIX

THE following night it rained.

Heat had burdened the day until the air felt as if it would curdle. The sun went down and evening draped itself around the cottage like a hot, damp towel. Vampire mosquitoes swarmed around the building, drawn by the promise of fresh blood. The deck, therefore, was out of bounds and the only option was to remain inside with the doors and windows wide and the screens firmly closed. There was nowhere to be comfortable and no amount of folded paper fans or cold, wet cloths brought relief. I took a cool shower, then, an hour later, showered again. Within minutes my skin was slicked with a salty sheen. It was pointless going to bed. I tried to read but couldn't focus. The ceiling pressed down on my chest, making me labour for every drawn breath.

Then came the first echoes of thunder. It began as a sequence of gentle stirrings, distant and prolonged. Turn by turn, dry flashes of electricity followed each rumble, cracking whips of white light across the skies but bringing no relief. When the first drops tapped on the iron roof, building rapidly to a drum roll, it felt like a blessing. The next thunderclap exploded directly above the lake. Lightning followed instantly and this time the flash tore the clouds apart and rain fell in torrents.

The storm rampaged for nearly an hour.

Forced, now, to close the doors and windows, I was held prisoner. Cataracts gushed in straight sheets from overloaded spouting, thrashing the dust below and churning it to pools of mud. One flash of lightning sounded like gunfire. It was followed by a creaking then a crash as a neighbouring tree was split by fire. The smell of burning hung on the air. I thought the cottage would be struck next, or a tree would land on it. I thought the roof wouldn't hold up to the pounding rain, or the walls would cave in. I tried to glory in the power of unleashed primal forces charging through the forest like warring beasts. I did try. Then I thought, sod this, piled cushions over my head and prayed it would all go away.

Eventually the electrical storm did recede, taking the deluge with it. It left a steady, healthy rainfall to feed the streams and swell the lake. When I was sure it was over I opened the doors to let in the cooling air and leaned on the deck rail, offering my face up to the night sky. There's nothing like the touch and the smell of fresh rain to wash the spirit clean.

The downpour had calmed but its rhythm was now made irregular by the tortuous zigzag journey through branches. All around me I could hear drips and splashes as droplets pooled their weight in leafy cups before spilling down to the level below. Each drop sounded its own note in the cascade, high or low, like the run of notes from a xylophone. I laughed and thought, yes, that's exactly what it was. 'Xylo', meaning wood. Xylophone — wood sound: the trees were making their own music. I moved down the steps so I could better hear, from deep in the bush, the giants playing their own tune.

Then I heard a different note.

Not the sharp staccato of raindrops; this was a sustained keening, ending in a sob. Another followed. It was the tremulous weeping of a violin, the music I had heard before, only this time the melody was slow and mournful. Each note hung upon the air as if it were falling with the rain, gliding softly from leaf to leaf. I reached out, trying to catch the sound, constructing note upon note to form the tune. Slow and sad, it was, as if the tears from the sky were of its own making.

Where was it coming from? It was impossible to see anything. The small clearing in which the cottage stood was illuminated by light flooding from the open door and window. Everything beyond was black, apart from the faintest shimmer on the surface of the lake, and even that was obscured in the mist of raindrops pattering the surface. You see, I did need that torch. And the boots and the raincoat, although I was already wet through.

The beam threw a yellow circle onto the mud. What had been pathways through the bush were now bubbling streams and I had to squelch along the edges to make any headway. Outside the music seemed to be coming from everywhere at once. I turned slowly to gain a bearing, slipped, struggled and grasped at slimy branches. This was all familiar, somehow. The dream — that's what I had done in the dream. Only this time it was real, or was it? For a moment I faltered and the two worlds eclipsed each other until I was no longer certain of anything.

Then I started forward, following the bobbing disc thrown out by the torch. It slid along the ground ahead of me and made attempts to escape by shimmying up tree trunks. Then there was a glow through the trees. The light and the music seemed to converge and all at once I found myself heading for the woolshed. The tune grew louder as I reached the building and a wedge of yellow light jutted out across the mud with music flowing over it and filtering away into blackness. I switched off the torch and reached for the door.

Inside was a cocoon woven from the soft glow of a lantern. It was a golden aura that closed off the dark edges of the room and brought the tableau at the centre into sharp focus. He sat on a wooden stool, his back toward the door. Even if I had been visible to him, he was so spellbound by his own creation that nothing from this earthly place could have touched him. With the fiddle tight between shoulder and jaw, the muscles of his left arm revealed the tension of his gliding fingers. The bow hovered, a note held poised upon the air and there was such sadness and such tenderness as string met fibre. Then his right shoulder rose and dipped, the bow sweeping back and forth to make a sweet sound in the stillness of the night.

I stood motionless until the last note dropped away and his arms lowered, carrying instrument and bow to their resting place on his knee. For a moment he did not breathe, and I dared not. When I did it was a gasp. Connors jumped from the stool and spun round, hunched, like an animal caught in a sprung trap. I found my voice in spite of his fear, or maybe because of it.

'Oh, God,' I whispered, 'that was the most beautiful thing I've ever heard.'

For an endless moment he stared, his body poised for fight or flight. Then, slowly, he stretched upright and his shoulders relaxed.

'Jesus, would you look at yourself. You're like a drowned ferret.'

There was nothing to say, so I stood there, dripping a small circle onto the floor. He placed fiddle and bow in the centre of the table, then turned to flip the light switch. The room sprang to life around us.

'I'll get you something to dry yourself on. I was going to make some tea.' He returned in a moment with a bundle of towels. I hadn't moved. I think my mouth was still wide open. He flung one of the towels over my head then put a light under the kettle and rummaged on the draining board for a clean mug. I had obviously been rained on a lot more than I realised. My jacket was soaked through and the boots waterlogged and loaded with mud.

'That was one hell of a storm,' I said.

'I've seen worse.' He looked over his shoulder, his eyes fixing on me accusingly. 'You weren't afraid, were you?'

'Me? No, of course not.'

'Here, sit and get this down ye. And for God's sake dry yourself. I won't be responsible for you getting pneumonia.' He placed the mug on the table.

Obediently I perched on the chair he had thrust behind me. I took a sip of the tea. It was hot and strong and brought me to my senses. I made some attempt to towel my hair. It was comfortable in here. A corner of the building had been partitioned off and fitted up as living quarters with sink and cooking stove, table and bed. There was another door through which he had gone to get the towels. I guessed it led to a bathroom.

'Liam, isn't it?'

'That's right, Liam Connors.'

'And I'm Regan.' He nodded. 'What was that you were playing?'

'A slow air. "An Droighnean Donn", in the Gaelic. It means "The Blackthorn". It's a love song. "My love is like the blossom of the sloe that grows upon the blackthorn."'

'Oh,' was all I could think of to say, so I sipped the tea for something to do.

He started to put the instrument back in its case.

'Oh, no. Please. Don't stop. Play some more.'

'I don't play for the entertainment of others.' He continued to loosen off his bow. 'Music's a personal thing.'

I placed my mug on the table. 'I'm sorry. I didn't mean to cause offence. If it's that personal I'd better leave you alone with it.'

For the first time his eyes softened. 'No, it's me that should be apologising. It's just that I'm used to being on my own. I'll give you another tune if you drink your tea. But no more slow airs if that's the effect it has on you.' He nodded at my dripping fringe and mud-streaked legs.

Resetting the bow and adjusting the tuning, he lifted the instrument to his chin, tucking it beneath the fuzz of beard. This time he broke into a jig so fast the notes tripped over each other as they came tumbling from his fingers. I was forced to put the tea down in order to slap my legs in time with the dance. My feet beat out the rhythm, mud splattering the floorboards, until the last, drawn-out note brought the tune to an end. I clapped and cheered and told him it was wonderful. I'm not sure, but he may have smiled. It was hard to tell what went on underneath all that facial hair.

'And what sort of a jig was that? Was it a jig?'

'Yes, a pair of slip jigs, nine-eight time. The first is called "The Butterfly", then "Hardiman".'

'And the first tune you were playing, that was an air?'

'A slow air, it's called. Played in free time.'

'It was very sad.'

'Yes, there's many a sad tune come out of Erin. But then there's much sadness born there.' He finished putting his fiddle back in its case.

'Is that where you're from? Southern Ireland?'

He snapped the catches down firmly but gave no answer.

'What brought you here?' I asked.

'I needed work. Sullivan needed a handyman. That's all.'

I was beginning to get a feel for the boundaries of his conversation. Just steer clear of people in general, Ireland in particular and anything personal.

'What's he like to work for?'

'He's all right. Pays me what I'm due. Keeps himself to himself.'

Yes, I thought, you two would get on fine together.

'He spends a lot of time in the pub,' I said. 'Or so Maggie was telling me. She's the barmaid.'

'Yes, I've met Maggie.'

'She was telling me a bit about the family history. Strange

happenings up in these hills. You ever noticed anything strange up there?'

'No, can't say I have.'

'Apparently one of them, Anne, who was married to the first Sullivan, she died up in the hills. Had an accident and bled to death.'

'You don't say?' His gaze was firmly fixed on the instrument case, fingers still touching the clasps. But there was a slight shift in his shoulders as a wave of tension tightened the muscles of his arms.

'Yeah, like the locals are still spooked about it. Maggie says that no one ever comes here. Is that right? Doesn't he have any visitors?'

'I wouldn't know. I'm usually attending to my work.'

'It is Ireland you're from, isn't it? The Sullivan family came from Ireland, or at least the first one did. Michael Sullivan, the one that was married to the woman who had the accident. Eighteen hundred and something he arrived. I guess that would make him a pioneer. He's got this big monument in the local graveyard, in fact there's quite a few of them there. Though not all—'

'Is that so? Well, it's getting late and I've got work to do first thing.' He stood up. 'Will you be finding your own way home or shall I walk you in that direction?'

'No, it's OK. I left all the lights blazing so it shouldn't be hard to find. And I've got this torch. I bought it today in case of emergencies and impromptu concerts.'

'Well, goodnight then.'

'Yes, goodnight.' And before I knew what was happening, I found myself once more outside in the rain.

There were no dreams that night, or if there were I had no memory of them. I woke late, feeling refreshed, hungry and ready for work. Sometime during the night the rain had stopped. The sky was clear blue but the sun burned high and hot, turning the bush into a steam bath.

The urge to work had become a pressing need so I studied the pictures on the wall. Fortunately there was no sign of any leaking at the studio end of the deck, so the paperwork had survived without damage. A concept of form had emerged, as I had hoped and trusted it would. As the drawings were to scale with the actual wood, I could now consider what rhythms and proportions to apply to adapt the concept to the three-dimensional block.

I had already prepared the wood by removing some of the outer layer with an adze. Using the drawings as a reference, I marked where the first cuts and hollows would come. The next task was to manoeuvre the block down onto the floor again and carve into the first spaces using the adze and saw. This process would be repeated over and over. Place the block on the bench, draw the wood, develop the design on paper, then transfer the design back to the wood again, ready for the next layer to be removed — the design leading me to reveal the shape within the wood, the grain and texture of the wood dictating the next adaptation of the design.

The first stages are the most exhausting as there is so much lifting and lowering and the tools used for the first shaping are heavier. As the form emerges the work becomes refined, the cuts smaller and more delicate. I do a lot of thinking before each step. I need frequent pauses to consider and, often, redefine my motivation and perspective. Sometimes I spend hours agonising over my emotional relationship with the form before I'm ready to proceed. Whoever said art is a relaxing therapy was talking a load of crap. It is physically, mentally and emotionally exhausting.

It was during one of those periods of contemplation that it suddenly hit me. I was considering what it was like to be isolated within the fabric of the wood, when it dawned on me that I was. Isolated, I mean. Alone with my block of wood. Apart from Connors and Sullivan, two dogs, a few thousand trees and some sheep. But no, really, I was cut off. No one I knew, friends, family, contacts in the art world, had any idea where I was. I had made no plans to go away, cancelled no appointments, told no one what I was doing. I had simply disappeared, literally, overnight.

I thanked God for the cellphone. Then I thanked God for voice mail as I patched into my answerphone. It had been only three days yet there was a queue of messages all wanting something from me, some just wanting to know where I was. Some I could ignore, others I rang back. Fortunately most of them were also out so I was able to leave reassuring communiqués without actually telling anyone where I was and why. A rest, a new phase of work, a refreshment of the soul, see you in a few weeks, love to all, goodbye.

But it made me think. There are so many threads connecting our lives with the lives of others. And so many of those threads cross and recross each other. Networking, I think, is the current term. But oh, how easy it is to slip through that net. To simply disappear. And no amount of recording or information sharing or electronic gadgetry would be able to track me down. Not one of the people who knew me would know where I was and how to start looking for me. Oh, there was Jason, of course, but I don't suppose it would have occurred to him to tell anyone. Besides, he would have to explain why I had left so suddenly. With all the phones and emails and whatever, I had managed to vanish without a trace. But that was what I wanted, wasn't it? Well, for the time being, yes, it was. And at least I had let everyone know I was OK, so no one needed to come looking for me.

Then it was back to work.

Bramble came by in the afternoon and I took time out to talk with her. She was not overly impressed with her new water bowl — dogs don't appreciate such refinements I learned — but the biscuits were a great hit. She taught me how to play fetch the stick, not an easy task in a bush clearing where the ground is littered with bits of broken twigs and branches. I marvelled at her ability to locate the correct piece. I even surreptitiously marked it with a notch to make sure she wasn't cheating on me but, no, she got it right every time. But of course, how dumb can you get? It wasn't the stick she was seeking out, it was the scent of my skin. The sudden comprehension of that intimate and tender act of friendship touched me so deeply that I stood there, among the fallen branches, and cried. Though I did wonder why I was so easily moved to tears.

For the next few days I was adrift in a timeless world, allowing the work to take me where it would. I laboured hard and when not in the studio I walked in the bush and up through the pines, my sketchbook and colours always to hand. This was also work, but of a different order.

I needed to be in contact with the wood and to know it as a living substance. I needed to know the trees as living entities, a different order of consciousness, but one I could connect with. And I needed to absorb that contact at a subconscious level for it to come back to me as inspiration. That's what inspiration is, I think: you allow art and meditation to blend together for long enough and pow! You get a result.

I played music when working, Mahler mostly. In the evenings I wandered around the lake or moved listlessly through the cottage. I did try to read, but was unable to focus on the page. Sometimes I sat out on the deck watching the moonrise and listening for Connors' music. He did not always play, but when he did I wondered if he knew I was listening. And during the hours of darkness that followed I was sometimes unsure which world I walked in.

Some nights after the rainstorm I again woke in front of the mirror as Connors' violin broke through the dream. Was it his playing that called me back? Or was it the sadness of the tune that drew me away? There was something out there, some consciousness that was not the bush or the pines, which had made itself my companion. Perhaps it was Anne Sullivan herself calling to me to save her broken body? Or was Connors leading me to damnation with his devil music? It all became part of the one reality, impossible to tell where one thing ended and another began.

Then there were the missing hours.

I put it all down to mental exhaustion, which, of course, made no sense. Yes, I was working hard, but I always do when I become immersed in a project. Nothing unusual about that. I'd done a lot of walking, true, but that was supposed to be a healthy form of exercise. In other ways I was actually resting: no parties, no late-night drinking sessions, no emotional stress, early to bed and, usually, late to rise. I should have felt fantastic when, instead, I felt constantly tired. But how else was I to explain away the holes in time?

The first one happened like this. I had just returned from a morning ramble through the pines and was ready for some lunch. The hot weather had continued and I felt dusty and clammy and spent ages standing under the shower. Then I padded, barefooted, into the bedroom, towelling off my hair and thinking about what to eat. Sitting on the edge of the bed I studied my reflection. Big decisions were to be made. To cut or not to cut? My hair was looking shaggy, a roughly chopped mop of two-inch spikes, the tips bleached almost white in the sun. I thought it looked great. On the other hand, who was here to see it? If this heat continued it would be more comfortable with an all-over shave. Perhaps I could leave a few bits at the front and the neckline to grow and shorten the rest . . .

Suddenly I felt as if I were falling, and jerked upright. Like the other awakenings, I was staring at my own reflection. Only this was daytime. I shivered, even though sunlight was pouring through the window, and pulled the towel around my shoulders. I was still sitting on the bed but the room looked different. The light had changed; shadows seemed to have jumped across the floor. I couldn't think how I had fallen asleep sitting upright, but that's what must have happened. What was I doing, anyway? Ah yes, my hair, that's it, I was thinking about my hair. I ran a hand through it. It was completely dry. I had got out of the shower a moment ago and it should still be dripping. How long had I been there? I looked through the window. The sun was low over the treetops and the afternoon was nearly gone.

SEVEN

THE sun slipped below the tree line and the room lost its light. I felt suddenly cold. Pulling a sweater over my head, I moved out onto the deck and sat on the steps trying to figure out what the hell was wrong with me. Not sleepwalking, surely? I'd never done that before. Yes, I had been working but I wasn't that stressed out. Was I? When Bramble wandered up and nosed my hand I clung onto her neck, burying my face in her shoulder. Warm tears wet both of us, smearing the dust in her coat. That was something else I don't normally do, cry for no reason. Get mad, yes, but not all this snivelling.

'I'm sorry girl, I can't be doing with this. I've got to get out of here.' I ducked inside, sluiced my face with cold water then, grabbing my purse and car keys, I ran for the truck.

'No you can't come. Go find Badger, go on. I'll be back later, I promise.'

I went to the bar. It was the only place I knew and the only place I knew anyone, if you could call one conversation with the barmaid knowing someone. But I needed to be where there were people.

The place had changed character for the evening. Yellow strip lights flooded the room, making it seem bigger and closer at the same time. The air hummed with the buzz of a dozen conversations and a country blues singer filled in the gaps via the CD player. Maggie was there — different sweater, same lurid pink lipstick. She was pulling mugs of beer from the pump and laughing with the customers, but she spotted me as soon as I entered and her face lit up. Thank God, I thought, and ran to her as if she were my salvation.

'Regan, hi, what's up? Is something wrong?'

'I need a beer, that's all. No, everything's fine.'

'Well, you don't look fine. Here get this down you. I'll be with you in a moment.'

'Thanks, I'm just thirsty. Been working, you know how it is—'

But she had gone, wiping the bar top and taking orders from a cluster of men at the other end of the counter. I took a long pull at my glass and realised how dry my mouth and throat were. My lips were cracked as I licked the foam from around my mouth.

Looking around I recognised one or two of the lunchtime crew but they were outnumbered by an older crowd that included a few women so I didn't feel so out of place. People sat at tables in twos and threes. One of the women was playing darts with a man in a police uniform, tie loosened off and hat thrown down on the table. Two young girls sat in a side booth, giggling, their heads close together, their legs long and bare beneath matching leather skirts. By the time Maggie came back my glass was nearly empty.

'Wow, I guess you did need a drink. Here, let me get you another. Sorry I had to leave you. This is usually the busiest time of day. People come in straight after work and some of them like to eat here.'

I had noticed the smell of cooking meat hanging in the air.

'You're not the cook too, are you?'

'No, that's my dad. Fancies himself as a chef. Are you hungry?'

'No. No thanks. I couldn't eat right now. The beer's fine. Listen Maggie, you know we were talking about the Sullivan family, their history? You said some of the locals might know more about it. Is there anyone here I could talk to?'

'Possibly, yes. Why, what's happened?'

'Nothing, it's just . . . Well, I found some old grave markers and wondered if anyone knew anything about it.'

'Well, there's old Trevor Benson just come in. He might know something. Hey, Trev, there's someone here wants to meet you.'

A barrel of a man in shorts dragged his hat off as he picked his way to the bar. He used the hat to wipe the sweat and dust from his head where a few wisps of white hair still defied the course of nature. His skin was pale and burnt red except where time had melded freckles into patches the size of cornflakes. He blinked at me with no sign of curiosity, and then focused on the beer pump.

'This is Regan, Trev. She's new round here. Interested in local history.'

He watched Maggie fill a large jug, then hand him a chilled glass.

'She's staying out on the Sullivan place.'

Trev whipped his head around to stare at me with red-rimmed eyes. 'Ya don't say. Well I'll be—'

'Can I shout your drink, Mr Benson? Perhaps you wouldn't mind me joining you for a few minutes?'

He continued to stare at me. His eyes were pale and watery; he looked like a startled rabbit. He didn't answer, but when I moved towards a side table he followed like a dog at heel, clutching his jug and glass.

'Is that right now?' he asked as we settled at the table. 'Staying at John Sullivan's, are ya?'

'Yes, that's right. Not at the house, though. I've taken the cottage for the summer. Apparently it belongs to his son, Jason.'

'Well I'll be . . . Ya don't say.'

'You do know the Sullivans then?'

'No more 'n anyone else. John comes in here most nights. We usually exchange a word, ya know, the weather, stock. Not that he's got much. Stock, that is. Barely keeps the place ticking over and most of that's down to his hired help.'

'That's the hairy one. Connors, isn't it?'

'Well, it is at the moment but they're always moving on. No one stays long.'

'Why is that?'

'Blowed if I know. He's a good enough boss and it's not what you'd call a heavy workload. But you say you're staying there. Some sort of farm worker, are ya?'

'No, I'm just a guest'

'Well I'm . . . That's a first. He's not one for visitors. They always kept themselves to themselves.'

'Who do you mean by "they"?'

'Well, John and his son Jason. And there used to be his father too, the boy's grandfather. He died about twelve years ago. Getting on by then, of course.'

'So you knew him. What about Jason's grandmother? That would be Jane, wouldn't it?'

'No, I never knew her. She died a long time ago, I was just a little lad. Why all the interest in the family?'

'Well, I found some gravestones, all Sullivan wives, Jane, Mary and Anne.'

'Ah, yeah. They say they've got the women buried up there.'

'Those three, anyway. What happened to the others?'

'There weren't any others. Not a good place for women. Never has been.'

'What do you mean? What happened to them? I heard Anne had some kind of accident.'

79

Trevor Benson took a long swallow of his beer and reached for the jug to top up his glass, then looked around nervously. It was early evening and, according to what Maggie had said, about the time when Sullivan would arrive for a drink. We were sitting either side of the table and I had a clear view of who was coming in and out while Benson had his back to the door.

'There's stories, but that's all they are. Tales to frighten the kids, keep them from trespassing on Sullivan land. It's like I said, they don't like intruders, never have done. But they're good people, always help a bloke in trouble. Ya can't say a bad word against 'em.'

'Who was Anne? Where did she come from?'

'That I don't know. Local girl she was, but the family would have been immigrants like Michael Sullivan himself. He came over from Ireland and bought up some land. Not as much as there is now, of course. But he was a bright young fella, did well for himself. Built 'imself a house. Oh, not the one that's still standing — the first one was just a shack. But it was a beginning. Found 'imself a wife and settled down. She was a spinster, well into her twenties, which was late to marry in those days. Women left home young. Fathers glad to get them off their hands. Not that there was anything wrong with her, ya understand. Only that she was bookish. Did a lot of studying and helped out at the school. Young Michael was a smart young man, could afford to be choosy, and with all the pretty young things around he chose the schoolmistress.'

'And she had a son?'

'She got pregnant straight away like they did in those days. No need for all this family planning then. New country. They needed young 'uns to work the land. But the little one didn't live longer than a few weeks. Nothing unusual in that then, but they say she wasn't the same after, turned her a bit strange. Still, wasn't long before she had another kid, David. And then young Michael's mother came out to join them, which was just as well.'

'Why was that? What happened to Anne?'

'It's like I said. She'd turned a bit strange. Reckon they thought the second baby would put things right, but it seems it got worse. Took to riding off into the hills. She'd leave the kid and go off all by herself for hours at a time. Often gone all day. Then one evening she didn't come back. Michael was worried, tried looking for her but nothing he could do in the dark. He was out again first light. Then, when her horse come home without her, they got up a search party. By the time they found her it was too late. They reckoned she'd fallen from her horse and hit her head on a rock. Probably lain there hours, unable to move. Lost too much blood. They say the earth was soaked with it.'

'Yes, I was told she bled to death.'

'Who can say what happened. That was before my time, before anyone's time that could tell you now. It's just what they say. After that young Michael took to himself, him and his son, David.'

Trevor swung round in his seat as the bar door opened. No doubt he expected to see Sullivan, as I did, but it was Connors who came in. He hesitated when he saw me, as if he were going to speak then thought better of it, nodded awkwardly and walked up to the bar.

'The son who lived was David Sullivan.' I was trying to remember the inscriptions on the grave markers. 'It was Mary who married him, wasn't it?'

'That's right, against all good advice, or so it's said.'

'Why was that?'

'As I say, it was a strange set-up. Kept to themselves. No one went near the place, apart from work hands that is, and they were all strangers passing through. Farm had grown by then, and they were well off. Young David finished his schooling and worked the farm with his father. Never mixed with the locals, and no one thought he'd marry. He were well past his mid-thirties when he came courting Mary Price. She was no spring chicken either.

Youngest of a big family and had stayed on to look after her father when her mother died. Then David came on the scene and next thing they were announcing their engagement.

'He had the new house built for her, the one that's standing now. It was grand for those days, but I reckon they could afford it. He furnished it with the good stuff his grandmother had brought over from Ireland. She'd be gone by then, of course, but the old man was still there. I think he lived right up to just before the war.'

'Mary had a baby, didn't she? Thomas?'

'Well, you've done your homework, haven't ya? Yeah, that was Tom Sullivan.'

'So what happened to Mary?'

'They say she went looking for Anne's ghost. That's all talk, of course. But yes, she did start wandering about in the hills. It must have been lonely out there for her with just the two old men. And I reckon it was something about the land, too. It gets to people, women especially. They're a bit less down to earth than men, I reckon, more inclined to let themselves get caught up with ideas. Anyway, she took to wandering off. And when she went missing they all said it was Anne's ghost that called her away.'

Trevor sat back and topped up his glass from the jug. Then he looked at me sharply. 'Why all the interest? You seen nothing strange up there, have ya?'

'No, nothing. Just curious, that's all.'

'No, well you don't want to start imagine things. That sort of nonsense causes no end of trouble.'

Trevor took another pull at his beer while I sat holding mine. My chest felt tight and I was thankful for the coolness of the glass. The room hummed around us; I could hear Maggie's voice rise above it and occasionally bursts of laughter came from a crowd near the bar.

I became aware that I was being watched. I turned my head, ever so slightly, hoping that Liam Connors wouldn't notice. But

there he was, sitting at the bar, staring at me. He nodded. I gave
a quick smile and turned back to Trevor.

'Was Mary dead too when they found her?'

'Oh, no, no. But she'd been out all night in a rainstorm. Wet
through and cold as stone. They carried her home and put her
to bed. Pneumonia'd set in. Died a few days later and buried
before anyone knew. Of course they all blamed Anne, or the
land itself, which doesn't make a lot of sense. But you know how
people are.'

I was aware of Liam Connors' gaze on me; the tiny hairs on
the back of my neck lifted. I could just see the edge of him at
the corner of my eye.

'And what about the other grave?' I asked. 'Jane's?'

'That's right. I was just a lad then. But I remember there was
talk.'

'What did they say happened to her?'

He shook his head. 'I was too young, didn't understand what
was going on. But no one knows for sure, anyway. There was an
inquest, of course, not that that made any difference. She died,
that's all.'

'I see,' I murmured, although I didn't. 'And did you know
Jason's mother?'

'Ah yes, young Sarah. Pretty little thing. Bit odd, though.
Involved with all that New Age stuff, she was, bit of a hippy.
People were surprised when she married John.'

Just then the door opened and Sullivan himself came in. He
hesitated when he saw me, but then came over to our table, his
hat twisting in his hand.

'Good evening, Regan. Didn't expect to find you here.'

'Just having a drink,' I said, which sounded really stupid.

'Gidday, Trevor, how's the family?'

'Yeah, good as gold.'

'Good. Well, I'll go and er . . . and . . .' He backed away to the
bar while I turned back to Trevor.

'You were saying about Jason's mother.'

'Ah, no. Can't tell you any more.' He darted a sideways glance towards to the bar. I turned to see that Sullivan had joined Connors and, although they had struck up a conversation, Connors was still looking steadily at me. I was the one who turned away.

'Oh, come on Mr Benson, there must be more to the story. You said the place was bad for women. What about Jason's mother? What happened to her?'

'No, I've said too much already. History's one thing, tales for dark nights and campfires. But it's that bloke's mother you're talking about,' he jerked his head in the direction of Sullivan, 'and his wife. I'm not gossiping, especially with him standing behind my back. He's a good bloke and this is a tight little community round here.'

'I thought you said he keeps himself to himself?'

'And so he does. But he's never harmed anyone. The Sullivans are a rum lot, but they're good people. Never crossed on a deal or underpaid what land or stock was worth. And a Sullivan's always the first to put his hand in his pocket when a man's in trouble. They don't mix, that's all. Makes folks suspicious and that's why the stories grew.'

He downed the remains of his beer and got up from the table. 'You'll have to excuse me now, have to be getting on home.'

Trevor Benson dusted his trousers down with his hat, then waved it towards the bar in a goodnight greeting to Sullivan.

'Look young lady, people were always dying in those days. The mystery to me was how they survived at all. You just be careful, OK?' And with that he turned and walked to the door.

I was conscious of being on my own again and of Connors still watching me, although I was determined not to look again. It was getting to be uncomfortable so I returned my glass to the other end of the bar. Maggie was still serving a steady stream of new arrivals and I waved to her as I headed for the door.

'Hey, Regan,' she called after me, 'come back when I'm not so pushed. We'll have a proper visit.'

Of course I dreamed that night.

My dreams were becoming as vivid as my waking life was becoming nebulous. It's not real, we say, only a dream. But I can't see how a dream is anything but real, or at least the subjective experience is. If you think about it, everything that ever happens to you happens inside your head. Sights, sounds, smells, they are all just scraps of information collected by our senses. It's our brain that unscrambles the signals and translates them into a picture. Hopefully this has some resemblance to what's going on outside in the physical world, because if it doesn't they call you insane.

Dreams happen inside your head too, only they come from somewhere else. Sure, they come from your imagination mostly, or from your subconscious or whatever. But not always. In any case, wherever the images come from, they're all events that you experience. Dreams and thoughts and feelings, they're all real, but they relate to different levels of reality. So, is your experience of them any less valid because it isn't happening in the physical world? The way I'd begun to dream seemed to be related to some kind of happening that wasn't of my making. Dreams have different textures. Mostly it's just stuff that's going on inside my head, though that's weird enough, but sometimes you get the feeling that it's more than imagination. And isn't imagination itself a kind of reality?

Sometimes when I dreamed at the cottage it was like there was another world pushing its way through into mine. And there were other times when what was happening was more real than anything I'd ever known. Certainly, what it was doing to me was real enough.

Anyway, that night I had another dream and I don't think it was all my doing.

I am walking through the hills looking for Anne.

The night is very dark and windy. A heavy sky obscures any moon there may be, but occasionally stars show themselves through breaks in the clouds. The wind pushes and tugs at me, turning me this way and that, causing me to stumble and slide on stony paths. There are long sweeps of hillside where the trees grow in sparse clumps, leaving broad avenues where I scramble up one side and tumble down the other, mud-streaked and bruised.

Anne is there, somewhere up ahead. I know she has fallen from her horse, but it is still possible to save her if only I can reach her in time. She is moving away from me, not lying on the ground but walking slowly, ever so slowly. Though I cannot see her I know she is wearing a long dress and a cloak that drags over the grass as she moves, leaving a trail to mark her passing. She moves with a steady grace, unhurried and with no concern for the elements or the passing of time. Her loosened hair writhes and coils, twisting upward on the wind. But, no matter how hard I try to run, no matter how I scramble on all fours, slip and snatch at the long grasses, stumble to my feet only to falter again, I cannot catch up with her.

Somewhere in the distance a horse whinnies, its distress carried on the air. And I am certain I can hear a fiddle. Maybe he could help me find Anne? But I would have to find him first and there is no time. She is moving away from me, gaining ground, and I have only the trail of her cloak to show where she has passed.

The grass is crushed where she has walked, I can see that quite clearly even though the darkness is unrelenting. There is something shimmering in the swath of broken grasses as if her cloak, in the wake of its passing, has laid down a tracery of light for me to follow. And I try, I try so very hard to keep up, but I know I am losing her. In the end I fall to my knees, heaving lungfuls of air, my hands pressed into the trail she has left behind. And as I lift my palms they glisten with wetness. I now see what it is that lights the path.

Blood.

Anne's own blood is washing the earth as she moves across the land.

I woke early, sunlight filtering through a misty haze, the grass heavy with dewfall, and wandered down to the lake. The surface was still and silent. There were wild flowers growing at the water's edge, foxgloves and some sort of yellow daisy, and I picked a handful, shaking the dew from their petals. Suddenly I knew why they were there.

Briefly returning to the cottage to collect a jar and fill it with water, I took the road back around the lake and up through the trees to the clearing. The name on Anne's gravestone stood out sharply where I had cleaned it a few days before. It took only a moment to clear away the weeds and grasses and arrange the flowers. The makeshift vase looked clumsy, but it would do until I found something more fitting. Any trace of a mound in the earth had vanished decades ago but a few smooth pebbles gathered and laid around the stone would mark out her territory.

It wasn't much to do for her, perhaps, but it was something.

EIGHT

THE next few days at the cottage were clearly divided into separate compartments. After that my memory seems to run together like wet paint streaking down a canvas. There was the work, which, at first, was all encompassing. Hours of intense concentration when I forgot to eat or drink and only the sinking of the sun reminded me that I had other needs.

Between bouts of working I needed to maintain constant contact with my source material. I'd spend hours wandering through the bush and the pines, adrift on the tides of the life force as it flowed through the living land. I came to know the trees. Their voices were constant, their leaves and branches never still, their mood changing with the shifting of the wind. And always there was a presence, something else that made me feel I was not alone.

Then there were dreams, dreams of walking, going to meet someone, perhaps the same someone who was watching me. But I never arrived. I always woke up, and often I'd find myself in front of the mirror. I put it all down to being stressed out. When I was more rested, things would get back to normal. That's what I told myself.

Bramble was my friend, though a fickle one. She took to

spending the nights sleeping on my sofa and the afternoons sunbathing on the cottage deck. She walked with me through the bush, though occasionally she would take off as if something had startled her. Usually I'd find her back at the cottage. Some days she needed my undivided attention, other times they'd run out on me, she and Badger, on some secret mission that took them away for hours. She always turned up eventually.

Badger had responsibilities. He spent a lot of time with Liam Connors, riding around in the little tractor, guarding the toolbox, barking at the cows — men's work. Sullivan didn't seem to mind both his dogs defecting, or if he did he never said anything, but they always seemed to know when he was going rabbit shooting.

I don't know how long I'd been there when the accident happened. That particular day the work had been progressing well. I had left a lot of the original block in its raw state, allowing whatever lived within it to appear as if emerging from its natural element. Something was growing from the wood; something that at first startled me, then left me amazed. I was now working on the finer details, sensing the soul of the thing that was coming to life, and allowing it to find its independence.

The phase of the heavier tools was long over and I had been using small gouges and chisels, the heel of my hand acting as mallet for such sensitive stokes. Some areas needed refining. I prefer to use an edge of broken glass for this, even though it means wearing goggles. Restraint was the key: now the end was so near it would be disastrous to rush. So I worked the glass as if it were a feather and scraped away layers as fine as whispers.

I had worked longer than I had intended, straining my eyes to labour until the last fire of the sun had brushed the lake with molten copper. I was aware of gunshots in the distance and forced myself not to wince each time they sounded. I know I don't eat animals but I'm not some New Age freak. Bugs Bunny and his extended family had caused enough damage around the place to justify a cull.

Eventually I realised it was too dark to work and I was too tired to eat. I dusted the wood shavings from my clothes, shut the door against the fast approaching night and poured a glass of wine. A hot bath, that's what I needed; a hot bath laced with something rich and creamy and smelling of exotic flowers. And another glass of wine. I drained the first and forced myself out of the sofa before I got so comfortable I missed the bath altogether.

As I got to my feet something threw itself against the door. There was a wild scratching and the latch rattled and jumped as if it were about to fly open.

'Who's there? What do you want?' As if some thug in a black ski mask was going to push a copy of his CV under the door. I looked around for something heavy, but anything resembling a weapon was outside on the deck with the intruder. Now wasn't that a sensible arrangement? I could see the headlines, 'Famous artist stabbed with her own chisel'.

Another blow at the door and more scratching. Demon claws, tearing at the woodwork. And then a familiar whining.

'Is that you Bramble?' A bark, then the scratching redoubled. 'OK, OK. I'll let you in. There's no need . . .'

But she would not come in. Instead she leapt back, paws splayed out in front and her back end bouncing as if she would bound away.

'Do you know what time it is?' I tried to say, 'I can't play now, I'm going to bed.' But my voice was drowned in a volley of barking, culminating in a growl. Then she collapsed in a heap at my feet and whimpered.

'I give in. You've got my full attention. You want me to go somewhere, right? Just wait a minute, let me find the torch.'

Moments later I was scrambling through undergrowth trying to keep up with a dog who was in too much hurry to bother with pathways. She would crash on ahead for a few metres, then come back to check I was still following. The yellow beam would catch her panting mouth and heaving flanks. Then she'd be off again. My hands were lashed by springing branches and I could feel a long scratch on my leg starting to bleed. When I finally caught up with Bramble she was in a small clearing, standing over something. I crawled through the last of the trees and stood upright, fighting for breath. All I could see was a hump of something black, almost lost against the shadowed earth.

'What's is it? What have you found?' Bending down I played the light on the black mass, and then reached out my hand. It was warm and soft and, thank God, it was still breathing. Bramble came forward and nuzzled the small body.

'Badger? Is that you, Badger?' I found his head and stroked his ears and neck. As I moved down his shoulder he yelped and I snatched my hand away. My fingers felt wet and sticky and there was a metallic smell as I wiped the smears down my shirt. I was scared. What was I supposed to do? Bramble had come to me for help and all I could do was be scared.

'Listen, you stay there. Stay with Badger. I'll go get someone. No, you stay, there's a good girl.'

I stumbled back towards the cottage, though what I was going to do there I had no idea. Perhaps the phone. But who would I call? Thankfully I'd left the light on so at least I could find the way. But everything had slowed down and my legs were weighted with lead. Then I could see another light beyond the cottage. Of course, the woolshed.

'Help! We need help here!' I had to stop and fight for breath before I could shout again. 'Connors! Liam! — please help me.' Before I had taken another half-dozen steps there was a second light bobbing towards me through the trees.

'I'm here, I'm here. What going on?' His shirt was flapping open and he was clutching one shoe.

'It's Badger. He's badly hurt. She scratched at the door and he was lying there and there's blood all over my hands.'

'All right, all right, now calm down.' He balanced on one leg, doing acrobatics with his spare shoe. 'Now, where is he?'

'I don't know. Back there in the bush somewhere. I didn't know what to do so I left Bramble with him and came to get help.'

'Then call her, she'll answer to you.'

I turned back to the trees and yelled her name. A moment's silence, then a trio of sharp yaps, not too far away.

'Good girl!' Liam called. 'You stay there, you hear me. Stay girl, just keep talking to us.' Then he was leading the way and we were thrashing through the tangled palms toward Bramble's whimpering. It could only have been a few metres before she was nuzzling my hand. Liam dropped to the ground, setting down his own torch, his hands moving over the hump of damp, black fur.

'Now hold the light steady. Let me see the damage. Gently now, there's a good boy.'

Badger let out a yelp. I flinched and bit my lip.

'I said hold the light steady. Here, bring it nearer, onto the front shoulder.' I focused the spotlight on a mess of fur matted with red. There was something white and jagged sticking up out of it.

'What in Jesus' name have you done to yourself, lad? This is bad. We can't deal with it here.' Liam rose to his feet, wiping stained hands down his trousers. 'How far are we from the roadway?'

I swung the beam around the clearing. 'The track's over there.'

'Right, go fetch your truck round.' I blundered off to find the lakeside path, Liam calling after me, 'And bring a blanket or something we can lift him on.'

I pounded along the track. It was only a short way to the cottage but the light from the doorway seemed to be retreating as fast as I was running towards it. Eventually I made it to the door but panicked when I thought I couldn't find the car keys. Of course they were still in the middle of the table where I'd left them. Then I nearly forgot the blanket and had to run back inside to snatch the rug from the sofa. The truck started first time, even though I dropped the keys twice. I'd forgotten how to find reverse, then the headlights wouldn't work and the windscreen wipers kept coming on instead. Somehow I managed to manoeuvre the vehicle round to where I could still see Liam's flashlight and scooted under the branches with the blanket.

'Now, we're going to have to move him into the truck. And we're going to have to be very quick and very gentle.'

Using the blanket as a stretcher we shifted him onto the back seat of the car. Badger yelped with every jolt and I could feel the pain shoot through him.

'I can't do this. We're making it worse. Can't we leave him here? I'll get some water and stuff, clean it up.'

'It's a surgeon he needs. And a surgery. Now, there's a vet not too far away and we'll take him there. That's the best we can do for him.'

'Shouldn't we phone, get the vet here?'

'It's only a few minutes away. Be quicker to take him.'

'But we're hurting him.'

'Trying to save his life is what we're doing. I'll sit in the back and try to hold him steady. Now, let's get out of here.'

Bramble leapt in after me and jumped over to the passenger seat. There was no time to argue with her so I let her stay and swung the truck out onto the road and round the lakeside.

'Steady there,' Liam shouted from the back. 'You're throwing us all over the seat. There'll be time to put your foot down when we reach the main highway.'

After all that bungling the journey took no time at all. It was only a short drive past the pub and the store when he told me to turn right.

'It's along here a' ways, through that gate. You can see the house from here.'

As I turned in at the gateway I slammed my hand down on the horn and left it there. It must have woken everyone in the district. Lights flicked on all through the house, and as we pulled up the door was flung wide and a man came running out. He was short and round and was wearing only pyjamas. Blue and white striped they were, and I thought of Christopher Robin and wanted to giggle. Then I wanted to slap myself for being so stupid and then I wanted to scream at him because Badger was hurt. But it was all right because Liam was already out of the truck and talking with the vet, who crawled into the back seat. Both the dogs were quiet now. Animals do that, don't they, when they know it's a vet? He seemed to know them, anyway.

'Well Badger,' he said, 'what have you been doing to yourself? Oh, I see. Oh, you poor fellow. Right, we'd better get him inside and take a proper look. I'll fetch a trolley. It'll be easier to move him.'

Bramble and I jumped down from the truck and joined Liam.

'Name's Harry Warner. I've had him out to the sheep a few times. Seems to know what he's doing. Perhaps it would be better if you and Bramble stayed here.'

Like hell we would, I thought, but there was no time to dispute the matter as Harry was already coming back and the two men lifted Badger out of the back seat. This time Badger made no sound and I began to think we were too late. I trailed after them, with Bramble at my heels, through the waiting room to the surgery door. Liam turned as I was about to enter.

'There's no need for you to come in. Wait here.'

'But I want to see—'

'Sit down will you, woman!'

And I did. And so did Bramble. We sat side by side on a rough wooden bench and waited for what seemed a century but could not have been more than five minutes. She kept looking up at me as if I was going to make it all right. The weight of her trust was unbearable.

Then the door opened and Liam came out. Up to then he had been calm and in control. Now there was a change, perhaps a shift in his stance or something about his eyes. I don't know. But somewhere, beneath all that hair, he looked shaken. Of course I thought the worst had happened.

'Harry's going to operate straight away.'

'Badger's still alive then?'

'Yes, but it's not good. It's his upper leg bone, where it joins the shoulder, it's fractured.'

'But how—?'

'It seems he's been shot.'

The word reverberated around the room and I heard it but could make no sense of the sound. Shot. What did that mean? How could he get shot? There were guns, yes. Rabbits, they were shooting rabbits. Not *they*. *He*. *He* was shooting rabbits. Sullivan.

'Sullivan shot him?'

'We don't know that. Even so, it must have been an accident. Harry needs me to give him a hand. You'd best be getting back now and I'll let you know.'

'We're staying right here, aren't we?' I looked to Bramble for support but she was sniffing around the corners of the room. So I, alone, stared at him in fierce defiance. He stared back. There would have been no giving way had Harry not called from the inner room; Liam answered by turning his back and closing the door in my face. I sat down again, preparing for a long wait.

It was a bleak room in which to spend a night. I studied the poster explaining all the breeds of dogs and cats, and found out all about feline enteritis, kennel fever and the most up-to-date methods of controlling fleas and intestinal parasites, to say nothing of ear mites.

Bramble gave up waiting and went to sleep on the floor. It

could easily have been her. Shot. Just saying the word brought pain: it was like being punched in the stomach. How could you shoot a dog and not know? The animal must have howled in pain. Didn't he hear it? Didn't he even notice they were missing? The night just went on and on. I didn't have a watch or clock to measure it by. There were sounds beyond the closed door — the hollow hum of half-heard voices, barely audible thumps and the clanking of metal — all of which told me nothing.

I grew so used to staring at the blank door that when it eventually opened I was taken by surprise. Liam's clothes were streaked with blood and he was wiping his hands on a towel. I was too afraid to ask and he simply nodded at me. Harry followed, still wearing his pyjamas with a green plastic apron and a matching cap. They brought the stink of disinfectant with them.

'Well, I think he'll do.' That was Harry. 'He's still recovering from the anaesthetic but he's stable. Fortunately, he hadn't lost too much blood and the bone was shattered but only in the one area. It was a glancing blow. The bullet hadn't actually penetrated. It could have been a lot worse. Even so, the limb will have to be pinned for a few weeks and I doubt he'll be able to run far again. Shame for a working dog.'

'Working dog?' Liam laughed. 'That pair of clowns never did a day's work in their lives. No, he'll do fine.'

'Well, he's not out of the woods yet. We'll see how things are in the morning. I'll let you know if anything changes, so if you don't hear, give me a ring about lunchtime.'

'I will do. And thank you once again.' Liam reached out his open hand and they shook and held wrists, the way men do when they've shared some heroic episode. 'Thank God you were here, Harry, I don't know what we'd have done.'

'I'll see you tomorrow, then.'

'Right.'

All through this I had stood by, made speechless by fear. Bramble and I followed meekly as Liam led the way back to my vehicle and I clambered up, fired the engine and worked the gears. For the past few hours I'd been cowered by the horror of events. Now I was back in charge. Fear had given way under the tide of relief, and anger started to boil up inside. I gripped the wheel as if it were Sullivan's neck.

Liam looked shattered and neither of us spoke. I moved the truck off the road, onto the station track, then through fields and up to the pine plantation, plummeting down through the trees.

'Just drop me off by the path,' he said. 'It's only a few paces through to the shed.'

'I'm not dropping anyone anywhere until we've paid that bastard a visit.'

'Hey, no. Jesus, you can't go barging in there now. Leave it till the morning.'

'Well I'd hate to spoil his beauty sleep, but his dog nearly died out there and I think he deserves to know about it.'

'Look, it was obviously an accident. We don't even know if it was him that fired the gun.'

'Well, who else was taking pot shots at rabbits then? How long had the dog been out there? Why wasn't he out looking for him?'

'You know those dogs, they go their own way.'

'Not when their master's out bunny hunting they don't.' I slammed on the brakes and skidded to a halt in front of the house. I can't remember what I had in mind. Perhaps I was going to knock his teeth out. But I can remember hammering on the door and yelling.

'Sullivan, Sullivan, wake up! Where's your bloody dog, Sullivan? Shouldn't you be out looking for him?'

'Come away, will you now? There's nothing to be gained by making a scene.' Liam had grabbed me by the sleeve and was trying to drag me back to the truck.

'He's not getting away with this. Do you hear me, Sullivan? You're not going to turn your back on this one.'

That's when the door opened. Sullivan was still dressed and a light came from the back of the house. He stared at me vacantly.

'Your dog, Sullivan? Where's your damned dog?'

'What about the dog? What's happened?' He swayed against the doorframe, trying to focus, and then turned and wavered down the hallway towards the kitchen. I struggled free of Liam's grip and stormed after him.

'You shot him, that's what you did. You shot your own bloody dog and for all you care he could be dead.'

Sullivan had slumped onto a chair, his hand round a whisky bottle that was already partly empty.

'That's right, you have another drink, Sullivan. Forget all about it. Why the hell should you care what happens to a dog? It's not as if it's your responsibility.'

'You have to understand, Mr Sullivan, she's very upset. It's been a long night.' Liam was still trying to pull me out of the house. 'Will you come away now, woman? You're only making things worse.'

'How could anything be worse than that pathetic sod? Look at him. So drunk he doesn't even know what I'm talking about.'

Sullivan did look bewildered, turning helplessly from one to the other of us. Liam stepped forward, trying to get between us. I don't know what he thought I was going to do.

'It's Badger, Mr Sullivan. He's been injured. It seems there was a shooting accident.'

'Badger? Oh, no. Where is he?' Sullivan looked around as if he expected to see the dog in the room.

'He's with Harry Warner. He's fixed him up for now, but we'll know better in the morning how things stand.'

'Shot, you say?' He looked confused and . . . what else was it? Yes, that look had crossed his face again. It was fear, raw fear. But I was too fired up to care what was happening to him.

'Yes, apparently some joker mistook him for a rabbit.'

'Regan found him, and it was a bit rough on her—' Liam continued.

'Yes, well some people actually care what happens to injured animals.'

'— and there's nothing more anyone can do for tonight. So, we're sorry to have disturbed you.'

'Disturbed him? Yes, I must say he looks bloody disturbed—'

'So will you come away now?' This time he took a firm hold and dragged me down the hall.

'— people like you shouldn't be allowed near animals. Or humans for that matter.' I was still shouting when Liam pushed me out onto the deck and slammed the front door.

'Will you shut the fuck up!' he yelled. 'There's enough harm done for one night without you adding to it. Now get in the car. I'll drive.'

Bramble was waiting in the passenger seat, having chosen to remain politically neutral. I climbed into the back, obedient but still spitting fire, while Liam started the engine, reversed the truck and drove around the lake towards the cottage.

'Surely you're not going to let him get away with it?'

'It was an accident. Look, I know he's an alcoholic and I know he's irresponsible. And I'll grant you he shouldn't be left in charge of a lettuce patch, let alone a working station. But he wouldn't deliberately hurt an animal. Besides, I'm not at all sure it was him.'

'Oh, don't talk rubbish. Of course it was him.'

'The one thing he's trained those dogs to do is to keep behind him when he's firing. And he would never take a shot unless he knew where they were. Besides, when I heard the shooting it was late. Too late for him to be out. He'd be downing the bottle by then.'

'Well, who could it've been if it wasn't him?' I asked.

'I don't know. Poachers maybe.'

'What do you mean, poachers? There's nothing here worth

poaching. If you thought it wasn't Sullivan, why didn't you go after them? Surely you realised someone was shooting at something?'

His shoulders tightened as he gripped the wheel. He drew breath as if to speak, but there was only a long silence while I counted, five, six heartbeats. Then he breathed again and when he did speak his voice was soft and precise. 'Yes, I'm well acquainted with the sound of a gunshot.'

Something had gone wrong with this conversation. I'd gone too far, or perhaps I was trampling on sensitive ground. Whatever it was, Liam was somewhere else. Then the truck bumped over a rock and swerved and his attention was forced back to the steering wheel.

'Sorry,' I said, 'I just thought . . . But it's part of your job, isn't it? Looking after things?'

'Well, after that little drama back there I wouldn't count on still having a job.'

'That's ridiculous. It was me who was mouthing off at him. I can understand him turning me out. But not you. You don't think he'd really sack you, do you?'

'I don't know what he's likely to do.'

'Don't worry. I'll talk to him, explain everything.'

'I think you've said enough. Just leave the talking to me.'

We pulled up outside the cottage and Liam jumped down, Bramble scrambling past him, leaping onto the deck. I stepped down slowly, feeling the blood rushing to my face.

'I seem to have made a bit of a mess of things, don't I?' I said. Then for some reason I burst into tears. Not dainty little sniffs, but great, big, howling sobs. Liam stood in front of me, hands clutching at the empty air. He tried to say something but when he opened his mouth nothing came out. Then, full of trepidation, he reached out and took hold of my shoulders, holding me at arm's length as though I were a piece of wet laundry and he didn't know which line to peg me out on.

100

'Look, the dog's going to be fine,' he whispered.

'It's not the bloody dog,' I howled. 'I don't even like dogs.'

'Oh, is that so?' Gently and awkwardly he stepped nearer and pulled my head into his shoulder and I buried my nose in his shirt. I thought it would be all dirty and sweaty. Instead it smelled of freshly laundered linen, like the sheets my grandmother smoothed on my bed when I used to stay with her in the summer. He just went on holding me awkwardly. That made me cry even more, and at that moment I hated him completely and his hairy face and his shirt that smelled of my childhood.

'I'll fix everything in the morning,' he said. 'Sullivan probably won't even remember us being there. A good night's sleep is what you need. Look there, I think you've got a house guest.' He nodded towards Bramble, who was waiting patiently by the door.

'She shouldn't be staying here. She's not my dog. I don't even like dogs.'

'Yes, well, you try telling her that.'

NINE

THERE were no dreams.

I slept deeply through what remained of that night and the following morning, eventually drifting to the surface in a room awash with the golden light of midday. I lay in bed feeling warm and at peace, watching the ceiling reflect the dance of sunbeams on the lake. I could have lazed there indefinitely but indolence is inevitably overcome by the need for coffee, and a shower.

Bramble was still asleep on the sofa. She opened one eye as I passed, flipped her tail and went straight back to sleep. The sofa seemed to be her favourite spot. Last night she had insisted on staying with me but again refused to go into the bedroom, although I would have welcomed her company.

I spent ages under the shower before returning to the kitchen. According to my watch, which I had stopped wearing and now hung on one of the cup hooks, it was gone twelve. I wondered if Liam had rung to see how Badger was. Perhaps I should go over to the woolshed and find him, though I couldn't imagine he would welcome a visit from me after the way I had behaved the night before. Then there was Sullivan. Ouch! Maybe it would be better if I just kept out of everyone's way.

I was putting the kettle on, still swathed in a huge towel and dripping footprints over the floor, when there was a gentle knock at the door.

'Yes, who is it?'

'Connors here, um, Liam.'

Bramble was instantly awake, and as soon as the door was open an inch she forced her nose through to pounce all over him, tail working like a propeller.

'I'm sorry, I seem to have come at a bad time.'

'No, that's OK. I've just got out of the shower. Yes, I suppose that's obvious. I was about to make coffee. Would you like some?'

'Shall I make the coffee while you make yourself decent?'

What a wonderful expression, I thought. 'Make yourself decent.' As if I could.

'Great idea. I use coffee beans. You have to put them in a grinder . . . oh sorry. Yes, I expect you know how to make coffee. Yes, well, I'll only be a few minutes. Mine's milk and two sugars.'

Slipping into the bedroom, I listened for sounds of progress from the kitchen while towelling off and pulling on shorts and a T-shirt and fluffing up my hair. By the time I emerged the cottage was filled with that special morning fragrance.

'Thanks for doing that.' I took the mug from him. 'Um, wonderful. Yes, you do know how to make coffee.' It was good, strong and sweet; the first gulp kicked me into life. 'Any news of Badger?'

'Yes, that's what I came about. I rang Harry just now. Says the dog's doing fine. We could go and see him if you like. No. Well, to be honest, I'd like to go see him but I've not got my own transport. It's not far from the pub. I thought perhaps I could buy you a beer in return.'

'Can Bramble come?'

'Sure, why not?' He was silent for a moment, sipping the coffee and studying the toes of his shoes. 'How's the work going?'

'Oh, fine. The first piece is finished, just needs oiling. I was going to do that today.'

'Don't suppose I could have a preview?'

'Yes, of course.' It slipped out before I thought what I was saying and immediately wished I'd bitten my tongue. First viewings should be for tried and trusted friends who know your work and know how deeply they're allowed to dent your ego. Too late now, but . . . Well, what the hell. I led the way out to the deck and removed the cover sheet from the bench. He stared in silence for a long time.

'Of course, it might not be your thing,' I muttered.

Silence. He started to walk around it slowly, twisting his body to view from every angle. Then he turned to move in the other direction.

God, he hates it, I thought, probably thinks I'm mad. I bet he'll say it's nice just to be polite.

'It's not representational, of course. I mean, it's not supposed to look like something in real life.'

No response. He kept looking and circling while I cringed in the corner. People who don't understand art should never be allowed near a studio. I bet his only experience of sculpture was a set of flying ducks his mother had over the mantelpiece. He stood still, sniffed and pulled at his earlobe. If he's Irish he must be Catholic. Bet he has those statues of the Virgin Mary at his bedside. Bet they're made of plastic. And glow in the dark.

Then he nodded, slowly. He looked directly at me, about to speak. If he'd said it was nice I think I would have hit him.

'It's breathtaking. And completely different from your work in the *Manscape* exhibition. The way the figure emerges from the raw wood as you move around it, then it's like it's being reabsorbed again, as if it's surfacing from its own element. It's taunting us, saying I'm not of your world. You can sense a part

104

of me but you'll never really know what I am. Look at that face. There's intelligence there. But it's not like anything we know.'

His hand reached out, tracing the line of grain with his fingers. It felt electric, as if he were touching a part of my mind.

'The way it's turned in upon itself — aware of us, but it doesn't need our approval, so primitive it makes us irrelevant. There's a kinship here with some of the ancient Celtic forms, you know, the pagan concept of intelligence within nature. Yet this is totally of *now*. And *here*, this place. No wonder you spend so much time wandering about in the bush.'

For the first time in my life I truly understood the meaning of the expression 'gob-smacked'. The muscles of my face had ceased to co-ordinate, leaving my eyes bulging and my lower jaw unhinged. I was powerless to control anything. I tried to speak but only a few strange sounds came out.

'Did you say this is the first piece? There's going to be a series?'

I nodded.

'Then I feel really privileged that you've allowed me to see it.' He moved around the figure again and shook his head. 'You know, I'm just blown away by this. I can see where your influences come from. There's certainly something of Noguchi in the rawness of the wood but the style is unmistakably your own. It's amazing.'

'You know my work?' I'd found my voice.

'Mainly from magazines, I'm afraid. But yes, I went to *Manscape* when it was showing in London. And I saw some of your pieces in Melbourne, in the University Library. You know you've come such a long way from *Skyliners*. How did this all happen?'

'I, er . . . It was the trees,' was all I could manage.

'Yes?' he prompted, waiting eagerly for some profound statement of artistic motivation.

'I came here. And . . . and I saw trees.' I sounded like a

gibbering idiot. 'I mean, I saw them. Not just trees. They are alive. I can feel them thinking. Well, not thinking, exactly. But there's a sort of consciousness, an awareness.'

'Sentience, do you mean?'

'Yes, that's it. Sentience and, well, they're like a related group. Sort of like a colony of bees. Or ants. But not like that. With trees each one is different. But they know each other. They can think all together, like in a chorus.'

'Yes, well trees are living things. They emanate an aura, a sort of energy, like all things. It's like everything in nature has a spirit or a soul and it can be sensed by those who are in harmony with the Earth.' He gulped down the remains of his coffee. 'Which you are, of course, even if you don't know it. Still,' he did an abrupt turn about, leaping down from the deck and heading for the truck, 'we'd better be off to see that dog before Harry goes out on his sheep rounds.'

But there was more I wanted to tell him.

'There's something else out there,' I whispered. 'It knows I'm here. It watches me.' But Liam Connors was already standing by the truck and I don't think he could have heard me.

It was still early in the afternoon and lunchtime drinkers, draining their glasses before returning to work, watched us as we walked up to the bar. It was good to see Maggie again. I had called in a few times since my first visit and she always stopped to talk. I think she enjoyed a break from male company. So I could see she was surprised, and a bit put out, when I arrived with Liam. She gave nothing away as she took his order, but when turning to pour our drinks she caught my eye. I forget who once said that the spoken word had ruined the art of conversation but a lot can be said with a frown or a raised eyebrow. On the surface it translated as, 'What the hell are you doing with him?' and 'Just having a drink, that's all', but there was a strong undertow of meaning in that silent communion. She stood two cold glasses in front of us and wiped the counter over with a cloth.

'How's the dog then?'

'You heard about it?'

'Of course I heard about it. This is a small place, you know. If someone sneezes at one end of the street you feel the draught at the other. So what happened? I heard he'd been shot.'

I was drawing breath to answer when Liam flashed me a look of cold steel.

'We don't know what exactly happened,' he said. 'But whatever it was, it was an accident.'

'Well, I should hope it was, poor thing.' Maggie bridled. 'Is he going to be all right?'

'Yes, he seems to be fine.' I managed to get in first this time. 'We've just come from Harry's place. He's keeping Badger there for a few days. At the moment he's all bandaged up and can't even stand. I expect he'll need a lot of looking after when he's allowed out. Can't see Sullivan making a good nurse, though, can you?'

'I think we'll go sit over there by the window.' Liam snatched up both our drinks and, before I could protest, walked away from the bar.

I gave Maggie a shrug and followed him to a corner table. A few of the drinkers watched us cross the room. There were some exchanged looks and raised eyebrows, more face dialogue, before they concluded we were of no further interest and turned their backs. Meanwhile Maggie came around the bar with a bowl of water for Bramble, who obviously drank here regularly. She slurped it eagerly, splattering the dusty floorboards, then ambled over and flopped down under the table.

'I suppose I ought to apologise for last night.'

'You were upset,' he said. Then he looked straight at me and his eyes softened. 'You did well for the dog. If I'm ever in trouble

I'd hope to have you on my side.'

'What about Sullivan? Have you seen him?'

'Yes, I had to go up to the house this morning. It's as I thought — he didn't remember much about anything, only that we'd been there and there'd been some problem with Badger.'

Liam fell silent for a few moments. His fingers traced the condensation as it ran down the outside of his glass. Then, as if reaching a major decision, he said, 'You know, he's a strange one, that Sullivan.'

Now, how was I supposed to respond to that? There I was, sitting across the table from the weirdest man I had ever encountered.

'What do you mean by "strange"?'

'Well, he was really upset when I explained what had happened to Badger. I'd anticipated that he would be, naturally. But it seemed to go much deeper than that. It was like he was badly shaken. And scared. Yes, that was it, he was scared. Yet he said it was probably poachers and nothing to worry about. He was anxious to know how the dog was faring, of course, so I thought he'd want to go straight to the surgery. But no, he'd have nothing to do with it. That's when I came to you for a lift.'

'Oh, I see. Well, it sounds to me as if he doesn't give a shit about the poor, damned dog.'

'No. No, that's the strange thing. I'm sure he was genuinely concerned. Said Badger must have the best care. No expense to be spared. Harry's to send him all the bills. Then, when I said Badger would be home in a few days he said he couldn't have the dog in the house. He's to go to the woolshed with me and I'm to be his nurse.'

'Huh! At least he hasn't given you the push.'

'Far from it. Practically begged me to stay and tend the animal. And he's offered me a lot more money if I do.' Liam drained his glass, then gazed into it as if hoping to find an explanation.

'Doesn't he even want to see his dog?'

'No, apparently not.'

'OK, I grant you that is weird.' I stood up, taking both glasses. 'Thirsty weather. I'll get this round.' I moved away before he had a chance to object.

'Same again please, Maggie.' I was aware of her eyeing Liam over my shoulder. 'Seen anything of Sullivan lately?'

'What? Oh, yeah. Part of the furniture. He's in here every night.'

'What about last night?'

'As always. Came in about sundown for his usual couple of beers. Though I dare say that was just for starters. The serious drinking doesn't begin till he gets home, or so they say.'

'So he would have been here about eight, nine o'clock?'

'Yeah. Why? What's so important about Sullivan's drinking hours?'

'Oh, nothing. Just wondered.' I slipped the money onto the bar and scuttled back to our table with fresh glasses.

'Here's to you!' Liam took a long drink of beer, leaving a fringe of froth along his moustache. As he stared out the window I looked at his hands wrapped around the wet glass. They were large, the fingers long and bony, knuckles jutting out like small pebbles. There was no seemingly permanent line of blackness beneath the nails, like you see on the hands of workmen. Liam's nails were white and neatly trimmed. I looked down at my own hands. They, too, are working hands, covered with tiny white scars. All the scars are old, of course, from my student days. When you work with sharp tools you soon learn not to cut yourself. Apart from the pain, blood stains the wood: hours of work can be ruined by a dripping wound. Then there were Liam's hands. A bit rough, cuts and scratches, a raised callus where he'd swung a hammer. But that was all recent, the cuts barely scabbed over. He might be a casual labourer now, but Liam Connors and hard physical work were not what you'd call old friends.

'You know a lot about art,' I ventured.

'Is there any reason why I shouldn't?' Was it possible to say anything to this man without offending him?

'No, of course not. It's just that not many people do. It helps to have someone around who understands what you're trying to say. Thank you.'

He nodded. And then I think he smiled. At least his eyes did.

'I'd read a lot about you, of course,' he said, 'but you're not in the least what I expected.'

'Oh? In what way?'

'Well, for one thing, I thought you'd be a lot taller.'

That's when I took a swipe at him and knocked the remains of my beer all over the table.

After I'd cleaned up the mess and said goodbye to Maggie I found him waiting outside, staring at the wall. I went to see what was so interesting, and found he was looking at a brightly coloured poster tacked to the boards.

'Wow, a gypsy fair,' I said. 'What's that all about then?'

'They're travellers. Go all over the country.'

'I've never seen them before.'

'Well, you wouldn't. Not in a big city. But in country places, where they can bring their vehicles through and find a field to set up, they make a regular annual visit. They're mostly people who've got tired of the pace of life, trying to find a different way of being. There's all sorts of stalls and craftsmen, you know, handmade things. You'd enjoy it.'

'I guess I would. How come you know so much about it?'

'Well, I travelled along with them for a bit. Got to know a few of them. Friends like.'

'You're just full of surprises, aren't you?'

I drove back with Liam sitting uncomfortably beside me, staring straight ahead. The few animals looked up as we passed but mostly we were ignored.

'Sullivan doesn't seem to do much about the place. Does that leave a lot of work for you to do?'

'Hardly any. It's more like the station's a hobby, only he pays someone else to do it for him.'

'So what do you do all day?'

'Oh, there's always some jobs that need attending. I've been fixing up fences and sorting out the sheds. There's lots of old tools there, not been used for years,' he said.

'What about the animals?'

'Just a few sheep and cows. Some hens behind the house.'

'Don't they have to be milked or sheared or something?'

That almost made him laugh. 'Nothing has to be milked. They're beef cattle. All they need is health checks and feeding. I call in Harry if there's any of them looking troubled. And the feeding's something they take care of themselves most of the time, as do the sheep. It's just a matter of moving them from one paddock to the next. When the sheep need shearing or dipping, Sullivan calls on one of the lads from over the way to give a hand. Joseph, he's got a good pair of sheep dogs. Put you two to shame, don't they, Bramble?'

Bramble leaned over from the back and licked Liam's ear. She nearly fell off the seat as I turned onto our track, up and over the hill and into the pines.

'But you must know something about the animals to be able to look after them.'

'I do. I used to work on farms during the holidays.'

It was purely on impulse that I swung off the track, turning right and onto the edge of the pines. I seemed to have come this far with Liam and there was part of him that I felt I could trust. I tend to trust people on impulse. It's an instinct that usually backfires on me, but I figured that if he understood my work maybe there were other things he would understand.

'Where are we going now?' he asked.

'Come on, there's something I want to show you.' I jumped down from the truck and found the path through the trees to the clearing.

'Ah, the gravestones. Yes, I have come across them.' He stood over Jane's marker.

'I thought you probably had. But have you read them? I mean really looked at them, the dates?'

'Can't say I've given it much thought. They were all young, I suppose, but I would think life wasn't easy in the early days. Lots of people didn't make it.'

'It wasn't that long ago, not really. Well, not for Jane, anyway. And why were they buried here? There's a cemetery just up the road. I've had a look round. Plenty of Sullivans in there, some of them a lot older than these. Michael Sullivan's there. He was the first to come from Ireland. Anne was his wife. Yet they buried her here.'

'Well, she died a long time before him.'

'Yes, that's just it. Three women. All married to Sullivans. Three successive generations. All three had just the one son. And they all died when they were about thirty. Don't you think that's odd?'

Liam was quiet. He went on looking, moving from one stone to the other. 'I grant you,' he said eventually, 'it is strange.'

He bent down, tracing his finger over the letters of Anne's name. Then he moved over to the other graves and studied them for a while. 'Someone's been cleaning these up.'

'Yes, that was me. I felt someone ought to do something for them. It's like they've all been abandoned. There's no one that cares about them any more.'

'And what about the flowers? I suppose it was you put those there? Why that grave in particular?'

'That's Anne. I sort of . . . Well, it may sound silly but I feel I know her. It was hearing about the way she died. She was out

112

here, up in the hills somewhere. It was a horrible death and she was alone. And then Mary followed her. They say she died looking for Anne's ghost. I don't know about Jane.'

'And as a consequence you feel you have some kind of rapport with Anne?'

'I told you it sounds silly.'

'And you're sure that's all it is?'

'Of course. What else?'

'It's a grim tale right enough. Easy to get caught up in it. Tell me, why did you bring me here?'

'I thought you might know something, you being from Ireland. I mean, is it some sort of Celtic tradition, burying young women in the backyard?'

'No. I'm sure the holy fathers would take exception to that.'

And then something happened in his face. It was as if another idea, or a memory, had invaded his thoughts, throwing his mind into conflict.

'Yes, what is it? You know something, don't you?'

'I don't *know* anything. It's just . . . well . . . the name Sullivan. There were stories.'

'What sort of stories?'

'No I can't say, I don't recall exactly. Besides, you've got an overactive imagination and I won't be feeding it on half-remembered scraps.' He moved back to Anne's grave and examined the stone again, then the others. 'You say you found Michael Sullivan? What was the date on his stone?'

'I think it was 1913. But I worked out he was quite old by then. Apparently he emigrated from Ireland when he was a young man.'

Liam shook his head slightly and stood looking at the ground.

'You do know something. Tell me, for God's sake.'

'I'm not sure. I'd need to ask. There is someone who might know, but he's halfway round the world.'

'Could you phone him?'

'It's not that easy, not the sort of thing you can deal with in a long-distance phone call. He might have to do some research. I wish I had access to the Internet. As if anyone around here would have a computer.'

'You're not going to believe this.' I started running toward the truck. 'Come on. Back to my place.'

Of course, talking him into it wasn't that easy. He put up endless objections while I set up my laptop on the table. I could see he was itching to get his hands on it so I let him scan through the set-up and programs. He seemed to know what he was doing. It was quite new and still had a sheaf of techno-babble leaflets with it, which Liam studied with great intensity. I think, in the end, it was the technology that won him over.

'OK, I'll ask. I have this friend who has access to collections of old local folk tales. But that's all they are, mind you — tales, rumours thought up by superstitious people who created mysteries to feed their own fears.'

'Like me thinking the Sullivan women were all victims of an axe massacre?'

'Yes, something like that. What I'm saying is I might have remembered it wrong — there may not be anything. Even if he finds something it would have been a long time ago, nothing to do with here and now. And more than likely it'll be a load of nonsense.'

'Yeah, right. I'll control my imagination.' But you want to know too, I thought, don't you, Liam Connors? You know there's something going on here.'

He accessed the email program, clicked the mouse on the new mail icon, then sat pulling at his beard and staring at the blank message window.

'Well, go on then.'

'Look, this friend. It's a bit delicate, you see, my contacting him. And it would be better if it were kept private.'

'Well, who around here is going to want to know about your friends in Ireland? Oh, I see. You mean me. Fine, I'll go and make us some tea.'

From the kitchen end of the room I could see the concentration on his face as he watched the screen. His eyebrows creased together like the wings of a dark bird and his hair stuck out in wild tufts where he had raked his hands through it. I had to admit he was looking less like Rasputin and more like Albert Einstein. For a two-finger typist he was fast, certainly no stranger to a keyboard. Meanwhile I was clattering mugs and making a fuss of opening a box of teabags.

Just as the kettle boiled he said, 'Right, now, it's in the out-box. We need to plug into a phone line to send it.'

'Oh, I hadn't thought about that.'

'No problem. There's a phone at the woolshed. Leave the tea, we'll come back for it.'

A few minutes later we were at his place listening to the dial-up tone. I stood behind him, making a great show of averting my face from the screen. He hesitated, seeming on the brink of a fatal decision, then, with a sigh of submission, he took hold of the mouse. I happened to glance over just as he clicked on the send button and saw the message window vanish.

'There,' he said, as the screen went black, 'it's all done. I'll switch off. I don't know how long it will take to get a reply, if we get one at all. Better leave it two or three days.'

Back at the cottage we drank our tea and talked of other things. At least I talked, mostly about art, which seemed a safe subject. He wasn't really listening, though, deep in thought, as if already regretting what he'd done.

After a while he left and I was alone with the laptop.

Yes, I know you're not supposed to read other people's mail, but it was my computer. To be fair, it was at least an hour before

I switched it on. Even then I looked up some old notes I'd made about various wood merchants and checked some exhibition dates before I took a quick glance at the email program. I thought I ought to check the sent items box to make sure the message had been sent. There was nothing there. But it was there, I'd seen it. And I saw him send it. He must have deleted it. I clicked on deleted items. That, too, had been emptied. Whatever he'd sent, whoever he'd sent it to; the retained copy had been wiped off without a trace.

TEN

CHRISTMAS came around, as did Jason. In fact they both arrived unannounced at the same time, so I was thrown completely off balance.

Badger had come home swathed in bandages. Bramble was naturally overjoyed and expected him to play as usual. It took a lot to convince her that he was confined to quarters with Liam. Obviously her visits to the invalid had to be restricted but, as she had moved in with me, it was easy for us to drop by the woolshed. Liam and I soon fell into a routine of morning coffee and afternoon beer. It was all part of the rhythm of the day and Bramble knew when it was time to bully me into taking a break.

Liam and I talked, mostly about the dogs. He seemed to know a lot about animals and their behaviour, which, I suppose, was only to be expected from a farm labourer with an intimate knowledge of the arts and computer technology. Once or twice I persuaded him to play a tune for me. It was then, through the music, that I was allowed a glimpse beneath the carapace. What I saw there was something tender, something that knew kinship with pain. But mostly we both worked hard at keeping it all very light and superficial. Often he would take Bramble out with him while I was occupied. Badger slept the day away in the woolshed, allowing his body to heal. And I worked.

The second piece had made its beginning. The first had been about the consciousness of trees. The new sculpture was about something else, that other energy of which I was becoming increasingly aware. Small eyes watched me all the time. There were thousands of creatures roosting or burrowing on the hillsides and around the lake. I was an intruder on their territory, some large and terrible danger to their perilous lives. But that wasn't it.

At first I thought it was the trees and welcomed the sensation as a sign that I was on their wavelength. It wasn't until the second piece was under way that I realised that what I was tuning into was more individualised and specific.

And I sensed that it was growing more aware of me. All this probably sounds crazy now. I can only put it down to the creative process. I was exhausted, yet I had never experienced such a need to work: my mind was driven and my body forced to follow. I suppose it was a sort of obsession, but all I could see at the time was my work.

This was the most important thing I had ever done and I could not let go. So I cut and carved and witnessed the changes my hands brought about. I tried to make sketches as usual, but they seemed to get in the way. Whatever was happening this time, it was at a subconscious level and being transferred straight to the tools. I felt like a channel, as if a window inside me had opened up and light was pouring through. The only way I could understand the vision was by shaping the wood.

And I waited for the Watcher to make itself known. It was there in the day when I walked through the bush. It was there at night and, in some ways, the dreams seemed more real. Even when I couldn't recall the dream, I would know it had been with me. I would wake to my own reflection in the mirror, my face gaunt from exhaustion, eyes rimmed with red.

Was I afraid? I should have been. Yes, in a way I suppose I was — afraid, yet exhilarated. This intelligence, or whatever it was, was the key to my work. I needed it. I knew that.

I never stopped to wonder why it needed me.

The days had maintained their own rhythm. I worked and I slept and I walked through the trees. There was only the estate and the countryside around us, Maggie's bar and the shop where I bought food. It was like living in a miniature world under one of those glass domes: I could see out and others could see in but there was no point of contact. The rest of the universe was irrelevant to my existence.

So that was why I nearly missed Christmas.

The first I knew about it was the noise and the smell of engine fumes as Jason's bike skidded to a halt outside the cottage. I was under the sheltered end of the deck, cursing at a saw blade that had become jammed in a wave of grain, and had to leave what I was doing. He kicked the bike stand down, swung the camera round and clicked at me. When I realised what was happening I quickly retreated to throw a cloth over the wood block I was working on.

'Merry Christmas!' he shouted

'What the hell are you doing here?'

'I bring peace on earth and goodwill to all mankind.'

'Oh, fuck off, Jason, I've got no time for this.'

'You can't be working. It's Christmas. Even the peasants are allowed a day off.' He came up on the deck and walked inside, arms laden with packages, all professionally gift-wrapped in gold foil and tied with silver ribbons. 'Come on, put down your tools and see what Santa's brought you.'

'Are you serious?' I trailed after him. 'Is it really Christmas?'

'December the twenty-fifth. All day.'

'Oh, hell. I'll have to ring my parents.'

'Never mind that now, you have to open your presents. Here, sit down.'

He elbowed me onto the sofa and tipped the parcels onto my lap. Immediately the camera came into his hands and he started clicking. I'd forgotten how annoying that was. Or perhaps it wasn't before.

'Come on, open, open.'

I gave in. And it was fun. I finished up with a lapful of nonsense. A Father Christmas hat with a white bobble, a box of balloons in rainbow colours, a squeaky toy Santa (that would please Bramble), an oil burner with a bottle of frankincense, chocolate Christmas trees, a penknife with my name on it, a bottle of my favourite liqueur, a Japanese fan. The fan was beautiful, delicately carved from wafer-thin cedar wood that wafted its bittersweet scent into the air. But nothing too expensive, except maybe the penknife, which looked well made. Nothing I could justifiably reject for fear of committing myself. He had chosen well. And I was enjoying the game, laughing along with him.

'Jason, this is so silly. And you shouldn't be here.'

'Of course I should. I came to visit my father. I just wanted to make sure you were OK. Where's the beer? How's the work going?'

'It's going fine. In the fridge. One piece finished, the second started.'

'Can I see?'

'No.'

'Oh. Here, you want a drink? You look tired.' He bent over me, concern momentarily clouding his smile. 'I can see you're working too hard. You need a break — it's just as well I came.' The smile was back. 'I'm barbecuing our lunch up at the house. Come and join us. It would please Dad.'

'Can't. Too much to do. And while we're on the subject of Dad, what was all that bullshit you fed me about your father renovating this place for backpackers? This is your cottage, Jason. You did all the renovating.'

He hesitated a moment, suddenly serious. 'Yes, it is mine. If I'd told you it was mine you would never have come, would you? Be honest. But I knew it was what you needed. It was my fault that your workflow had dried up. There's something about this place that feeds the soul. I hoped it would resurrect your creative spark. The least I could do was to give you this, if only for a little while. And it worked, didn't it?'

'Yes, you're right, it worked,' I said. But I wasn't going to let up. 'This is where you went to, wasn't it, when you disappeared for days on end? You were here, weren't you? Why didn't you tell me about it? Why all the secrecy?'

He fell silent for a moment, looking a bit sheepish. 'This is mine,' he said, 'something for myself. We spent days here when I was little, my mother and I. She loved this land, the trees. This was her special place. She often brought me here and I'd have her all to myself. It was a place where she was happy. She hated the house.'

'What about your father? Where did he fit in?'

'I can't remember him much. They quarrelled sometimes. Mostly they were apart. She liked to be alone, spent a lot of time in her room.'

'Is that why you brought her dressing table down here?'

'Dressing table? Ah, yes. The mirror. I wanted to have it near me.' Jason went into the bedroom and I followed him. He stood in front of the glass and gazed into his childhood. 'She would spend hours brushing her hair. It was long and gold-coloured and she would pull it all over one shoulder and stroke it with the brush. But her eyes would be fixed on some distant place. She'd tell me some things she saw, as if she were looking through a window. But not everything. She always kept some things back.'

'What did she tell you?'

'Oh, about the hills and the trees. Things she would see when she went walking.'

'Did you walk with her?'

'No, I was far too small. Only three or four. I would never have been able to keep up. She would be gone for hours.'

'So what did you do when she was roaming the hills?'

'I used to hide in her room. I went on hiding there, even after she didn't come back. I wanted to be close to her, I suppose. I would burrow into her wardrobe and wrap myself in her clothes. Her special smell was on everything she touched. It was a way of bringing her back. My father used to get angry. I guess he felt guilty.'

'Guilty? Why?'

'I think he felt he'd failed me, that everything was his fault.'

'Is that why he let the place fall apart? Why he started drinking?'

Jason smiled suddenly, and pulled himself away from the mirror. It was as if he had come back from another place. 'Who knows why people do things?' he said. Then he turned and strode out of the bedroom. 'Lunchtime. Lunch for my father and my best friend. Us men are having steaks but I brought something special for you, something with cashew nuts and truffle mushrooms. You won't be able to resist, I promise.'

'I'm not sure how your father would feel about that. My coming to lunch, I mean. I've been avoiding him. We had a sort of argument a few days ago, though I think he might have forgotten about it. But I've been feeling awkward ever since.'

'Really? And what were you arguing over? Me, I hope.'

'Well, no, it was Badger's accident. I virtually accused him of attempted murder. He has told you about it, hasn't he? No?'

'No, he never mentioned the dogs, though I was beginning to wonder where they were. What's happened to Badger?'

So I had to explain it all to him and where Badger was now. 'Bramble went out earlier. They're probably both over at the woolshed. That's why you haven't seen them.'

'Oh, well that's OK. Dad asked that chap to join us for lunch. Connors, is it? He'll probably bring the dogs with him. And I know he'd really like you to come too. He's looking forward to seeing you.'

'Well, if you're sure it will be all right. Just let me find a clean shirt. Can't go to Christmas dinner like this.' I quickly shuffled out of my grubby vest and squirted myself with some body spray. I had to ask sooner or later, it might as well be now.

'By the way, how's Sally?'

'Sally?' He looked puzzled. 'Oh, that Sally. I don't know. I haven't seen her since you left.' Then he went outside and kick-started the bike.

Sullivan stood up to welcome me. He had a glass in his hand, of course, but it was Christmas.

'Ah, Regan, I'm glad you came. Jason said he mightn't be able to drag you away. A happy Christmas to you.' He took my hand and bent to kiss me on the cheek. It felt uncomfortable, as it always does when people you hardly know insist on greeting you with a kiss. However, he did seem genuinely pleased that I was there. Our last encounter might never have happened.

'Now, can I offer you a drink?' he asked. 'Jason's made this hot weather punch. It's spiced, like mulled wine, but chilled. Rather good, really.'

I watched Sullivan as he fixed my drink. Like me, he had made an effort with a clean shirt. And like me, his face looked thinner. In fact he looked physically ill and dishevelled despite the fresh clothes. His eyes were hollow and dark ringed and his hands shook as he handed me the glass.

'Jason's made a bit of an effort. Said since we had guests around the place we ought to have a proper Christmas.' The deck certainly looked different, impressive even. It had been swept and dusted and there were fairy lights strung across the railing. A table had been set up for lunch. It spoke of grander days. Precious family silver and chinaware sparkled on a white cloth squared with careful folds. A crystal bowl of roses had been placed in the centre.

'Is the old man looking after you?' Jason called out from a pile of bricks and metal grids that I recognised as a hastily rigged-up barbecue. 'I need to get this thing started — it takes a while to settle down before you can put the food on.'

'Anything I can do to help?'

'No way. Barbecue is a man thing. No women allowed. You sit right there and entertain Dad.' Jason was enjoying this and I wondered how long it had been since he last spent Christmas at home.

Sullivan and I made polite conversation and sipped our festive booze. He was quite pleasant actually — gracious, I think, is the word. He asked me about my work, about what it was like to live in the city. And he asked a lot about Jason. What was his life like, what did he do, how did he live, who were his friends? His son lived in an alien world. It must have been a long time since Sullivan had last ventured beyond the local bar.

Jason kept looking up at us, smiling and waving and brandishing cooking irons. Look at me, he seemed to be saying, are you still looking? He reminded me of Sebastian. Sebastian's my younger brother, indulged by everyone and always the centre of attention. He would contrive to have the whole family form an audience to witness one of his performances, making sure we were all positioned at some vantage point. Then he would show off his latest skateboard flip, or his tennis backhand or whatever. We would humour him, of course, and talk among ourselves whilst pretending to be amazed by his prowess.

'Are you still looking?' he would call.

'Yes, of course we are.'

Jason waved again. Suddenly the nine years between us, that age difference I always maintained was irrelevant, split us apart. It was as if the ground at my feet had cracked wide open and I was watching him from the other side of a deep abyss. What I saw was a blond-haired, blue-eyed child and I wondered how the hell I had ever managed to get myself involved with him.

The sound of an approaching engine was a blessing. The little red tractor thing came putt-putting along the path, Liam gripping the wheel as if he held the reins of a chariot, his wild hair tugged by the wind. The dogs sat up behind him, their ears flapping, noses savouring the air.

Jason was far too involved with his culinary art to pay much attention to Badger. Sullivan went down to meet him and I wondered how he was going to react to the dogs. But Bramble bounded all over him, paws on shoulders, and he hugged her like a long-lost friend. Then she spotted me and Jason. Everyone got the same doggy treatment, including Liam who had just brought her.

Badger was a different matter. Liam lifted him to the ground where he managed to take a few steps. Sullivan approached him tenderly, kneeling down to stroke his head and whisper gently. I'm sure his mouth trembled and when he stood he brushed his eye with the heel of his hand. Blankets were fetched and Badger was installed on the deck in comfort; each dog was presented with a bone. Bramble had to make the rounds again, showing everyone her trophy.

Liam was introduced to Jason and they shook hands, formal and distant. Then Liam turned to me.

'A good morning to you, Miss Porter, and a fine Christmas morning it is too.' *Miss Porter?* I thought, and what's with the thick Irish brogue all of a sudden?

Liam and Sullivan joined me on the deck and talked of farming things. The dogs chewed their bones and Jason played with the barbecue and clicked his camera while I mellowed out on the festive punch. Despite my misgivings the little gathering was turning out to be quite pleasant. Except that, well it was nothing really, but I did notice how attentively Sullivan watched Jason. Even when he spoke directly to Liam or me, he was alert to his son's every move.

Eventually lunch was ready. We sat around the table while bowls of salad and buttered new potatoes were produced to go with the pile of charred meat. I was served something unique and delicious as promised.

'Enough of the punch,' said Jason, 'I have a couple of bottles of a very special red to go with this. A friend of mine runs a little winery north of town. This is by way of a limited edition. Regan, I know you'll love this. Have a taste, Dad, see what you think. Now what about you, Connors? I expect you're a beer man. I can get you a beer if you'd prefer.'

'No, don't trouble yourself. I'll try the wine for a change.' Liam dutifully took a sip and grimaced. 'It's very nice, thank you.'

'Sure you wouldn't prefer a beer?'

'No, no this will do fine.'

'I was meaning to thank you for the work you did on the deck. You've made an excellent studio for my friend Regan. She's an artist, you know, quite famous. Works in wood.'

'Oh, is that so?' said Liam. 'My uncle was a wood carver. Used to make chair legs.'

'Chair legs, eh?' Jason smirked behind Liam's back. 'Well, you two will have a lot to talk about then, won't you?'

I could feel blood flushing my face. How dare he talk to Liam like that, the patronising little brat? And what did Liam think he was doing by playing up to him? Chair legs, my arse! And I bet he knows far more about wine than Jason does. I was about to explode when Liam gave me a covert wink and twitched the corner of his mouth. I bit my lip and let them play out the game. Then I had this awful feeling that it wasn't a game, not for Liam anyway. He was hiding behind a fool's mask, only it was Jason who was made to look foolish. What are you hiding from, Liam Connors? I wanted to ask. But he went on playing the part and somehow I'd consented to collude with it, though God only knew what I was allowing myself to be drawn into.

The meal progressed, with Jason taking sideswipes at Liam and Liam playing the ignorant peasant. Sullivan drank copious amounts of wine and looked as if he would have fallen asleep at any moment if his eyes had not been permanently fixed on Jason.

Christmas lunch was turning into the Mad Hatter's tea party. Alice, having wandered into it by accident, was trying not to giggle. Sullivan made the perfect Dormouse. Jason, master of ceremonies, was the Mad Hatter. And Liam? He must have been the March Hare. I wondered if we'd all have to change places at three o'clock.

'Why is a raven like a writing desk?' I blurted out.

'What's that?' laughed Jason.

'I said, why is a raven like a writing desk? It's a riddle. You have to guess the answer. Only there isn't one.' My ice cream slipped off its spoon and landed with a splat all over my lap, which made me laugh out loud.

'I think you may have leaned a little too heavily on the punch, Regan,' said Jason. 'Perhaps I ought to make some coffee.' He left the table and went inside. I looked over at Liam and, for a moment, I thought he was crying. Then I realised he was shaking with suppressed laughter, big tears rolling down his face and into his beard. I'd never seen him laugh before. But, of course, he was the only one who knew what I was talking about.

Just then Jason returned to clear the dishes. 'What's the joke? Have I missed something?'

That set us both off again and this time even the dogs joined in.

After the party broke up I elected to make my own way back. It was a long walk around to the other side of the lake, but I needed to clear my head. Jason walked with me to the edge of the trees.

'Are you sure I can't give you a lift?'

'Yes, I'm sure. When are you going back to town?'

'I'll probably leave tonight. I've done my filial duty and there's a Boxing Day lunch party on Jerry's yacht. I'd hate to miss it. Everyone will be there. Except you, of course. Sure you won't come along?'

'No thanks, I've got other plans.'

'Well, I'll see you then. Happy New Year.'

'Yes, Happy New Year, Jason. And good luck.' I said it as if it were something final.

ELEVEN

As Jason returned to the Christmas feast, I took the path that went the long way around the lake, a route I had never taken before. But the afternoon was warm with a gentle breeze blowing off the surface of the water and shadows were beginning to smudge the pathway. It wasn't really a path, just rutted tracks where farm vehicles occasionally passed. Thick grasses grew in tufts between the tyre marks, entangled with wild flowers and alive with the hum of bees.

Trees lined up in ranks to my right, rows of tall pines all standing to attention as if they were on parade for inspection. Not that I would have had the temerity to reprimand them for being improperly dressed, even though their lower branches were a little brown and straggly. I was heavily outnumbered. Besides, I was sure they were whispering about me, a small murmur carried on the breeze from treetop to treetop.

A squabble broke out among the flotilla of small birds bobbing on the water. There was a flurry of wings as they broke from the surface and chased each other, squawking across the path.

The sun stroked my arms and the wine still sang through my blood, flooding my veins like warm nectar. I felt lighter and walked freely as if I had laid down a burden. The tall pines tipped their heads as I passed and I nodded and smiled and gave a royal wave, thanking God there was no one to see me.

But then I wasn't so sure.

It was there, a flicker at the edge of my mind, just like when you catch something out of the corner of your eye and you're not even sure that anything was there at all. Only it was. A slight flutter of a thought, like a feather ruffled by the wind. The shadow of a shadow. I looked around, as I always did, but knew there would be nothing to see. There never was. As I walked on, it kept level with me, moving higher up the slope where the trunks drew tight together and shadows formed dense, matted clumps of magenta. I reached out to it. This was something I was learning to do, to visualise a part of my mind stretching out like a groping hand. I was feeling in the dark, feeling for . . . what? Another hand? Another mind? And I did touch something, as I thought I had done before. Only this time I was certain. And the something was also reaching out for me. There was a momentary shiver of contact, a consciousness that washed through my head in a wave of grey light. A shadow, yes, but so much more than a shadow. It was watching, that's all, just watching. Then it let go, ebbing back into the tree line, but watching still.

I was learning well.

The pines broke rank and gave way to bush, thick and tangled, like an unruly mob after the disciplined plantation. Jason must have walked here as a child, with his mother maybe, or after she had gone. I thought about his face as he talked of her. Poor Jason. Poor child.

When I reached the cottage I went straight to the mirror, looking deep into the glass and far away, trying to see what it was that she saw. I tried to see her face in his and the long rope of golden hair. But there was only me. I felt suddenly lonely.

So I tipped out the contents of a holdall and hunted down my mobile phone. Of course the battery was flat, so it was early evening before I was able to make a call. My parents sounded really pleased to hear from me and they seemed to think it was perfectly natural that I had forgotten all about Christmas.

Sitting out on the deck to watch the early evening sky, I found I was holding the penknife that Jason had given me. It was quite beautiful; he must have had it made specially. The handle was warm rosewood with my name set into it in mother of pearl. There was a long chain attached with a clasp at one end so that it could hang on the belt loop of my jeans and be slipped easily into a pocket. I pried one of the blades open and found it honed to a keen edge. Instinctively I reached for a log and started cutting away curls of wood. Not the best wood for carving, too soft, and this quick-grown stuff is unevenly grained.

I wondered what Liam was doing and if Bramble was still with him. It seemed that this Christmas thing had taken him by surprise too. At first he had been uncomfortable, but once he'd got into his humble Irish workman act he seemed to be enjoying himself, though he did rather overdo it. Not that Jason had noticed. He was too busy showing off. And Liam had shown a sort of gentleness towards Sullivan. Compassion, that's what it was. Compassion for an old drunk and contempt for a young fool. At least I had made him laugh.

I looked at the piece of wood I was hacking at and found it was shaping itself into the head of a dog. It looked a bit like Badger, so I worked on it for a while longer until the sun went down.

A whole day's work had been lost, so I was up with the first light of dawn and out in my studio. It was a glorious morning and not to be wasted, but I could feel the heat building behind the horizon and by midday it would be too hot to move. Lately, although I felt I'd been working hard, I'd begun to put in less and less time on the actual sculpture and more time studying the subject matter, which was also a vital aspect of the work. But, as a result, the progress of the piece had certainly slowed down over the past few days. I determined to move it forward that morning and set to while the dew was still clinging to the grass. I had been hard at it for several hours before Bramble decided it was time to go and visit Badger.

I found Liam chopping wood at the edge of the clearing. When he saw me coming he lodged the axe in a length of trunk.

'Happy Boxing Day,' I called. 'Strange sort of Christmas, wasn't it?'

'Strangest I ever had.' He wiped his hands down his trousers and came to meet me.

'I made something for you. It's a sort of belated present.' I held out the little wooden dog. 'To be honest, I only made it last night. But I suppose it still counts.'

He took the carving and turned it in his hand, stroking the ears and nose. 'Well now, that is something. A Regan Porter original. And you made it for me?'

'Well, sort of. I started making it and when I saw what it was going to be I thought you ought to have it.'

'I think it's the best gift I've ever had.'

He didn't look at me again but went inside to put the kettle on. I went to say hello to Badger, who was looking much brighter and obviously frustrated by his inability to return Bramble's physical assault. I distracted her by throwing a stick until coffee arrived.

'So what else did you do last night?' he asked.

'Phoned my parents. Lots of apologising. I didn't even send them a card.'

'Were they upset?'

'No. I think they're used to me by now. I'm glad I rang them, though. It was good to talk.'

'What are they like?'

'My parents? Oh, they're great. My father's a lecturer at Otago University. Economics.'

'Your mother?'

'She teaches piano. Tried to teach me when I was little. I

think she had hopes of me being the virtuoso performer she never was. But I wouldn't practise and I used her sheet music for drawing paper. And poor Dad couldn't understand why his little girl needed to play with mud. Eventually they gave up and sent me to art school.'

'It must have been difficult for you.'

'It was more difficult for them. But they'd do anything for me. They're like a pair of bewildered sparrows who've hatched out a cuckoo and don't know how to feed it. Thank God they have my brothers.'

'Older? Younger?'

'I'm in the middle.'

'Ah, that explains a great deal.'

'Does it? And what about you? Do you have a family?'

Liam drained the last of his coffee and set his mug down. 'I was going to take Badger for a walk. You want to come with us?'

'But he can't even cross the yard yet.'

'True, but I have a cunning plan. Wait there.'

I watched Liam disappear round the corner of the woolshed. He was back in a few moments, pushing a wheelbarrow. 'Look. I found this cushion from an old car seat to pad the bottom. Fit for a prince, eh lad? Come on your majesty, let's try it for size.'

Badger got the hang of it straight away. We must have made a bizarre spectacle, the family out for a Boxing Day stroll, with Liam pushing the pram and Bramble running on ahead like an excited kid. He saw it too, and when I caught his eye we both started to laugh. It was good when he laughed, made him seem almost human.

'So what was all that about yesterday?' I asked.

'What was all what about?'

'All that not knowing about wine crap.'

'Did I do that?'

'Oh, come off it, you know you did. Why pretend to be something you're not?'

He frowned, thought for a moment. 'He's an odd one, that Jason. I don't feel comfortable around him and it's obvious he doesn't think much of me. He comes home to find a stranger with his feet under the family table. He wanted to make sure I knew I was only the hired help. It wouldn't do to put his nose out of joint if I want to keep my job, even if he does act like a jumped-up little prick.'

'Yes, I see your point, but don't you think you were overdoing it? Look, I knew what was going on, Liam, you were taking the piss. If anyone was having a dig it was you.'

He gave me a wicked grin and walked on, taking a pathway up through the bush. After a while I said, 'You were right, it wasn't him.'

'Who wasn't what?'

'It wasn't Sullivan who did the shooting. I asked Maggie and she said he was in the bar at the time.'

'Ah, the lovely Maggie, did she now?'

'Besides it was the wrong sort of gun. Sullivan takes a shotgun when he goes rabbit hunting. The dog would have been full of pellets. The vet said it was a bullet that passed right through the shoulder, so it couldn't have been him, could it?'

'I suppose not. Don't know much about guns myself.'

We fell silent again. I had spent so much time alone in the bush that it was strange having someone with me, although I admit I did feel comfortable with Liam, despite his prickly armour. He didn't seem to want anything from me, there was no pressure.

I looked around, alert for that familiar sensation of being observed. No, it was either not there or it had backed off: at least I couldn't feel that familiar tingle on my spine. Perhaps the Watcher did not approve of me having company.

The morning was reaching its height. Cicadas screeched non-stop until the sound cut through my head. I could feel the ends of my hair sticking to my neck and a trickle of sweat running down my back. Liam manoeuvred the wheelbarrow around tree

134

trunks, his arm muscles tightening into hard knots; I think it was proving harder work than he had envisaged. Eventually the path widened into a clearing and there was my giant friend. I ran up and laid my hands on the trunk in greeting.

'Liam, come here, let me introduce you to the Lord of the Forest.'

Liam came up as I asked and laid his hands on the tree, leaning his head against the dry bark.

'Can you feel the energy?' he said. 'It's like standing next to an electricity sub-station.'

'Yes, I know what you mean, I've felt it here before.' I slid down to sit on the roots, leaning against its body. 'You talked about trees once, said they were filled with some sort of Earth energy. You said it could be sensed by some people. Is this what you meant?'

'The ancients were more in touch with the natural world. They were aware of the life force all around them, in the trees, the earth, running water. They saw these things as living beings, minor gods if you like. That's how they worshipped God — through nature.' He sat down beside me. 'They would find places where the energy was strongest, a pool, a rock, a special tree like this one, and come to say a prayer or ask for a favour. They would make a small sacrifice, a piece of bread, some wine. Lots of pieces of jewellery have been found in streams, bronze bangles and brooches. Gifts for their personal gods.'

'Perhaps we should make an offering,' I reached for the bottle we had tucked into the wheelbarrow, unscrewed the top and poured some of the water over the roots. 'There you are, Tree, it's not much but you're welcome to share what we have.' I took a long drink myself and handed the bottle to Liam.

'You'd have made a fine pagan,' he said. He gulped the water down, and then shared the rest between the dogs, cupping it for them in his hands.

'You don't sound much like a Catholic yourself, or is it Protestant?'

'Neither,' he replied. 'The Church is no master of mine. It certainly put an end to pagan worship. Locked God up in a prison of stone, it did. Laid the creator on an altar with a railing in front to keep the people out and a priest standing guard to bar the way. For over a thousand years now it's held my country in fetters, crippled their minds and bled their bodies dry while it filled its own purse. No, the Church is no master of mine.'

I was startled by his bitterness and the hatred in his eyes. I waited for his next words with no idea how to respond. Instead Liam jumped up and grabbed my hand, hauling me to my feet.

'Come, we're supposed to be walking the dogs,' and he snatched up the barrow handles and swung around onto the path, setting off at a breathless pace. I struggled to keep up with him, watching his shirt stretch across his shoulders as he bumped the wheel over jutting roots. Fern fronds slapped my face and the midday heat drew beads of sweat from my skin.

After a while Liam's pace slowed, his shoulders relaxed and I felt it was safe to speak again.

'You were saying how the ancient people knew about the energy in trees. That's something I've always been able to relate to. You know, pagan ideas about the forces in nature. Do you know something about that? Can you tell me some more about the trees?'

He was silent for so long I thought he hadn't heard me. Then he said, 'Well, if you think about it, to the Celts, in fact most other races throughout history, the trees were essential for survival. The forests provided building materials for their shelters and the fuel for fires to cook their food and warm their bodies. They carved weapons from wood for battle and for hunting. Later they fashioned yokes for the plough beasts and put up barns to store the harvest grain. Then, when they discovered the secrets of metal work, they needed fuel to fire the furnaces. Trees were to them what electricity is to us, the power that sustained their lives. Is it any wonder they believed that trees had magic powers?'

136

'Yes, I can understand that. But they used tree magic for healing and stuff too, didn't they? How did that work?'

'That depended on the tree. There were the Seven Trees held sacred by the ancient Irish, all part of the Druid beliefs.'

'And what were they?'

'Let me see now. Mistletoe was the most revered. All heal and golden bough it was called. It ruled the winter solstice, Christmas time, or Yuletide as it was then.'

'People kiss under mistletoe berries, don't they?'

'Yes. Originally the berries were used in love incenses and potions, but they're very poisonous. Mistletoe isn't strictly a tree, grows on the bark of the apple tree, which was also sacred to the Druids. Apple is useful for healing, gets rid of warts.'

'Like, an apple a day keeps the doctor away?'

'Of course. Where do you think some of those old sayings come from? You heard the old superstition of "whistling up the wind". Well that's another sacred tree, the alder. Whistles made from alder wood were played to entice air elementals.'

'And what are they?'

'Elementals? Oh, they're the personified energies of nature, creatures of fire and water and earth. Now the ash tree you would understand. It has a very straight grain, ideal for carving magic wands.'

I loved the idea at once. I could make a magic wand, etched with pentagrams and stuff. I could already see myself on a hilltop at sunrise, waving it about and chanting magical incantations. But Liam was still speaking.

'That's mistletoe, apple, alder and ash. Then there's willow. You know the Irish are famed for their poetry and story telling. Willow groves were considered so magical that the priests and tribal leaders, the poets and bards, all sat among the trees to gain eloquence and inspiration.'

'I know oak trees are supposed to be special.'

'That's right, the oak has been considered sacred by just

about every culture that has encountered it. But it was held in particular esteem by the Celts. It was called the King of Trees. It can be used in spells for strength and protection. Magic wands were made of its wood. Oak galls, known as serpent eggs, were used in magical charms and acorns gathered at night held great fertility powers.'

'One more. You said seven.'

'Ah now, that'd be my favourite, the rowan. Some call it mountain ash or witchwood. It's sacred to the Goddess Bridgit. It's such a graceful tree with its bright red berries to feed the birds in autumn. The berries have a tiny pentagram, that's an ancient symbol of protection. Sticks of rowan used to be carved with runes.'

'They're like Norwegian letters, aren't they?'

'Norse, to be strictly accurate. I must take you to see Fleur, one of those travelling people I was telling you about. They'll be here in a few days. She'll show you the runes. And tell your fortune if you like.'

'Hey, that would be cool.'

We were still tramping through the bush, heading back down towards the lake.

'What about these trees?' I said. 'Do they have magic powers?'

'I'm sure they do. But that's beyond my knowledge.'

'And what about the new trees, the pines?'

He stopped to look around at me, his face feigning shock and horror. 'There's nothing new about the pines. I'll have you know that pine trees covered the hills of Europe long before man was even thought of. The Druids called it the sweetest of woods.'

'I always associate it with disinfectant and school toilets.'

'And so you should. It's always been used to purify. They used to mix the dried needles with juniper and cedar and burn it to clean the home and purify the area for worship. The cones and nuts can be carried as a fertility charm. Any evergreen has special life-giving qualities.'

'And how come you know so much about all this?'

He smiled and winked and said, 'It's all part of being a humble Irish handyman.' I should have known better than to ask.

We were nearly back home by then. I was exhausted. He walked so fast, despite the wheelbarrow, that even Bramble had slowed down.

'Look, we've got to pass the cottage to get to the woolshed,' I said. 'I could pick up my laptop. There might be a reply from your friend by now.'

'On one condition. You must promise to come to the fair with me. I'd like you to meet my friends. Besides, I think you need a break. You look awful.'

'Oh, thanks very much.'

'Well you do. Look at you. You must have lost a stone in weight that you can ill afford. There's no colour in your cheeks and your eyes look like you haven't slept for a month.'

His words felt like a sharp slap in the face. I knew he was right and for some reason I felt guilty about it. Perhaps that's why I agreed to go.

'Day after tomorrow then. I'll call for you in the morning. We'll take your truck.'

Back at the woolshed Liam sat with the computer. From the opposite side of the table I was able to see his face and watch the tiny eye movements as his gaze flicked over the screen.

'Well?' I asked.

'Yes, I have a reply.' A long silence.

'And?'

'And I'm trying to read it.'

Then his fingers clattered over the keys and another long silence. His eyebrows dipped together and he chewed at his bottom lip. I was in agony, trying to sit still and say nothing. Just when I was beginning to think he would never move, he clicked over the keyboard again and shut down.

I jumped up and ran round the table to look at a blank screen. 'So? What did it say?'

'There was a letter for me. And yes, there was some information. It was on an attachment, which I've saved as a document file. You'll find a folder marked "Sullivan".'

'But what does it say.'

'A lot and nothing. You need time to read it and think about it. As I said, it's something and nothing. Old tales, scraps of information — that's how these stories arise. People making something out of a string of coincidences and exaggerations. But it might tell us something about the man, why he's how he is.'

'And what about the women?'

'Now, you're not to read too much into it and go off half-cocked. Just go home and look at it this evening and we'll talk about it in the morning.'

Of course I switched the laptop on as soon as I was through the door. As before, the message had been deleted and the deleted items folder emptied. That's as I expected. However, I found the new Sullivan folder easily enough and in it were two files. I read them through, then fetched a glass of wine and read them again. The line had moved quite a way down the bottle before I clicked on 'shut down'.

TWELVE

WHAT I found in the first file was copied from a newspaper. There were two articles in fact, printed two years apart, both from the *Limerick Times*. The first was dated 15 March 1863.

Sullivan. It is with deepest sorrow that we announce the passing of John Sullivan, eldest son of Patrick Sullivan, whose death was announced late last night. Mr. Sullivan was born in County Limerick in the year 1800, on his father's estate, where he had resided throughout his life.

It is reported that his widow, Katherine Sullivan, and his eldest son, Thomas, were at his bedside during his last hours. Mrs. Sullivan, mother of his younger son, Michael, was Mr. Sullivan's second wife.

A private family funeral will be held on Friday at the private chapel on the Sullivan estate and will be followed by the formal reading of the will. It is expected that all lands, deeds and entitlements will now pass to Thomas Sullivan, Mr. Sullivan's eldest son from his first marriage to Emily McCormack.

Michael Sullivan, who is at present overseas, is still to be informed of his father's demise.

The second press cutting was from 1865.

A reception was given last Friday by the Ladies' Church Guild to mark the imminent departure of Mrs. Katherine Sullivan, widow of the late John Sullivan, for the Antipodes. The reception was held in the function rooms of the Royal Castle Hotel where Mrs. Sullivan was presented with a painting of Limerick City by local artist Sean Barrden, as a memento of her home town and in recognition of her good works among the underprivileged of the City.

Mrs. Sullivan is due to sail aboard the *Lady Grace*, departing from Liverpool next month. She will be joining her son, Michael, who left Limerick five years ago to settle in New Zealand. The citizens of Limerick wish Mrs. Sullivan a safe passage.

The other file contained what was obviously the main body of Liam's friend's investigation. This is what he'd sent.

How to find a Sullivan in late nineteenth-century Limerick? Dead easy, like finding a piglet in a farmyard. The place was littered with them! Ha, ha!

Anyway, I thought it might be easier to start at the other end of the question by trying to find a Michael Sullivan who went to New Zealand. That did narrow it down considerably. Thank God for the Internet and genealogy links. It's absolutely amazing. You can access passenger lists for most of the vessels leaving the U.K. for the New World during that century. Of course the famine ships were crowded and records weren't too accurate. But from the information you gave I gathered we were looking a bit later than that so I moved straight to 1855 onwards. Came up with five Michael Sullivans.

The first, who was travelling on an emigration ship and claimed to be a baker, didn't fit the profile -- some question of a criminal record. But I kept him in reserve. Three were married men with a wife and several children, so I discounted those. However, I hit the jackpot with the fifth shot.

The S.S. 'Lady Egidia' left Greenock, Scotland on 12th October 1860, bound for Otago. In all, 438 emigrating passengers boarded, mostly Scottish, but quite a few from Ireland, including one Michael Sullivan. According to the passenger list he described himself as a farmer from the County Limerick. Although many were claiming assisted passage and travelled steerage, this Michael had paid the full fare and had a bit of comfort, although there were no private cabins. Apparently the voyage lasted 104 days and they arrived at the end of January 1861. Sadly the ship was 32 souls lighter (there was an inquiry about the competence of the medical officer). Your Michael Sullivan arrived in one piece so you should be able to track his progress from there.

Having got a name and a date it was then easy to extract references from newspaper articles of the corresponding period. That's how I came up with the press cuttings (see the other file attached). From there I was able to research the family from local records and of course the university archives. Putting it all together it does form a picture and a very strange one it is.

As far as Michael was concerned, being the youngest son of a wealthy landowner, his choices were limited. Obviously it was Thomas who was about to inherit the family jewels, or in this case all the land, which would have left Michael out on a limb. Traditionally the Army or the Church were the only recourse for the youngest son, but in the 1800s Australia and New Zealand offered an attractive alternative to many young adventurers from upper-class families.

The first thing I found was the record of Thomas's mother, Emily. Apparently she and John Sullivan were married in 1826. She died three years later of fever, according to the death certificate, following the stillbirth of her second child. She was aged 27. John remarried in 1830, this time to Katherine, who outlived him and followed her son, Michael, out to New Zealand.

And that's all there was. Which, in those days of large and extra large families, was in itself unusual. It seems the Sullivans have never gone in for intensive breeding, just the one or two children, all of them sons. And this Emily died fairly young, though that wasn't unusual for the time.

However, you did say you remembered something about a family in which the women died after having produced an heir. So I started searching our folk history data and came up with some weird stuff. But first let me tell you about John Sullivan, what little there is to tell, which, in itself, is rather odd.

The family owned vast acres of land in County Limerick, to which John Sullivan was the sole heir. His father, Patrick, died, leaving the young man with estates of farms and woodland, and a sizeable sum of money also. John lived there and managed his inheritance. He married twice, had two sons and then he died. And that, apparently, was the sum total of his life. He never travelled, or went in for politics as most landowners would, took no interest in civic matters, joined no committees, no social life, not even the local hunt. Nothing. His second wife was very active among the ladies of Limerick, involving herself with various charities and good works. Probably the only way the poor woman got out of the house.

What John did do was grow rich, or even richer than his father. And that's where the stories started, because no one could account for his wealth, or indeed the wealth he'd inherited. The Sullivans just accumulated land and money and had always done so. There were, of course, all sorts of speculation (no need to tell you about the Irish imagination). But the question remains unanswered. How did the Sullivans make their money? One can only assume that the land itself was very well managed. Large areas were sectioned off and let out to tenant farmers and cottiers and these would net a considerable rent. And therein, as they say, lies another tale.

The Famine struck, as we all know, in the mid-1840s, and of course County Limerick fared as badly as anywhere else, worse in some ways. Now, we have to remember that this wasn't like your usual famine in which there's a shortage of food. In Ireland there was plenty of food, just no potatoes. And as the poor ate only potatoes it was the poor who died, while the field next door was ripe with grain to feed the cattle and export to England. Of course many landowners, especially those who weren't actually present, continued to demand their rent, leaving the poor nothing with which to buy food. When the rent money was used to keep body and soul together and they couldn't pay up, they were evicted to die on the roadsides. The Church, as usual, was of little help, being more interested in counting souls than bodies.

There were, however, some landlords who showed concern for their tenants and did what they could to alleviate the situation. It could well be that John Sullivan was of that mind, which would account for the survival of his tenants and workers. But that's not the version told by their descendants, and the story that's been passed down is a strange one. It's said that the potatoes grown by the tenants on the Sullivan estate didn't succumb to the blight. The people who lived on his lands, and there were several hundred, all survived, well fed and healthy.

Now, they could have told tales of John Sullivan's generosity, or the leprechauns and fairies leaving baskets of food at the doors, or St Patrick himself bringing loaves and fishes. That I would understand as being the typical Irish way of embroidering a mystery onto an explanation. But the potatoes on the Sullivan estate didn't succumb to blight? When the spores came overnight, carried on the wind, and every potato plant in the country was black and rotting in the ground by morning? No, I don't think so. There's something not right here.

And that was about the sum of information I've been able to find on the life and times of John. So I started looking back further, at stories, folk tales, local gossip, and yes, I found just what you were looking for, a recurring theme.

Young women married into the family, produced an heir and then died suddenly. There are numerous stories, or maybe numerous versions of a few stories, scattered over several centuries. Nothing officially recorded, nothing that can be authenticated, just tales whispered by the hearthside. 'It was a dark and stormy night and the rain beat on the old castle walls . . .' You know the sort of thing. All manner of tales about accidents that befell young mothers. Strange and sudden illnesses. Suicides. Search parties up in the hills.

It was said that a team of brothers kidnapped their sister and kept her prisoner to prevent her marrying the lord of the manor. There's even a gypsy's warning to a bride, 'Marry the Sullivan gold and your wedding dress will make your shroud.' Naturally she was dead within two years, leaving an infant son. I can send you copies of all this, but, as I say, I doubt if anything can be substantiated.

What records do show, however, is that the Sullivan family had possessed the same plot of land for at least 1200 years, probably long before that too, and the boundaries had widened year by year as new fields and woods were acquired. County records refer to a castle or some form of fortified structure which disappeared long ago, but there's an ancient stone circle still standing. A large house was built in the fifteenth century and it had been subsequently extended and refurbished. Apparently in its heyday it was quite a grand establishment with servants' quarters and stables. Not that it was ever used for entertaining on a grand scale and certainly was never occupied by a large family.

Unfortunately nothing of the family fortune remains today. It seems that the son and heir didn't live up to expectations. Young Thomas Sullivan 'went to the bad', as they say, after his stepmother left for New Zealand. He never married but continued to live in the house and there were more tales; this time it was drinking sessions, gambling and loose women. The farmlands first went to waste, then were sold off piecemeal to finance his chosen lifestyle. He died a bankrupt shortly before WW1 and what little was left of the property was sold off against his debts.

Eventually urban sprawl ate up the countryside. The house stood empty for years, then was pulled down in the eighties to make way for a shopping centre. A motorway now runs through what were the grounds. The stone circle is still there, of course, being an historic monument, and the conservation people have charge of it. I think it's open to the public at certain times of the year.

And that's about all I've managed to find up to now, but it's a fascinating family history. I'm intrigued to learn what

prompted this 'urgent investigation' as you put it. I'll try to
find out more. In fact, I just might take a trip over to Limerick
and see what else I can dig up.

I closed down the laptop and headed straight back for the
woolshed. Did Liam seriously expect me to wait until tomorrow
and discuss this calmly over morning coffee? He saw me coming,
probably heard me, too, crashing through the ferns. He stepped
back from the woodpile to wipe his face on a discarded shirt.

'Oh, you've read it then?'

'Of course I've read it. What the hell is going on?'

'Probably nothing. As I said, it may be all stories and
coincidences. The result of overactive imaginations. You have
to understand it's a different culture, a different psychological
make-up, that creates that kind of mythology.'

'And what sort of psychological make-up created those three
bodies up the hill back there?'

'Look, I told you not to jump to conclusions. People die all
the time. There's nothing to link what went on in Ireland with
those women here.'

'Isn't there? Well, you seemed to think there was or you
wouldn't have sent someone looking for evidence half a world
away.'

'It was just . . . it rang a bell, that's all.'

'That's all, is it? A family of recluses? Generations of women
dying mysteriously? Then the same thing starting up here? Three
times at least, and probably four.'

'Four? And who's the fourth one?'

'Jason's mother, of course.'

Liam swung away, whirling his shirt through the air like a whip
and sending puffs of dust spiralling up from the beaten ground.
'Jesus Christ and all the saints in heaven, will ye listen to the
woman!' He rounded on me, his eyes flashing sparks of rage.
'Don't you ever think before you open your mouth? You know

148

nothing of Jason's mother. You know nothing about the women up there! You don't know what they died of or who buried them there or why!'

'Yes I do! Anne fell off her horse and bled to death. Mary stayed out all night and caught pneumonia. They both got some sort of postnatal depression that sent them wandering off into the hills. Strange illnesses, he said. Accidents that befell young mothers. Think about it, will you. Michael comes to New Zealand. He marries Anne and they have a son, David. A year later she's dead. David marries Mary and they produce another heir, Tom. She dies before she's thirty. Tom marries Jane, then John's born and she dies. John marries and Jason is born, an only child and he's been without a mother since he was four years old. That's what you call a coincidence?'

'I never said there was nothing to it. But you can't go round accusing people of . . . of . . .'

'What? Murder?'

'There, you see. You put words to a thing and you make it real. I'll grant you something odd is going on. But I don't know what and neither do you. There could be all sorts of reasons.'

'Like what for instance?'

'Well I don't know, something hereditary, a genetic defect.'

'In that case it would have been the men who died. The women weren't Sullivans till they married into the family. What's your next brilliant theory?'

'I don't have one,' he stumbled over his words, 'but when I do it will be based on fact not female hysteria.'

'God, you're an arrogant bastard.' And with that I stomped off towards the lake.

I wasn't going to go back when he called after me. Only he didn't. Nor would I give him the satisfaction of turning around to see if he was watching me. No option but to walk on, fists clenched so hard the nails dug into my palms. My breath was tight in my chest and I could feel the heat of blood pumping in my neck and face. I wasn't going to cry even though my eyes were stinging. It's so unfair that anger always brings tears. It's undermining and humiliating. Now I couldn't look back. How could I with the face of an hysterical female? I wouldn't give him the satisfaction, the supercilious, chauvinistic . . .

I took my righteous indignation and stampeded it through the bush with the air boiling all around me and only the trees on which to vent my fury. My mouth was dry with resentment and too much wine on an empty stomach. The sun blasted my face till the tears dried to salt. The world around me hummed and swayed and I couldn't feel the movement of my legs, only the blood pumping through my thighs and roaring in my ears. I squeezed my eyes to shut out the light and the sight of Liam's back sweating in the sun as he swung the axe, as he hurled bitter words. I stumbled through the leaves and over serpent tree roots that coiled around my feet. Inside my body it was dark and hot and the anger was drowned in a calm sea like the birth of night. And, as if it were night, I rocked gently, rocked gently on the dark water . . .

. . . and I woke. Thrown forward, I was snapped into alertness. As my arms flew out to save me I caught the wooden branches in my hands. Fingers twined among the leaves and brushed the little birds and the insects, all carved in oak, so pretty, so delicate as they twined around the mirror. And there, in the mirror, it was me, my face dark and smeared with dirt and heat. As time had shifted, so the colours had changed. The sun had gone and night-time creatures now hummed and croaked outside the window where the birds had been singing. But I was safe, unharmed. Only my leg felt strange: there was something on my thigh. Fingers traced the outline of sensation and my eyes followed. A long jagged scratch, deep enough to bleed. Enough blood to ooze down my calf and drip, slow drip after drip, onto the floor.

THIRTEEN

THE next day it rained. The sky was a cloth of seamless grey, tacked from horizon to horizon. I did battle with the block of wood while the steel roof drummed above me. I was here to sculpt, not go running through the bush to pay house calls on some arrogant sheep-dipper. Nor would I concede when he came to apologise. Only he didn't. The day was long and I sweated inside the plastic walls until skeins of sawdust clotted my skin. I expected any moment to see a khaki raincoat burst through the undergrowth and his muddy boots come clumping up the steps. But it never happened.

Had I overreacted the day before?

I would have found it impossible to fully justify my behaviour had someone been there to confront me. I'm not entirely sure I can explain it now. I dare say I could rationalise it as being the result of my intense involvement with my work. All that dredging about in the depths of my psyche, all that Jungian race memory stuff; not so much an act of creation as of retrieval. On top of that I was tired, stressed out and balancing on an emotional knife-edge. So I had taken it out on Liam.

Even then I wasn't clear on what the argument had been about. Was he right? Was I jumping to conclusions, getting caught up with something that was really none of my business? Ireland, all those women, centuries ago and half a world away. I had no personal involvement with them, so what was I getting so uptight about? In any case, it wasn't as if it was becoming an obsession or anything. I was merely interested, that's all. And what did I expect Liam to do? And why should it concern us anyway? So what if there were three graves up in the hills? So what if Anne Sullivan had bled to death and every time I moved the cut on my leg hurt like hell?

The early arrival of evening dimmed the corners of the studio and I was forced to stop. As I stood forever under a hot shower, my head felt light and separated and I remembered I hadn't eaten all day.

By the time I'd towelled off, the rain had ceased so I ate supper next to an open window, lighting a dozen candles and burning scented oils. Incense floated away on the night air like an offering. I could hear fiddle music carried to me by the wind, an invitation I chose to ignore.

The next morning the sun had returned and so had my sense of humour. I'd spent the whole of the previous day sulking like a spoilt child and he probably hadn't even noticed. Another day alone would achieve nothing, and anyway he was the nearest thing I had to a friend in this place, apart from Maggie. There would be a sort of triumph in making the first move. I would go over for morning coffee, just as if nothing had happened, as if it were the rain that had kept me away. But before I had a chance to act there was a tapping at the door. I knew it must be him, although at first I wasn't so sure.

'Bloody hell!' I gasped. 'What have you done to yourself?'

'Well, I thought, as we were going out, I ought to have a bit of a trim-up.'

'Who's your stylist? Sweeney Todd?'

'Sorry about that.' He fingered the little patches of blood-soaked paper on his cheeks. 'I'm a bit out of practice with a razor.'

'You look . . . different.'

The frayed mass of tangles had been scooped back and tethered at the nape of his neck where it again exploded into a wiry brush. A severe line of dark hair now framed a high forehead. The wild facial matting was trimmed into a neat beard and moustache, revealing pale cheeks beneath the wide, grey eyes. His newly visible mouth was full and soft, tinged more with blue than red. I realised with a shock that he was much younger than I'd thought.

'You haven't forgotten, have you? The fair?'

'No, no, of course not. I'll only be a few minutes.'

Of course I'd forgotten, but I wasn't going to tell him that. I darted into the bedroom and grabbed a sweater, rolling it into a ball and cramming it into a small backpack that I found kicked under the bed. I nearly trod on my sunglasses and threw them in too. Where were the car keys? And why was I panicking? I stopped to catch a breath, the pulse kicking in my throat. It's only a tatty craft expo, I told myself, hardly the social event of the year. But I fluffed up my hair and squirted scent on anything that showed.

'There, I'm ready,' gliding serenely across the kitchen. 'How far is it?'

'They've set up in a field just this side of town. About half an hour, but it's a pleasant enough drive. I thought we could take Bramble. Badger's comfortable enough and he could do with the rest.'

I'd forgotten how much I enjoyed driving that truck — a sort of empowerment, I suppose. There's something quite sensual about strapping yourself into the seat and taking the controls of a big machine, and I rode it like a stallion I'd personally broken in. Bramble was up on the seat behind us, pointing her nose out the window and flicking the back of my head with her tail. Liam also hung out of the window, crammed up against the door as if, in such a confined space, he needed to make a point. I glanced over at him a few times, becoming aware that he wasn't bad-looking in a dark sort of way. He smiled back but said nothing. Yesterday sat between us like an unexploded bomb.

'Have you thought any more about your friend's letter?' Well, someone had to say something.

'Yes and no. I mean, I've thought about it, but come to no conclusions.'

'Oh. So what do you think we should do next?' I was being so cool about this. I hadn't asked who his friend was or even why he'd deleted the emails. Dealing with this man was like walking on cracked ice.

'We don't *have* to do anything.'

I said nothing but looked straight ahead, kicking down on the accelerator, forcing the engine into a higher gear. There was a long silence in which I could feel him watch me grip the wheel.

'All right then,' he shifted in his seat, 'we'll see what else he comes up with from Limerick. Meanwhile, I could make some enquiries here. Find out more about the family history.'

'How could we do that? Ask the locals, I suppose. People hereabouts must know the Sullivans.'

'No, we've got to tread easy. If there's something amiss we don't want to go attracting attention. In any case, if it gets back to Sullivan that we're checking up on him we'll both be out on our ears.'

'Well, what do you suggest?' I asked.

'There's bound to be records, registrations of births and marriages.'

'And deaths.'

'Yes, and deaths. Then there's the local land registry of course, council records.'

'Won't that attract attention?'

'Not if I make up some story. Like, I had family in the area from way back. It would be natural for me to be tracing the name Connors among the early Irish settlers.'

'And what about a local newspaper? They usually keep some sort of archive. We could see if they have any old photographs.'

'I said "I", not "we". It would be better if you stayed out of it.' I was about to argue when he turned and looked at me. His eyes were sharp and hard as flint and I decided to leave further discussion for another time.

We could see the parking paddock from the brow of the hill. There was no mistaking the lines of coloured cars all glinting in the sun like strings of bright jellybeans. The town was nearby and people had turned out by the hundreds. Through the trees to another paddock, and there were the travelling people. A circle within a circle of houses on wheels, everything from camper vans to swish designer mobile homes towed by four-wheel drives. Then there were the houses grafted onto lorries, wonderful wooden structures like gingerbread cottages with high gabled roofs and leadlight windows. There was even an authentic gypsy caravan with wooden shafts resting, empty, on the grass and a hooped cover perched on top of huge, bright yellow wheels.

In this week between Christmas and New Year people were still in a party mood. I'd slipped a leash on Bramble, not so much for control but to help her feel more secure. Not at all used to crowds, she stuck to us like Velcro, trying to walk between my legs so I was constantly tripping up. I knew how she felt though: I'd been a virtual hermit for weeks, going for days, sometimes, without speaking to a soul. The sudden crowd burst upon my senses with all its noise and colour; children screeching and running past with streamers and paper windmills on sticks; young men colliding with each other, made clumsy by bravado and cans of beer. There were young couples, their arms twined around each other's waists, wrapped in their own dialogue to which the day was only a backdrop. But I wasn't alone and we both patted Bramble as an affirmation.

We drifted from stall to stall, each set out in front of the vendor's home. There were racks of gaily coloured clothes that hung like flags at a medieval tournament, tables piled high with jewellery and joss sticks, coloured glass and crystals to catch the sun.

Liam knew all about everything and everyone and there was a lot of hand shaking and backslapping as he met up with old friends. I had to be introduced, of course, and my head was swimming with new faces. 'This is my friend Regan,' he would say and there was a kind of warmth in his voice when he spoke my name so that I didn't feel like an outsider. They were an interesting assortment of people. Not real gypsies of course, but, as he had explained, people who were looking for a different way of living — ex-typists who now made hand-dipped candles, runaway bank managers stringing coloured beads into necklaces.

We made our way around the field eating junk food and drinking lemonade, meeting up with people and collecting all sorts of useless treasures. Liam insisted on buying me a leather hat, a belated Christmas present. He said it was a proper bush hat and that I shouldn't go walking with my head uncovered. I conceded he was right and wanted to wear it straight away, but first he had to pick bits of candyfloss out of my hair while we stopped to watch some Morris dancers. Then we witnessed an escape artist emerge from a sack bound with chains. It was like watching a butterfly struggle free from its chrysalis, and when he spread his arms to take a bow it was as if he were drying his wings in the sun.

We came upon a sad young man whose eyes were black bruises in a white face. He sat on the grass carving little wooden animals with hands that still trembled from whatever tragedy had led him here. Liam introduced him as Jethro, though I'm sure that wasn't the name he'd started out with. I picked up a roughly carved snail. It was awful: the shell was painted a lurid green and its face was lopsided.

Liam said to Jethro, 'Regan here, she does a bit of wood carving herself.'

'That's right,' I said, reaching for my purse. 'Oh, but not as nice as these.'

Jethro beamed as I handed over my five dollars. He wrapped the hideous thing in a sheet of tissue paper, making it precious, and I stowed it in my bag with great ceremony.

Liam shook his head as we walked on. 'No, you're nothing like I expected,' he said.

'What do you mean?'

'When you first arrived and I realised who you were I had an image of how you'd be. But you're not like that at all.'

We found Carl and Fleur's wooden house parked under a tree. The man was sitting by a makeshift bench, twisting silver wire into bracelets. He stood up immediately, laid down his tools and ran forward to grab Liam in a bear hug.

'Hey, Fleur,' he shouted over his shoulder, 'come see what the wind's blown in!'

A woman emerged from the doorway and her face lit up with a smile that rivalled the morning. She jumped down the steep steps two at a time and ran across the grass to Liam, who caught her, swinging her around in his arms. She was short and fair like me, but that was all. Fleur was well named, a snowdrop in a field of wild gorse. Short curls of white blonde hair framed her face like petals opening around a smooth bud. Everything about her was slender and fragile, her neck, her hands; she could not move without being graceful. Watching from the sidelines, at first I thought she was a young girl. Then Liam introduced her as Carl's wife and I noted the finest tracing of lines at the corners of her eyes. Carl was tall and wiry. His head was a shiny dome but strings of grey and black hair draped his collar and hung from his top lip.

Fleur took my arm and led me behind the table that held their display of silverware. It was like crossing the border into another country, a land where the travelling people sat and watched the ordinary folk parade by in their holiday clothes. Extra chairs were found and Carl went indoors to make tea, returning with enamel mugs and a big teapot. Then questions were asked and answered, all the usual where have you been and what have you been up to sort of questions. And then who was I and what did I do and how long had I known Liam. Liam was surprisingly open, telling them all about the sheep station that wasn't and how much work he didn't do. Bramble sidled up to Carl, who sneaked her a biscuit when they thought no one was looking.

'And are you still playing the fiddle, man?' asked Carl. 'Did he tell you he used to be a busker at the fairs? How long was it you were with us? It must have been six months. Best musician we've ever met on the road.'

'So what made you stop?' I asked Liam.

'Oh, you know, winter coming on and all that. By the time spring came round I'd found a steady job.'

'You'll have lunch with us, won't you?' asked Fleur.

'That would be just fine. And I wondered, Fleur, afterwards, if you wouldn't mind . . .'

'You want me to do a reading for Regan? And what does Regan think about that?'

I glanced at the board hanging next to the door of the van. 'Psychic Consultant,' it announced. 'Readings by Tarot and Runes. $15.00.'

'Yes, that's me,' she said, 'but pay no mind to that, it's just a quick fix for the punters. I can usually pick up something positive to say, but you can't be of much help on a holiday outing. The last thing they want to hear is the truth. But if you want me to read for you I'll do it properly. Though I should warn you, I'm not a fake.'

'I think Fleur can help you, Regan,' Liam broke in. 'I think you should listen to her.'

'Yes, but what does Regan think?'

'Yes, I'm up for it. Why not?' Although, from the way they were exchanging looks I wasn't too sure any more.

The inside of the van was like a warm lair made dark by wooden walls and heavy velvet curtains. It was surprisingly cosy, the chairs and sofa draped with tapestry rugs and swinging lamps made from coloured glass squares. Fleur and I sat on opposite sides of a table on which she had lit a single candle, throwing a circle of light around us that shut out the rest of the world.

'Have you known Liam for a long time?' I asked.

'No, only the six months he spent on the road with us last year. But you get close to people when you're living side by side every day. They become like family.'

'I only met him a few weeks ago. We didn't get off to a good start and I still don't know much about him.'

'Nor does anyone else. He showed up at the fair one day, driving a campervan. Asked if he could do a bit of busking to earn some petrol money. The punters loved him and so he stayed on, just tagged along like most of us do. Sometimes you know not to ask where people come from and why.'

'So you think he's hiding from something?'

'Tell me who isn't. But no, you're right, he's a fugitive if ever I saw one, but not from the law. No, he's running from whatever caused the pain.'

'The pain?'

'Yes, can't you feel it? He's been badly hurt. Sometimes it's so strong it's almost tangible.'

'Yes, I'll go with that. I suppose that's what makes him so defensive.'

'Don't be fooled by the barbed wire. Inside he's soft as butter. But there are wounds in there that can't be healed. Anyway,' she reached behind her and took a bundle of black silk from a cupboard, 'let's see why he's so worried about you.'

'Is he?'

'Of course. Why do you think he brought you here?'

She unwrapped the silk and took out a deck of cards, placing it on the table between us.

'Look, I'm not sure if I really believe in this sort of thing,' I said. 'Fortune telling I mean. Will it still work?'

'As long as I believe in it we should be OK.' A soft smile played around her mouth. It was often there.

'How did you get into it? I mean, did you have to take lessons or something?'

'My grandmother showed me, much to my mother's disapproval. She had the second sight, as they called it. I took a foundation course in psychology and then got a job in the personnel department of a multinational corporation. It involved talking to employees about their personal problems. Trouble was I could see what was really wrong with them. I couldn't help advising them to do things that weren't in the company's interest, like throwing in their job, cashing in their superannuation and buying a fishing boat. Eventually I took my own advice and went on the road with Carl. Would you believe he used to be a systems analyst?'

The cards, larger than normal playing cards and covered in brightly coloured pictures, were impossible to shuffle and cut as Fleur instructed. I fumbled and a few fell onto the table. She picked these up and studied them carefully before slipping them back into my hands. Eventually she took the whole deck from me and closed her eyes for a moment before laying three rows of three cards face down on the table.

'The top row represents you and where you're at in the present.' She turned the first card over. 'This card represents the inner self, your centre. Ah, *The Magus*, of course. He's a channel of divine power. See, he holds the magic wand through which he calls down the fire of the gods. He's a craftsman whose skill lies in the translation of the unknown into the known. That's the gift you have. It's the centre of your being, the force that drives you. And this,' she turned the next card, 'is what you show the world.'

'*The Fool*,' I read upside down. 'Now that looks more like me.'

'Now don't take the titles too literally. It's more about having the openness and naïvety of a child. I imagine people have difficulty in reconciling your art with your personal image.'

'What do you mean?'

'Well, you're not how most people expect artistic genius to be packaged. I'd have taken you for the bass player in a rock band.'

'Hey, I've always wanted to learn the bass.'

'And you do tend to walk blindly over the edge of a cliff, like this fellow is doing, never stopping to think before you act. Look at this next card,' she turned the third in that row, '*Strength*. See the young woman is holding the lion's mouth. She has control of a great force — at least she thinks she has. You're a powerful channel and there are energies working through you that are beyond your comprehension. Fortunately others recognise that in your art, even if you don't. Consequently your sudden rise to fame has left you a little bewildered.' She ran her fingers over the three cards, as if feeling for something.

'The reason Liam brought you here, at least the underlying cause of the problem, is that you're so involved with your work that you can't, or won't, see that what you're dealing with *is* beyond your control.'

'I do get very intense about it. I have to immerse myself completely in what I am doing. Like you say, it's a force that drives me. Something he wouldn't understand.'

'I think it's more than that. Ask me a question.'

'Will I be able to complete the project?'

She pulled another card out of the pack.

'*The Empress.* Something you create will come into being, but the fruit you bear may not be what you thought.'

She turned the next three cards.

'This line is about what is happening in your life at the present time. *The Five of Swords, The Nine of Swords* and *The Moon.* This is a troubled picture, Regan. You're surrounded by deception. No one is what they seem to be. And you're having disturbing dreams.'

'Yes, that's true, I am. I've told nobody.' But there I was, on the card, in bed and waking from a nightmare, swords stacked behind me.

'And *The Moon* here, something deep and primitive is being called forth. I don't like this.' Fleur was looking worried herself and I was beginning to think this wasn't such a good idea.

She pulled another card from the pack.

'*The Knight of Swords.* You're not alone. Someone comes to your aid but he may not prevail. Do you want to go on with this?'

'Christ, yes. Don't stop now.'

She turned the last row.

'*Judgement.* Deeds of the past being worked out in the present. And *The Seven of Wands*, that's swiftness, it's gathering momentum.' She turned the last card. '*The Hanged Man.* A sacrifice. Ask me a question.'

'What's going to happen?'

She took another card from the pack and laid it between us.

'*The Tower,*' she whispered, turning it towards me. Bodies were

thrown from a high building as lightning struck the roof. 'It ends
with fire and death.'

'Is that it then? What happened to the tall, dark stranger and
the win on Lotto?'

Fleur grasped both my hands.

'Regan, this is serious. You're in great danger.'

'Well, tell me what to do then.'

'Run. That's what you should do. Run now while you still can.
But you won't, will you?'

FOURTEEN

IN denial. That's what they say, isn't it? As if denial isn't something you do, but something you've inadvertently blundered into, like a frightened animal trapped in quicksand. Help, she's in denial, fetch ropes and boards, we'll pull her out. But by then it's too late and you get sucked down and down as your body is imprisoned, limbs numbed beyond feeling, immobilised, paralysed. No amount of reasoning can talk you through; no loving arms can drag you free. It fills your mouth so you can't scream. It clogs your ears, making you deaf to all warning, to every plea of wisdom and sanity. Down and down you go until it seals your eyelids, blinding you to the very substance of your self-betrayal. Denial. Seeping through the pores of your skin, polluting the blood and silting up the brain. And there you lie, rendered helpless by the weight of it all.

And that is how it was when we left the land of the gypsies and drove home. We had all said goodbye and exchanged hugs and promises. As they walked us to the truck Liam hung back and spoke with Fleur. He strode with shoulders hunched, hands in pockets, looking at the ground. But Fleur glanced towards me and placed her hand on his arm. I was too far away to hear any words but her face said urgent.

In the truck we were silent, each unsure of the other, until Liam spotted a bar and said we should stop for a beer and a sandwich. I knew it was time to talk.

'So, what did Fleur say? What did she tell you?'

'That I take my work too seriously and I need a holiday.'

'Try again.'

'All right, she said I was under some sort of stress and it was time I moved on.'

'In other words she said you were in danger and you should get the hell out of there,' Liam said.

'Something like that. Well, if you knew why are you asking me?'

'To see if you were listening. And are you going to?'

'Move on? Yes, when I have finished some more of the pieces. The agreement was for three months and I've been there nearly a month already.'

'And how many of the pieces are finished?'

'Well, one, you saw that. And I've made a start on the second. Sometimes things happen more slowly. It's not a production line, you know,' I said.

'No, I realise that, but I'm wondering if the reason your work has slowed down has anything to do with the hours you spend wandering through the bush.'

'Well, of course I do, that's what these sculptures are about. I have to get in touch with my subject, immerse myself in the environment.'

'And how deep do you have to go? I've watched you wandering up in those hills, hour upon hour sometimes, just standing staring at nothing as if you were mesmerised.'

'Oh, you've been spying on me, have you?'

'No. Yes. For God's sake, someone needs to look after you.'

'And that's why you took me to see Fleur? Beware the gypsy's warning? You're beginning to sound like those Irish folk tales. "Don't walk on Sullivan's land or your wedding dress will make your shroud."'

'Well, you said it.'

'Oh, come on now, I'm hardly likely to go marrying old man Sullivan, am I?'

'It might not be as simple as that.' Liam spoke quietly and I realised he was genuinely worried.

'So you do agree there's something strange going on?'

'Maybe. Whatever is or isn't wrong with the place it's certainly doing you a power of no good.'

'And what's it doing for you?'

'What do you mean?' he asked.

'Is it helping you to hide from whatever it is you're running from? Well, that's why you're here, isn't it? And don't tell me fence-mending is a significant career move. Maybe running away is your answer, but it doesn't work for me.'

'So why are you here then? Artistic inspiration, is it? Or has it got something to do with that young whelp you were trying to escape from?'

I gasped and pulled back, as if he'd actually slapped my face.

'No, no I'm sorry,' he stammered, 'that was out of order. This isn't going the way I intended. Look Regan, it's just that I'm concerned about you. No. No, it's more than that. Something's happening to you and it's scaring the shit out of me. Now maybe it has got something to do with this Sullivan business and maybe not. Whatever the cause, that place is destroying you.'

I lifted my glass from the table, took a slow, deliberate drink and said nothing. Then Liam, too, lifted his glass, tossing the remains of his beer down his throat. He looked at me with eyes as dark as slate.

'You won't budge, will you? You've not taken a blind bit of notice of anything Fleur and I have said.' He slammed his glass down on the table. 'God, you're a stubborn woman.' He spat the words at me and, snatching up his hat, stormed out of the bar.

I was determined to finish my drink in a leisurely fashion and not go running off after him. Besides, he wasn't going anywhere. I had the keys to the truck.

'Well, what happens now?'

It was the following morning. We were at the woolshed having our ritual coffee. I'd woken early and been working for a couple of hours; at least I'd tried to work but I was finding it unusually difficult to focus on the sculpture. It was as if the day away had disconnected me in some way.

'You're looking better. Nice to see you a bit rested. Sleep well?'

'Yes, you were right. I did need a break.' I had slept long and deeply. No, no dreams. 'So, what now?'

'Well, I've done all that needs to be done for today so I thought I'd take a trip back into town, see if I can ferret out some information. Then on the way back I've got an appointment with the sexton of the local church. I rang him earlier and he said if I could drop in round about five he'd show me the parish records. We'll see what that fetches up.'

'Right, I'll get my stuff.'

'I said I'm going. You're staying here. I'll have to take your truck, of course. You can keep an eye on the dogs.'

'Great. Thanks.'

'Come on, I'll walk you back to your place and get the car keys.' He set off through the trees with me catching up behind.

'Can you drive?'

'Of course I can bloody drive. You know that, I've driven the truck before. And, yes, I do have a licence. Your insurance will cover me I hope.'

'How the hell should I know? It cost a lot of money, so I suppose it ought to.'

'And stay near the cottage. I don't want you wandering up

in those hills. Do you hear me?'

I wasn't going to be put down by this exhibition of macho dominance so I started singing 'The Teddy Bears' Picnic':

If you go down in the woods today,
you'd better not go alone,
If you go down in the woods today,
it's safer to stay at home.

Liam spun round and jabbed his finger at me. 'And that's not bloody funny!'

After he left I made a serious effort to get down to work but couldn't concentrate. The second piece was emerging, but slowly. I had the major shape outlined and was now working with the smaller chisels and gouges to define the facial features. But something was missing and it was hard to resist the pull of the trees. I needed to walk, but Liam had insisted that I shouldn't go into the bush, and, as he was running all over the region to satisfy my curiosity, I felt obliged to do as he said. However, no one had mentioned not walking around the lake. Besides, it was about time someone had a word with Sullivan.

By the time I got to the house the sun was directly overhead. Sullivan was sitting on the deck, a glass in his hand, gazing into the distance. I don't think he realised I was there until the steps creaked under my foot, and then he looked up and stared at me as if he did not know who I was.

'Hi Sullivan, nice morning.'

'Ah, Regan, yes. Come up, come up.' He nudged a chair in my direction, then picked up a bottle. 'Will you join me?'

'No thanks. Perhaps some water? No, don't get up. I can find the kitchen.'

I found a clean glass, filled it and returned. By then I think he'd forgotten all about me and was quite startled when I emerged from the front door.

'How's Badger?' he asked.

'Oh, he's mending fine. He can walk around the yard a bit now. He's putting on weight, though, I'm sure Liam's spoiling him.'

'And what about you? Are you comfortable? Is there anything you need?'

'No, the cottage is wonderful. It's just, well, I thought I ought to drop by and thank you for inviting me to share in your Christmas.'

'It was a pleasure to have you here, but I have to confess the idea was all Jason's. And all the work too. Suddenly got it into his head that Christmas was a time to be at home celebrating. He never thought much about it before.'

'Not even when he was a child?'

'That was different. When he was small and his mother was here, she made it really something. She'd have the house all prettied up, greenery and bright lights. And the tree, of course, we had to have the biggest tree, with fairy lights and covered with glass balls and tinsel. Then she'd go shopping for him, practically cleared every store in town. She got me this Father Christmas outfit and made me dress up, the whole bit. Don't know who was more excited come Christmas morning, Jason or her.'

'And what happened when she . . . when she wasn't here any more?'

'I tried. And he tried too, poor kid. But it could never work. Everything I did seemed to reinforce her absence. It was like there was this big empty hole in the house, and the more I tried to fill it the bigger it got.' Sullivan reached for the scotch and topped up his glass.

'I can't imagine what it must be like to grow up without a mother,' I said.

'Can't you? Funny, I can't imagine what it would be like to have one.'

Of course, I'd forgotten. Or rather I hadn't thought it through. Sullivan was orphaned too, probably at about the same age. It was his mother up there in that clearing.

'I'm sorry, I wasn't thinking. I've seen her grave, you know. Jason showed me the first day I arrived. But I have been up there since. Jane, wasn't it?'

'Yes, Jane Sullivan. Though I can't remember her at all. That makes it easier, I think. The problem with Jason was that he could remember and he wouldn't let go.'

'He told me he used to go to his mother's room.'

'Yes. Sarah — my wife's name was Sarah — she said she needed her own space. That's the way she put it, one of those phrases she'd picked up. She was into all that New Age stuff, read endless books about eastern philosophy, crystal power, that sort of thing. Couldn't understand it myself. She got into meditation and said she needed somewhere — how did she put it? — "free from unsympathetic vibrations". So she moved into that room, practically lived in there when she wasn't at the cottage. Only Jason was allowed in with her — they treated it like a privilege, being in Mummy's special place. Afterwards he sort of held onto that room as if it would bring her back. Became like an obsession with him. I began to worry, after what happened with his mother. But eventually he seemed to snap out of it. Strangely enough it was Christmas that did it.'

'How was that?'

'Well, in spite of everything I'd tried to keep Christmas over the years. Always bought him something special. I think he must have been about ten that year. He used to spend hours looking through the family photo albums, looking at pictures of his mother and grandmother. But he started taking an interest in the photographs themselves, kept asking all sorts of questions that I couldn't answer. Then he took to getting books out of the library, all about camera techniques and developing and so forth. Anyway, I decided to get him a camera, not a snapshot thing but a good one. We blacked up the boxroom and set it up as a darkroom. It was like another world had opened for him.'

'So, that's how he got started. You gave him the most important thing in his life.'

'But there was no way I could have given him back his mother.'

I was walking a very narrow path here. I took a long drink of water, and then chose the words carefully. 'He doesn't talk much about his mother. But he did say she spent a lot of time in the hills, just walking he said. She must have loved this land.'

'We both did. But with her it was more than that. It was like she was entranced by it. It was after Jason was born — not an easy birth and she never really recovered. Oh, sometimes she'd be fine, like at Christmas and birthdays. She always loved celebrations, made a big thing of it and I was relieved to see her happy. But if I were honest I'd have to say she was too happy, you know, she'd . . . she'd go over the top, like she was a kid herself. Then other times she'd go inside herself, want to be left alone. Even moved into that cottage to get away from this house and me. Days on end she'd spend there. Sometimes she'd take the boy with her, but mostly she preferred to be on her own. And then she'd go walking, hour upon hour, and it seemed like she'd forgotten all about the child. Certainly she'd forgotten all about me.'

'It sounds like there was something really wrong with her. Didn't you think she might have needed help?'

'Well of course I did. Postnatal depression they called it at first, then a psychotic breakdown. The doctors came up with all sorts of labels but none of it made any difference.'

'So what became of Sarah?' I whispered it softly.

But he said nothing, just shook his head and closed his eyes tight against the world.

I slipped away silently and retraced my steps along the lake path, leaving him clutching his glass.

Liam had been gone much longer than I had anticipated and daylight was fading when I saw headlamps along the lake road throwing highlights across the water. Bramble bounded off to meet him and practically dragged him out of the seat. Even Badger struggled down the steps, his tail sweeping the sawdust. I was quite pleased to see him too; it was the only day I'd spent there without knowing he was around.

'Bramble, you're a brazen young lady,' he said as she slurped his face with her big, wet tongue. 'And you here too, Badger. You didn't walk, did you?'

'He did. We took it very slowly, mind. And he may need the wheelbarrow service to get home. I hope you're hungry, I'm making supper for us.'

'Starving. Nothing since lunchtime. I thought the sexton would never let me go. I'm probably the first person who's taken any interest in his paperwork for years.'

'I can have food on the table in ten minutes.'

'OK. I'll just nip back to my place and find a clean shirt.'

'Hey, Liam,' I called after him, 'bring your fiddle.'

I was being so very cool and self-controlled. When he returned from the woolshed I opened a bottle of wine and served up. It wasn't until we'd both started eating that I asked the question.

'So, did you find out anything?'

'Well, yes and no. It's a bit like the stuff from Ireland. Lots of accrued wealth with no explanation. A family that kept itself very much to itself, bred in small numbers and lost its womenfolk in tragic circumstances.

'First off I went to the council offices and asked about land registration records. The chap there was very helpful. I told him

I was tracking down my forebears who'd once owned land in the area before moving to the South Island. I said I believed the land had been sold to a family of Sullivans and if I could fix a date for the transfer of deeds it would help trace the Connors' movements.'

'That was good thinking.'

'Yeah, I thought so too. Apparently all the historic records are now under a department called Land Information New Zealand and have all been moved off to the city or somewhere.'

'Oh, that's a bugger.'

'No, that's good. The purpose being that all registration information can be accessed by computer, as can all the associated archive material. Much quicker than looking through rooms full of old documents. He did most of the work for me, all part of the service he said. Mind you, it's still that slack time in the holiday season — just a skeleton staff on, and I think he was glad of something to do. What's this I'm eating?'

'Chickpea and spinach fritters.'

'Oh. Right. Anyway, he invited me into his office and even made me a cup of tea. Obviously knew what he was doing because he tracked it all down quite quickly. Strangely enough there *was* a Connors who sold land to the Sullivans around about the turn of the century, a common enough name and nothing to do with me as far as I know, but it did give my story a bit of credence. He traced it forward and found that same section is still part of the Sullivan estate. He downloaded it all and printed it out for me. There's a pile of papers and maps that we'll have to look through. But from what I gathered, they simply moved in and started buying up land. First one large block, enough to make a decent farm, and then they added more acres every few years until quite recently. That was about it.'

'Oh. So then what?'

'I'd been there quite a time so I grabbed a sandwich and went straight to the local newspaper office. Opposite story there. They were short of staff and couldn't spare me the time. Which was again good, because they left me alone with the microfiche and I didn't have to make out I was looking for Connors.'

'So, did you find anything there?'

'Not really, although I was able to confirm the births and obituaries from the dates we already had.'

'What about Jason and his mother?'

'Yes, there was the birth of Jason in 1983. I searched all through 1987, which was when we figured she dropped out of the picture, but no mention of a death or anything. Then I scanned through masses of back issues from around the significant times but found nothing. It's like looking for a needle in a haystack, but, even so, I expected there to be regular mentions of Sullivans, seeing they were the biggest landowners in the area. All I found was a few articles about prize-winning bulls owned by a Mr Sullivan and other stuff to do with farming, all very impersonal. But the newspaper people did say that most of their early records, like stuff from the 1800s, have all been passed over to the museum. There it's been set up as an archive display along with loads of photographs. So that might be worth a visit.'

'You didn't go there then?'

'Well no, by the time I got out of the press office it was after four o'clock and I had to get back to see the sexton. Would you pass the salad?'

'You want some more fritters?'

'Yeah, I wouldn't mind. They're not bad when you get used to them. You want some more wine?'

'Please. What about the sexton, did he tell you anything?'

'Oh, the man's an archive in himself — he must have been there when they built the church. Mr Withers is his name and he looks like he's about to crumble into dust. But fiercely independent and defensive of his responsibilities. Insisted on unlocking the cupboard and getting the books out himself, even though it took him half an hour to find the keyhole and the old volumes weighed more than he did. I stuck to the same story of tracing the Connors, so when I said I was working on the Sullivan place that led us neatly into the Sullivan family history.'

'And, did he tell you anything?'

'Nothing new, but he did throw some light on things we've already discovered. He knew about the early times when Michael Sullivan first arrived. Apparently that man's quite a legend in these parts.

'It seems there were numbers of people fetching up and wanting to buy land. But Michael came with money and official letters and got straight onto this government chap who negotiated a good piece of property for him. Apparently Michael actually knew what he was doing. There were lots who didn't, middle-class dreamers who came for the adventure. They knew nothing of land or farming and bought up a few acres, not enough to grow a profitable crop even if the soil had been suitable. Despite all their struggles, most of them went under. Sullivan had money and hired the labour to clear the ground quickly and started raising cattle. Whenever one of his neighbours gave in, he bought their plot. Mind you, he gave a fair price, by all accounts, and helped them resettle as best they could. Some went back home, others stayed and fared much better by setting themselves up in business.

'Meanwhile the Sullivan estates grew and grew, as did their bank balance, until the 1960s when Tom Sullivan, that's our John Sullivan's father, bought up that last little patch of orchard. Got it from a newly widowed woman who needed money more than oranges. Paid her almost twice what it was worth. The Sullivans are well respected. Nothing can be said against them, it seems, yet no one knows much about them.'

'That doesn't help us though, does it?'

'No, but it does echo the story that came from Ireland. Also, now this is the interesting part, being with the Church and Church history, Mr Withers knew something about the burials. Shall I put the kettle on for coffee?'

'No, it's OK, I'll do it. Go on, what about the burials?'

'Well, there's definitely something odd there. The way the Sullivan men reacted when their wives died. And the women too. Something happened to them when they came to live here. It's as if the place affected them in some way.'

'It sounds like you're beginning to agree with me?'

'Yes, I admit you may be right. But I'm still not jumping to any conclusions. It may simply have been the isolation of the place and the way they kept themselves separate from the community. Enough to send anyone stir crazy after a while.'

He looked hard at me. I looked down at my plate, pushing the food around aimlessly.

'So, what about the men? What did they do?'

'Well, according to Mr Withers, Michael married Anne two years after he arrived here. Their first child died after a few months — a poor wee thing, by all accounts, and not expected to last long. Nothing unusual in those days. Anne immediately fell pregnant again and the mother, Katherine, was already on her way to join them.'

'That's what Trevor Benson told me. I met him at Maggie's place. Remember, you were at the bar talking with Sullivan.'

'I remember,' said Liam. 'I wondered what you were up to.'

'Asking if he knew anything about the gravestones, that's all. So what else did old Withers say about Anne?'

'Well, as Trevor probably also told you, Anne had a son, David, and after that she went a bit strange — at least that's what was said. Just as well the mother was there to look after the little one. Anne kept wandering off, spent a few nights in the bush and they had to send the men out looking for her. Eventually there was that accident with the horse.

176

'It seems Michael lost the plot completely when they found her. He insisted she be buried where she lay, even dug the grave himself. Now, it wasn't really on to do that. As you pointed out, there's a church nearby and there seemed to be expectations of a decent Christian burial. But by the time the local priest, or whatever he was, found out what was going on, the deed was done. When he tried to visit the grave Michael drove him off with a shotgun. It was after that Michael and his descendants started closing in on themselves.'

'Was there anything suspicious about her death? Who found her?'

'Who could say now? But it seems there was a whole bunch of people out looking for her and she'd been dead a while when she was found. Mary, now that's another matter.'

'I thought she died of pneumonia?'

'Not that simple.'

Liam pushed his coffee mug to one side, making room for a sheaf of papers he had brought to the table.

'Now, let's see if I've got this right.' He spread the pages, scanning the notes he had made. 'Yes, now Anne died in 1866. Michael survived until 1913 — he was eighty-one when he died. Meanwhile David, their son, married Mary in 1902 and she died in 1905, a year after giving birth to Tom. There's an official note of her death, but no death certificate.'

'No death certificate? But I thought you weren't allowed to bury people without . . . Oh, I see, of course it was another DIY job. Trevor said she was found wandering about the hills in a rainstorm and caught pneumonia. Called away by Anne's ghost, or so they reckon.'

'Something like that,' he agreed. 'It seems she'd taken to wandering about at night. Apparently there were problems after the child was born. Mary never seemed to recover her strength. Her eldest sister, who'd been widowed by then, moved in after the birth and helped look after the child. Apparently the Sullivan men weren't best pleased having an outsider, but the child and the house needed tending to so there was little they could do about it.

'When Mary was found, it was the sister who insisted the doctor be sent for. He diagnosed the pneumonia and didn't hold out much hope. She held on for a few days and only David Sullivan was with her when she died. The first the sister knew about it was when she found him carrying Mary down the stairs all wrapped in a sheet. He said he was going to bury her. Of course there was an almighty row. The sister wanted her put back in the bed and the priest sent for. But Sullivan would have none of it, wouldn't even let her see Mary's body. It was like he'd gone a bit crazy. So the sister, she gets on a horse and rides off to fetch help. However, while she's gone, David goes ahead and buries Mary himself.'

'Was he allowed to do that?'

'No, of course not'. By then there were proper laws in place concerning disposal of bodies. Home burials were definitely out of order unless a designated site couldn't be reached within a certain time.'

'Why was that?'

'Well, partly to do with the Church I suppose, but also for hygiene reasons. There were a lot of contagious illnesses still doing the rounds then, like diphtheria and cholera. I suppose you'd get diseases in the ground. Then it was a matter of rotting bodies contaminating the waterways and so forth. Plus they didn't want some unsuspecting farmer digging up the previous owner's granny.

'However, he went ahead and buried Mary anyway. When the sister returned with the police, both David and the body were gone. By the time they'd tracked him down it was too late, the deed was done. Of course the authorities weren't easy with this. The doctor was interviewed and confirmed that Mary had been ill and hadn't been expected to live. But as it had been several days since he had last seen her and, as there was no body to examine, he refused to issue a death certificate.'

'Surely they would have exhumed the body?'

'You'd have thought so. But somehow David managed to talk his way around it. Remember, he would have been quite a prominent figure by then. It was a tight community that relied on his generosity. And although his actions were out of order, there was no reason to suspect anything wrong with her death.'

'So nobody actually saw the body. No one really knew how she died.'

'No one — except David Sullivan.'

For a long time we sat in silence. The sun had set long ago and the room was swathed in shadows. I couldn't see Liam's face and was glad he couldn't read mine. Eventually I fetched a candle and set it in the centre of the table. A draught from the window caused the flame to stretch tall and thin, so that the circle of light fell on the papers Liam had spread around. He started to look through them again.

'There's nothing to say what happened to Mary's sister after that, or how the son was brought up,' he said. 'David never married again. He died in, let me see, here, 1940 aged seventy-five.'

'I suppose in the meantime Mary's son, Tom, got married.'

'That's right. This time it was Jane. Tom and Jane, of course, were John Sullivan's parents. She committed suicide when he was two years old.'

'Hell, no! Why? How?'

'Why? God only knows. How? It seems she tried to cut her wrists, then hung herself. They took her down from one of the big trees out the back of the house. This time of course the police were involved and there was an inquest, the whole bit. "Suicide while the state of her mind was disturbed", as they say. After the verdict, old Tom managed to get permission to bury her with the other two. Claimed it was an official family plot, that it had been consecrated and was all quite legal. Mr Withers reckoned that was all nonsense, but a powerful landowner like that, and it being such tragic circumstances, no one argued. Besides, in those days suicides weren't welcome on hallowed grounds so she couldn't have gone in the churchyard anyway. Probably saved a lot of embarrassment all round.'

'Did your Mr Withers know anything about Jason's mother?'

'I asked if he remembered her and he said he did. Very pretty girl, he said, bit strange. Didn't go to church.'

'Did he say what happened to her?'

'Well, I asked him, but he just muttered something incoherent and launched off onto another subject. Whatever he knows he's not telling.'

We drank our coffee in silence. Eventually I said, 'It's a clear pattern. Father to son. The wife has an untimely, probably violent death. Her body is given to the land. The land grows and prospers.'

'Yes, only the pattern's been broken twice.'

'How do you mean?'

'Michael was the younger brother of a second marriage. All the land and property went to his older stepbrother and whatever was going on should have continued in Ireland. Instead of that, it all fell apart there. At the same time the pattern started up again here.'

'So Michael brought whatever it was with him?'

'Could be. Either him or his mother who joined him. Though I can't see what she had to do with it.'

'You said the pattern was broken twice. You're thinking of Jason's mother?'

Liam nodded.

'I'm not so sure it has been broken. Because there's no gravestone doesn't mean there's no grave.'

This time he didn't argue with me. I said nothing about my conversation with Sullivan. That could wait for another time.

The silence hung heavy in the room.

'Hey, Connors, give us a tune for God's sake.'

So, while I made fresh coffee he rosined up his bow and thrashed out some jigs and reels, lifting our spirits as the notes skipped on the evening air.

It was only when he played the slow tunes that I thought again of the women. Anne, her life ebbing away into the earth; Mary, cold and beaten by the rain; and Jane, a final offering to the trees. Jason's mother, Sarah, what of her? But it was all so long ago, another age, another world. Just a curious tale for me to unravel.

Even now I don't understand how I couldn't see the connection. Denial? Oh yes, I was in denial all right, up to my ears and over my head. I was drowning in the stuff.

FIFTEEN

L IAM was around early next morning. He'd obviously come to
check up on me and didn't bother to pretend it was a social
call. I said I was going to the dairy and then might drive on into
town as I needed some wood oil and a new saw blade. He said
he was happy with that: I would be away from the place, he
said; it would do me good. He told me to make a day of it, find
a good restaurant for lunch and go shopping. He said I should
treat myself to a new dress and didn't understand why I fell about
laughing.

Of course I had no intention of doing any of that. I thought
it was time I did some investigating of my own and planned to
visit the museum and hunt out those photographs. Still, lunch
sounded pleasant and I understood there was a good art gallery
that might deserve an hour of my time.

First stop was the dairy for a few tins and packets of stuff, and
then I thought I'd call in on Maggie. I know Liam had said
we shouldn't go asking questions, but even I could use a little
discretion. It was far too early for the bar to be open but I could
see Maggie in there, going round with the vacuum cleaner.

When I tapped on the window she looked up and saw it was me, switched off the machine and came over to unbolt the door.

'Regan, how good to see you. Come on in.'

'Not if it's a bad time. You look busy.'

'No, it's an ideal time. I hate housework. Come on, I'll switch the coffee-maker on.'

Although this was an out-of-hours social call we took up our customary positions, me perched on a stool and Maggie behind the bar.

'So, how was Christmas?' she asked. 'Do anything special?'

'I had Christmas lunch with Jason and his father.'

'That sounds a bundle of laughs.'

'It was actually. Sullivan got smashed as usual, Liam and Jason nearly came to blows and I drank too much punch and made an idiot of myself. And you?'

'Just a quiet day with Mum and Dad. Still, it made a nice change to get away from this crowd. Though I expect they'll make up for it tomorrow night, with it being New Year's Eve. The place will be heaving and I'll be rushed off my feet. Don't fancy doing a bit of bar work, do you?'

'No thanks.'

'No, don't blame you. Still, Mum's on the mend now. She reckons she'll be able to help out a bit. Oh, and one of the young girls said she'd give me a hand — overspent at Christmas and could do with the extra cash.'

'Does that mean your mum's up to visitors?'

'Er, yeah, why not? Do her good. I've told her about you. I said you'd been asking about the Sullivans and she'd welcome any excuse for a gossip. Tell you what, come through and I'll introduce you. Then I can finish the cleaning while you're having a chat.'

'You sure I won't be disturbing her?'

'No way. She can only put up with so much of this invalid business.'

Maggie led the way through to the room behind the bar. It was a bright room full of flowers — flowered curtains, flowered wallpaper, flowered cushions — none of which had anything to do with the colour of the carpet, which in turn clashed with the paintwork. Every available surface was taken up with china ornaments containing more flower arrangements, the plastic variety this time. My eyes were so busy that at first I didn't spot the woman on the sofa, her feet on a stool and a halo of smoke drifting above her head.

'Hello dear,' she beamed, 'you must be Maggie's new friend. Rachel, isn't it?'

'It's Regan, Mum. Thought you two might like to talk while I finish the vacuuming. I've told Mum you want to know about the Sullivan family. There's not much that's gone on round here she can't tell you about. I'll bring coffee through in a minute.'

Maggie went back to her work and her mum pointed me to an armchair while reaching for the ashtray.

'Call me Bev, dear. I'll just put this out. That was the first of today's three. All I'm allowed now, since the op.'

'Maggie said you'd not been well.'

'No, I've had a bit of trouble. Not half as bad as giving up the fags, though.' She laughed as though this were the funniest thing that could happen to anyone. She had the look of someone who had been round and cuddly but had recently lost a lot of weight. Her hair was bright copper and in need of some attention at the roots. Scarlet lipstick smeared her mouth and I could see where Maggie would be in thirty years' time.

'You ever been in hospital, love? No, well they fixed me up and I'll be all right for a few more miles. They tried to tell me it was the fags that did it.' She mashed the remains of her cigarette into the ashtray. 'How can you run a pub and not smoke? Been breathing in other people's ciggies for years. Can't see what difference a few of my own's going to make.' Bev rocked with laughter again and I couldn't help joining in, although I really couldn't see what was funny.

'Maggie says you're staying at the Sullivans' place? That'll be a first. Friend of young Jason's, are you?'

'That's right. I'm an artist, using the cottage to do some work.'

'Well, that's nice. Though we don't get many tourists round here if you were thinking of selling. No passing trade. What's he like? Old John Sullivan, I mean.'

'Oh, quiet. Polite. Don't see much of him really. But I'm interested in the family history. There's some gravestones, you see.'

'The graves? What, you mean you've actually seen them? I've heard all about them, of course, and them having the women buried up there, but you never know what to believe, do you?' That set her off laughing again.

'I was talking to Trevor Benson. He told me some of it,' and I recounted the essence of what I'd learnt about Anne and Mary. Bev nodded to confirm the stories but could add nothing new.

'What about Jane?' I asked. 'I didn't have a chance to talk about her.'

'Ah, now, there's a sad lady if ever there was one.'

'Did you know her?'

'Me? No, she died soon after I was born. But her and my mum, they were good friends. Grew up together, went to school. Mum often used to talk about her. I think she felt a bit guilty about what happened, thought she ought to have done more. But as I said to her time and again, how could she have known how things would turn out?'

'It was Tom that Jane married, wasn't it?'

'That's right. Now him I remember, though I never actually spoke to him that I recall. He was John Sullivan's father, of course. Lived with his son right up to when he died. That would have been about ten, fifteen years ago.'

'So, likewise David would have been around when Tom married Jane?'

'Oh, very much so. I think that was half the trouble. Her stuck out there on that farm with only those two men for company, pining for a child she could never have.'

'But I thought she had a child. John, wasn't it? Jason's father?'

'Ah, yes, but that was much later. It was the first child I'm talking about. She got into trouble, you see. At least that's how they saw it in those days. Not like it is now with single mums parading their stomachs all over the front of magazines. Those days you were in disgrace, about the worst thing that could happen to a girl. Of course Jane was beside herself, and her being friends with my mother, well, it was her she confided in. Wouldn't say who the father was, though, not that it would have made any difference. If he could have married her he would have done. She was a beautiful girl, my mum always said, a catch for any man.'

'So what happened to the baby?'

'Lost it. She would have been about six months gone. Stillborn, it was, and that just added to her shame. People get so high and mighty, don't they? Saw it as a punishment, no more than she deserved. Yes, things were certainly different all right,' and Bev set herself off laughing again.

'So what happened to her?'

'Well, of course, it was like she'd been written off. No man would want her after what had happened. Damaged goods, brought shame on her parents — I expect they thought they'd be stuck with her for life. Then suddenly, out of the blue, she was marrying Tom Sullivan. Wealthiest bachelor in the district, and good-looking with it by all accounts. My mum said you could have knocked her down with a feather.'

'And were they still friends after she was married? Jane and your mother, I mean?'

'Well, Jane came to see her sometimes when she came in to shop. This used to be a much bigger place, you understand, quite a thriving wee community. Not many people had cars in those days and the town was a day's drive away by horse and cart, so people did most of their shopping here, Jane Sullivan included. She'd call in on my mother when she could. Mum never went there, of course. People didn't. Besides, Mum had married by then and had little ones of her own. I expect that made it harder for Jane.'

'Why? Wasn't she happy?'

'No, she wasn't. No good ever came of that marriage. Mum reckoned it was a child Jane wanted more than a husband, you see.'

'But she did have a son, didn't she?'

'Eventually, yes. Took his time coming, though. She was nearly thirty when the kid was born. Mum tried to keep the friendship going over the years but it was like the gap between their worlds got wider. And Jane, well . . . By then she'd become very quiet, Mum said. Like she'd closed in on herself. I suppose nowadays you'd say she was suffering from depression. Not surprising with her out there on the farm with only Tom and the old man for company.'

'What about after John was born?'

'She was no better. In fact things must have got much worse. Because of what happened, I mean. It was one of the farm hands found her. They said she'd tried to cut her wrists and when that didn't work she hung herself. They say there was a big pool of blood under the tree. The men that cut her down were covered in it.'

'And Tom buried her on their land?'

'That's right. There was no funeral or anything. Or if there was, no one outside the family was invited. Mum took flowers to the church instead. I don't think she ever got over it. They'd been close once and she felt she'd let Jane down.'

A quietness settled over the room. Bev looked into the distance, as if still listening to her mother's regrets for a friend lost. Then she shook herself and reached for her cigarette packet.

'Here, we can't have this. No good getting all mopy, is there?' She lit up and blew a column of blue smoke across the room just as the door opened and Maggie came in carrying a tray of mugs.

'Oh, Mum, that's the second one and it's not half past ten yet. You know what the doctor told you.'

'You're a nagger, Maggie. Make some bloke a wonderful wife.' She was shaking with laughter again.

Maggie looked at her straight-faced and said nothing.

'Oh, all right.' Bev took another long puff. 'I'll put it away for later.' She pinched the lighted end off and stowed the cigarette back in the packet.

'Sorry I took so long but I had to get the place sorted out before opening time. Hey, Regan, I heard you went to the Gypsy Fair with Liam.'

'God, you can't get away with anything round here.'

'I did warn you. Here's your coffee. That wasn't like a date, was it?'

'No, it was not like a date, or like anything else. We're just neighbours and he wanted to introduce me to some of his friends, that's all.'

'Yeah, right.'

This conversation was getting off track.

'I was quite surprised when Jason turned up on Christmas Day,' I said. 'He worked really hard at making it special. Mr Sullivan was telling me about how Christmas used to be when his mother was still around.'

'Was he now? Yes, it's sad,' said Bev, 'something you'd never get over, especially at Christmas. Dreadful business, that.'

'She wasn't from round here, was she, Mum?'

188

'No. Whole crowd of them turned up one day, looking like a bunch of leftovers from the sixties, all beads and flowers. They seemed harmless enough, all a bit daft if you ask me, but they frightened the life out of the Women's Institute.' Bev was laughing again and had to find a tissue to blow her nose. 'They rented an old woolshed off my brother for the summer, so I saw quite a lot of them. Well, truth be told, I made it my business to hang around. I remember Sarah was very pretty, long blonde hair — turned out to be Canadian, or something like that. There was some talk about them setting up a commune but it never came to anything. When they moved on, she stayed behind and moved into the Sullivans' place.

'They didn't get married straight away, though. In fact it wasn't until a couple of years later and the baby was on the way. Last thing people expected. Well, we all thought John was set as a bachelor. He must have been in his forties by then and she'd have been a lot younger and hardly what you'd call his type. Can't understand what they saw in each other, or why a young woman like that would want to shut herself away in that place. Still there's no accounting for people, is there?'

'How did it happen?' I asked, 'I mean, how did she die?'

'Die? She's not dead.'

'Not dead?'

'No. Is that what Jason told you?' That was Maggie.

'No, I just . . . I mean . . . she's *not* dead?'

'No, of course not,' Bev cut in. 'Mind you, she might as well be, as far as the family's concerned.'

'Why, what happened to her?'

'They took her away. You know, up to the house.' She jerked her head in no particular direction. Obviously I was supposed to know what she was talking about.

'Which house?'

'Harston House, of course. At least that's where she ended up. Got taken to the hospital first, of course, didn't she, Mum?'

'That's right. She was there for months, as I remember, but they couldn't do anything with her. Eventually John Sullivan had her sent to Harston House. Been there for years.'

'What is this place?'

'Private nursing home, they call it. Very posh by all accounts, more like a hotel. Well, they can afford it I suppose. But it's still a mental home.'

'Hang on, can we just back up a little? Are you saying that Sarah Sullivan, Jason's mother, had some sort of breakdown and has spent the last, what, sixteen years in a psychiatric hospital?'

'Yeah, that's what she's saying.' Maggie picked up the story again. 'Though I can understand Jason making out she was dead, poor kid. Fancy something like that happening to your mum at that age. Mind you, she always was a bit odd. Not like a proper mother.'

'You knew her, then, Maggie?'

'Oh, yes, we all knew her. I'd have been, what, twelve or thirteen. Jason was just little — don't think he'd even started school. They used to come down to the shop together or we'd see her in town. I remember she was real pretty, long blonde hair like you said, and she wore those long, floaty Indian dresses. Bit of a hippy, I suppose, though that sort of thing had really gone out of fashion by then. As I say, she was a bit odd the way she'd play with the boy. Like, she'd get overexcited, more like a kid herself. Then we wouldn't see her for ages and his dad would take Jason out.'

'So, what happened to her?'

'I don't know, but it must have been something major. The police were called, and then an ambulance, and she was taken into hospital. I can remember there was a lot of gossip among the other mums — you know the sort of thing, whispering and people suddenly changing the subject for no reason. What did happen, Mum?'

'You know as much as I do. Though there was plenty of gossip, people's imaginations running riot. She got sick and they took her away. That's all I know.'

'And she never came back?'

'No. As I say, she ended up at Harston House. Still there as far as I know.'

'And where is this place exactly?'

'Not far. It's off the main highway, just the other side of town.'

SIXTEEN

A ND there it was, just where she'd said. I drove straight
there after I'd left Maggie. It was shortly after noon when
I arrived.

A discreet sign announced the address but said nothing about
its purpose. I had expected closed gates set in a high wall, some
kind of security. There was a gate but it was wide open and
led onto a broad driveway winding through a gently sloping
shrubbery. There was no one in sight. Trees gradually gave way
to neatly trimmed lawns sculptured with rose beds. The house
was sublimely elegant, white weatherboarding and three levels
of leadlight windows.

Still no one in sight, so I left the truck next to a line of parked
cars and headed through what seemed to be the main entrance.
I was painfully aware of my clumsy boots on their marble tiled
floor and hoped I wouldn't have to climb that sweeping, wooden
staircase.

'Can I help you?' The voice echoed round the vaulted hall and
I nearly jumped out of my skin.

'Jeez, you scared the shi— Um, sorry. I was looking for
someone.'

'Well, I can probably assist you. I'm Janet,' she pointed to a badge bearing her name. It was pinned to a white shirt that had never seen a tomato sauce splat and never would. Her lipstick matched her nail varnish exactly. 'I'm the secretary and I also act as receptionist if we have visitors. Unfortunately, that's not as often as we'd like. Who is it you're looking for?'

'Well, I was told Mrs Sullivan was staying here.'

'Ah, Sarah, yes. And you are?'

'Er, Maggie, Maggie Connors.' That was quick thinking. 'She won't know me. I'm a friend of the family and I've been spending Christmas with her husband and son,' that was nearly true, 'and I thought I ought to get to know her.' Let Janet make what she would out of that.

'Sarah's probably over at the art centre — she spends most of her free time there. I'll just check if it's OK.' She moved to the reception desk and turned her back to me while she spoke into the phone. Then she said, 'Yes, Sarah is there. Henry's with her. If you'll come this way, I'll take you over.'

Obediently I followed a trail of perfume, trying to figure out how those stilettos managed to stay upright on polished marble. We passed through the back of the house where, thank goodness, there were people; I was beginning to wonder if Sarah and Janet had the place to themselves. They all looked fairly ordinary, some sitting on the deck reading or playing cards and a group on the lawn playing bowls. Janet entered a single-storeyed building and took me into an office where a man sat in front of a computer.

'Miss Connors, this is Henry, our art therapist. As I told you, Miss Connors has come to visit Sarah. I'll leave you with Henry. If you could let me know at reception when you're ready to leave.' Then Janet departed, her perfume wafting after her.

'Hey, grab a seat. You look worried.' Henry was a small man with thick glasses and blue paint on his chin. I decided he was OK.

'I've never been in one of these places before. I didn't know what to expect.'

'And you don't know what to expect of Sarah?'

'That's right. I've never actually met her, only heard about her from her family.'

'Well, there she is.'

Henry nodded at the wall which, I then realised, was an internal window looking out over a huge art studio. There was the usual clutter of workbenches and cupboards and easels with works in progress. But the room was empty except for one person.

She sat at one of the benches, her back towards us. Her shoulders were rounded and plump beneath the muslin print of her dress. I was thinking of her as a young woman, but of course she would be nearly fifty by now. But the hair was hers. It reached down to her waist, one long, loose plait that had once been light gold, now faded and intertwined with silver and white. There was no doubt: it was Sarah.

But it was all a bit sudden. Less than two hours ago I was searching for a hidden grave. Now here she was, resurrected and waiting for me. Having found her I had no idea what to say or even what I was doing there.

'She hasn't been told about you yet. When you're ready I'll let her know she has a visitor. That's if you still wish to meet her.'

'Yes. Yes I do. It's just that I know nothing about this sort of thing. How ill is she? I mean, is she likely to . . . you know?'

'It's perfectly natural to feel nervous,' said Henry, 'especially if you've had little contact with mental illness. This place is an asylum in the true sense of the word, a sanctuary from everyday pressures that our people are simply not equipped to handle. The dangers are all out there, not in here. Sarah's a charming woman. I'm sure you'll get on very well.'

'What should I say to her? Suppose I say the wrong thing and she gets upset.'

'Treat her like anyone else you're meeting for the first time. It's true that you may inadvertently hit on the wrong subject and she may become distressed. That's a risk we take every time we meet someone new. If that should happen, and it's highly unlikely, remember it's because Sarah's the one with the problem and you're not responsible for how she deals with it. I'll be in here, keeping half an eye on things. If you feel uncomfortable just walk away and come back to me. OK?'

'OK.' I tried to smile.

'Come on. I'll introduce you.'

I stood at the back of the room while he spoke to Sarah. Then he beckoned me forward and she turned to look at me. Her face held confusion and a trace of fear. But it was a beautiful face, despite the damage worked by time and torment. The years had added weight but taken nothing from the delicacy of her features, her skin retained the creamy freshness of youth and, though sagging round the jaw line, held tight across high cheekbones. Her eyes were a striking blue, small and round. She wore a long dress of dusty blue, one of those Indian things, and a collection of copper and silver bangles jangled on her arms.

'Hello Sarah.'

'Maggie Connors? Do I know you? Have we met before? I can't always remember.'

'No, you don't know me. I'm sorry to arrive unannounced like this. Bit of an impulse really. But Jason had told me about you—'

'Jason? You know Jason?'

'Yes, we were, well, we're friends.'

'And how is he? Is he all right?'

'Yes, he's fine. I spent Christmas with him and his father.'

'With John? You were with John?' A shadow of something changed her expression.

'Only for Christmas lunch. Is it long since you've seen them?'

'I never see them. It's best that I don't. Besides Jason wouldn't know me now. He must be nearly a man.'

'Oh, I see. Well, yes, Jason's twenty now. He's tall and very good-looking. He has your hair — in fact he looks a lot like you.'

'He does? Really? Twenty, tall and very good-looking.' She repeated this to herself as if trying to memorise the words. Then she smiled and for a while her eyes looked at some place far away. She came back to me suddenly.

'And do I know you? What did you say your name is?'

'I'm Maggie.'

'No, I don't know you. You're very pretty. And how do you know my son?'

'I met him while he was working. He's a photographer.'

'Yes, that's right. They showed me some of his pictures in a magazine.'

'Yes, he's quite famous. An artist really, only he works with a camera. His work is amazing. You have every reason to be proud of him.'

'I do, yes. And John? How is John?'

'Mr Sullivan? Oh, he's OK. He, er . . . takes life easy.'

'And you're Maggie.' She laughed, a nervous little giggle.

I tried to hide my awkwardness by looking around the studio. 'So you come here to paint?'

'Yes, whenever the room is available.'

'May I see what you're doing?'

'Yes, yes of course.' She picked up the board on which she'd been working. It showed a partially completed tree, its stark branches twisting against an autumn sky.

'But this is good, Sarah. Really good.'

'You know about painting?'

'Yes, a little. I can see where Jason got his creative talent. Do you have any others?'

'Yes, these are all mine.'

She drew a sheaf of papers from an art folio and spread them over the bench. Trees, all trees. Trees of every race and every season, all colours and characters. Some were charcoal sketches and pastels, some delicate watercolours, others vigorous acrylics. But all trees.

'These are wonderful.' I said and I wasn't bullshitting her. Sarah was obviously skilled and the paintings were expertly done. But the trees looked so alive that something was beginning to squirm inside my stomach.

'So, where did you learn to do this? Did you go to art school.'

'No, I learned here. They sent me to art therapy sessions. That's not really about painting, more about externalising feelings and inner conflicts. That's what they tell us, anyway. I found the sessions rather harrowing, although I think they helped me work through some of the bad things. It was all very difficult when I first came here, you know. But through that I started to enjoy the painting, so they arranged some proper lessons for me.'

'Well, you certainly have a special gift. And these trees, are they the ones I passed on the way in?'

'Oh, no. I never go near them, the ones I paint are inside my head. No, that's what I like about this place. The trees all keep their distance.'

'I'm not sure what you mean.'

'Things aren't always what they seem, you know. Not all trees are harmless.'

'And yet you paint them?' That knot in my stomach was tightening.

'Yes. They have a particular beauty. Still, they're not to be trusted.'

'And what about the paintings? Do you ever sell any?'

'Oh, no. I keep them for a while to look at. Then, when I feel satisfied, I burn them. It's better that way.'

Not sure how to respond, I changed the subject. 'I'm staying in the cottage. I hope that's all right with you. I know it's a place you used to enjoy.'

'You're staying there?' She looked alarmed.

'It's only for a few weeks. I needed to be on my own, you see. But if you're not happy about that . . .'

'No. No, that's all right. Just a few weeks, you say? And you're staying in the cottage, not the house? No, you should be safe enough there.'

I wanted to ask her what she meant, but was too afraid of what she might say. She said it anyway. 'The Sullivan property, it's not a good place for women. You would have felt it too, wouldn't you?'

'Felt what, Sarah?'

'It's always there. In the trees. When they whisper at night, you know it's there. Be careful. The land is always hungry.'

'I don't know what you mean.'

'Oh, I think you do. Did you find their graves?'

'The family plot, you mean?'

'Anne and Mary and Jane, like three sisters. He tried to kill me too, you know.'

'What?'

'John did. He tried to kill me. He said I was his best beloved. That's what he used to call me. Then he tried to kill me. Of course nobody would admit they believed me. I was mad anyway, you see, so it was easier to believe him. When you're crazy they pretend they can't understand you. But you can understand me, can't you Maggie?' She grabbed my wrist, her nails digging deep into my flesh. 'You know what I'm saying?'

Not daring to pull away, I desperately looked around for Henry. He saw what was happening and sauntered over.

'I think it's nearly lunchtime, Sarah.'

She let go immediately and smiled as if all were well. 'Goodness, we were having such a nice visit I forgot all about lunch.'

'Yes and it's time I got going too. It's been really good to meet you, Sarah. I'll come again if you'd like me to.'

'Yes, I would like that,' and she kissed me on the cheek. 'Goodbye, Maggie.'

'Goodbye,' I said.

And then, to my eternal shame, I turned away from her and left as quickly as I could.

I did believe her and yet I betrayed her like everyone else. I should have stayed and listened. God knows, that's the least she deserved.

SEVENTEEN

Tʜᴀᴛ night I dreamed about the mirror. I was looking into it, seeing faces. I saw myself, then Sarah, then other faces I didn't recognise, but all were women. Their features were constantly changing, one masking the other, then melding together to form only one face. I dreamed all that night and woke up sweating and thrashing in my bed.

I got up early and tried to concentrate on the sculpture. My mind was elsewhere, my thoughts not moving with the grain of the wood but trying to catch those faces. I felt twitchy and jumpy as if I'd overdosed on caffeine, though I'd had only one cup. The wood and I, we usually work together, but this time it would not co-operate. I was becoming irritable and that's probably why the chisel slipped. As it clattered to the floor I yelled, furious with myself, and a jagged line of red bloomed on my finger. I didn't need this and I should have known better. Any artisan worthy of respect should be able to control her tools and I'd thought my days of self-inflicted injury were over. I squeezed the wound, hoping no splinters had found their way into the cut. Blood sluiced out, sliding the length of my finger and falling in a shower of droplets, bright as berries, a cascade of scarlet against the grey morning. Dark circles formed on the decking where they fell and, where sawdust had drifted, it formed into clots.

I was back in the butcher's shop with my mother, her body pressed against the glass case of the counter while the man in the red-stained apron wielded his knife. When you're very young, and so much closer to the ground, ground-level smells feature sharply in your landscape: freshly turned earth, the playground tarmac melting in the sun. And there was sawdust. That's where I first knew the fragrance of wood and, though it has since become a permanent element in my life, to me it's still as exotic as incense. But not the blood; not the red stain that dripped from those pink and white carvings that scarcely resembled lambs and piglets. I knew the knife-wielding sculptor was responsible for the smell of death and I hated him for it. But I loved the smell of the wood. I scooped up handfuls that hadn't been contaminated and let it run through my fingers like gold dust. All the way home I held my hands over my face to inhale the aroma that lingered on my skin.

The pain cut through and dragged me back to my injured hand. I rinsed the wound under the tap and, for want of a better dressing, wrapped a wad of toilet tissue round it. This was hopeless. I needed to walk off this excess energy or agitation or whatever it was. I needed the serenity of the trees, needed their energy to counter-balance my own. What I didn't need at that moment was to be spied on, so I took the path round the far side of the lake; Liam would be off in the other direction seeing to the sheep or whatever he did.

As soon as I got into a rhythmic stride I started to calm down. The early sun struck straight at eye level but, as the path curved round the head of the lake, it cut sideways and threw long shadows over the grass. In the reeds water birds were squabbling. Early clouds were breaking up and sunlight was already warming my skin.

I moved to the edge of the path, my boot leather collecting

dark, wet patches where the sun had not yet cleared the dew from the grass. The coolness of silver droplets brushed over my shins and offset the hot throbbing in my finger. I breathed deeper, and a tightness, of which I hadn't been aware, uncoiled from my shoulders. My mind stretched and opened, eager to drink in the day.

And it was there again, that flicker on the edge of thought, that shadow that wasn't a shadow. It was waiting for me; I knew that, though how I couldn't say. But it was all right because it was really only the trees, wasn't it? The wind moving the branches?

Only there wasn't any wind.

It moved on higher ground, keeping pace with my own steps. Then it reached out and touched my thoughts as it had before. A gentle nudge. 'This way,' it said, 'this way.' Less than a whisper, less than a breath. But I heard it somewhere inside my head.

A broad trail cut off to the hill, wide enough to have been used by a farm vehicle but not recently as the grass was long and uncrushed. I followed the steep incline until the lake dropped away below me. Then another trail branched to the right, this one only a narrow passage through the undergrowth. Here the air was cooler and alive with insect scrapes and screeches. I pushed my way through fern fronds in a tunnel of indigo shadows. Roots rose in tortured coils then sank again beneath a sea of dank moss.

Abruptly the shadows parted, opening into a clearing filled with sunlight. There was an outcrop of large rocks and I sat down on one, wishing I had brought my water bottle. No matter, I scooped the dew from the grass with my good hand and licked the wetness from my fingers. It was cool and strangely sweet.

The rock I was sitting on was a large, flat slab, a few centimetres off the ground at one end and sloping up to half a metre at the other. Its surface was pitted and brown, stained by time and the elements but, as I ran my hand over it, surprisingly warm. I scrambled onto it and lay down full length, gazing up at the wisps of cloud fragmenting to promise another hot day. But what a place to spend the night, to bring a blanket and stretch out under the stars and watch the moon rise and fall. However, after a few moments I realised that hard rock does not make a comfortable bed and rolled over to sit up. As I did so, something jabbed in my thigh.

Reaching into my pocket I found the little penknife, the Christmas gift from Jason. I'd attached it by the chain and clasp to my belt loop. I flicked it open, carefully though; one cut was enough for that morning. At one time, when I was young and even sillier than I am now, I would have carved my initials on the rock. But you don't vandalise nature, do you? Still, it was a good stone on which to sharpen the blade. As I stroked it carefully over the rim of the rock the metal caught the sun, firing rays of blue and orange light into my eyes. When the knife was honed to a fine edge I tested it on a stem of grass and was satisfied.

Then a hollow pang in my stomach said 'breakfast' and I decided it was time to make my way down again.

Back at the cottage there was a reception committee waiting for me. Bramble came leaping forward, paws on my shoulders, and Badger thumped his tail. Liam sat on the deck steps twirling a twig in his fingers, his eyebrows pulled together in a dark scowl.

'Thank God you're all right,' he said. 'We were about to organise a search party.'

'Why? I'm fine. I just . . . OK, so I went for a walk.' I was a rebel teenager out after curfew, expecting him to growl me out. 'I'm not a prisoner, you know.'

He got to his feet and came up to me. 'No, of course you're

not.' His voice was so quiet. 'We were worried about you, that's all.'

He stroked my hair gently and his eyes were full of concern that was far worse than any growling. I almost died of guilt.

'Did you think I was out on the hills chasing Anne Sullivan's ghost?'

'No, I don't think it's ghosts we should be worrying about.'

'Don't you believe in ghosts then?'

'I think there are such things. Sometimes, though it's quite rare, a poor soul will be traumatised by the suddenness of their death, the violence of it perhaps, or sheer disbelief. They wander around lost trying to be what they were. They need help but they'll do you no harm.'

'Then why were you so worried?'

'There are bloodstains on the deck. Have you hurt yourself?'

'It's only a cut finger.'

'Here, let me see.'

He unwound the tissue. Some of it had stuck to the wound by then and he took me into the kitchen and re-washed it.

'You'd think there would be a first aid kit in this place.'

'Perhaps there is. I didn't think to look.'

He rummaged through the cupboards and located a red-crossed box.

'What else do you think causes ghosts?'

'I think they're mostly the remnants of events recorded on the energy fields of a place. It's as if the intensity of emotion around the event causes the image to repeat itself. Rather like the flare from a flashlight repeating on your retina, completely harmless. That's all speculation, mind, and I don't think that's what we're dealing with here. I believe it's something much more real and much more dangerous.'

'Like what?'

'I'm not sure yet.' He was fiddling with the little plastic strips on the plaster. 'So, where did you go this morning?'

'Round the other side of the lake and up the hillside. Did you know there's a small clearing there with some big slabs of rock in the centre?'

'No, I haven't been round that way much—' He froze, astonishment flooding his face. 'All the saints in heaven! Could you believe I could be so stupid?'

'Why, what's wrong?'

'It's you saying about the rocks. That stuff we had from Ireland. I was so busy looking for the family and the women that I skipped right over it.'

'What is it? Tell me?'

'A stone circle. He said there was a stone circle there. On the Sullivan estate. Of course that . . .'

He was still gripping my finger with one hand, the plaster held in mid-air with the other. He seemed to be working through some personal dilemma and a dozen expressions passed over his face.

'What's wrong, Liam?'

Then he looked at me with his grey eyes, his expression suddenly softening. He nodded. 'Yes. It'll be OK. It'll have to be. I've got some things to do now. Come over later, I'll fix us a bite of lunch.' He wound the plaster round my finger. 'And bring your laptop with you.'

And with that he abruptly departed, leaving the dogs to keep watch over me.

I was able to fall back into the rhythm of working and the rest of the morning went well. The dogs heard Liam returning and alerted me, so I gave him a few minutes before walking across to the woolshed.

'It's only soup and bread. I'm afraid the soup's out of a tin but the bread's fresh baked — I picked it up this morning when I went to get supplies for Sullivan. So, how was yesterday? Did you do some shopping?'

'No, but I visited some interesting places.'

'Well, I hope the day off did you good, though I can't say you look much better.'

'I didn't sleep well.'

'You look as if you haven't slept well for a month. Here, get some food down you. I'll say this, whatever's going on here it doesn't seem to affect your appetite.'

'Fresh air. Makes me hungry.'

'Well, eat up then.'

I knew not to ask questions and that, whatever he was up to, he'd get around to it eventually. If nothing else, he was teaching me to be patient. So I ate the soup and bread and then fresh peaches and waited while coffee brewed. When the table was cleared he set up the laptop, plugged in the phone line and accessed the Internet. Then he sat for what seemed ages, just staring at the screen, rubbing one hand over the knuckles of the other and biting his bottom lip. He didn't seem to mind me looking over his shoulder, so the hesitation wasn't about me this time.

Suddenly he took a breath and attacked the keyboard, firing a jumble of letters and numbers into the search box. I was still trying to decipher the address when the screen changed and the University College of Dublin came up. Again he tapped the keys and flipped through some pages, moving deeper into the website. It asked for a membership code, which he entered immediately. The next window asked for a PIN and there he stopped.

His hands hovered over the keys and then withdrew; he was back to rubbing his knuckles and biting his lip. Standing behind him I could see the tension building in his shoulders. Then he turned to stare at me, as if weighing me up. Was I worth the next step? Apparently I was, because he nodded, almost imperceptibly, then tapped in a number. He was through the security barrier and another page appeared.

'How the hell did you do that?'

'Special dispensation from the Pope.'

'No, tell me.' I thumped his shoulder, which he ignored. 'How come you've got a membership number? You have to be part of the faculty, have proper security clearance and everything.'

But he wasn't listening. His fingers skittered over the keys as page after page jumped onto the screen. He obviously knew exactly where he was going as he negotiated his way through the labyrinth of academic archives. The fancy designer web layouts gradually gave way to plain type text as he ran deeper and deeper into the maze until, abruptly, he stopped.

'That's it. I knew there would be something.'

All I could see was pages of text, but I did catch the words 'Ancient Ireland' and 'worship'.

'I'm going to download this and put it with those other files. You'd better put the kettle on again. I think I'll need more coffee if I'm going to pick the bones out of this lot.'

By the time I had set the fresh cup on the table beside him he was well down the page, highlighting and cutting out huge areas of text.

'What's that you're deleting?'

'Academic waffle mostly. But I'm getting down to the nuts and bolts of it.'

I'd nearly finished my drink when he scrolled up to the top of the file and sat back from the screen.

'There,' he moved his chair over so I could see more easily, 'you have a read of it. Dry as dust, of course, as most of his stuff is. But I think it's what we're looking for.'

I started to read out loud.

THE ASSOCIATION OF TREE WORSHIP WITH THE STONE CIRCLE

The pre-Christian tribes of Europe saw the natural world as imbued with an intelligent, living force, a spiritual power, which was manifested through features of the environment. This natural energy was then perceived to take on the characteristics of the place or object through which it was manifested, something that individuals could relate to on a personal and more meaningful level.

'Whoever the author is, he's no Stephen King. Is it all like this?'

'Bear with it. It gets better.'

European paganism is not alone in its reverence of the tree. Throughout the world, in almost every culture, man has been influenced by the presence and power of trees. Tree spirits were given respect in the folklore and mythology of many cultures. The Druids, particularly, believed that trees possessed mysterious powers, especially the rowan and the oak.

'But that's more or less what you were saying the other day, though I think you tell it better.'

'Go on. This is where it gets interesting.'

Each Celtic tribe had a sacred tree that was a symbol of wisdom and spiritual energy. This belief survives even today. Take, for instance, the Howth Oak, which grows at Howth Castle, Ireland. The St Lawrence family, the Earls of Howth, are associated with a particular oak tree. It is believed that when the tree falls the Howth family direct line will become extinct. This explains why, today, the branches are strongly supported on wooden uprights.

Trees were often associated with ancient stone circles. Although the identity of the builders of these circles has been lost in time, it is certain that the later pagan peoples believed in the power of the stones, adopting the circles for their own rituals. Trees were encouraged to grow around them in the belief that the tree spirits would guard the stones. Over time, the identity of these guardian tree spirits became merged with the circle itself, the focus of worship shifting so that the tree also became the object of worship. Many of these trees feature in legend.

One outstanding example is the story of the Kranon Circle, which still exists today, sited on a hillside a few miles from the City of Limerick. Sadly, as with many such relics, some of the stones were disturbed during the nineteenth century. However, the circle is still remarkably intact, comprising eighteen pillars, the tallest not above two metres. Once it stood on land that was part of a private estate. The property now having been dispersed, the circle has fallen under the protection of the appropriate authorities and may be viewed by the public.

'You're not thinking this is the same circle that was on the Sullivan land?'

'I'll bet anything you'd name that it is.'

'Surely not? There must be hundreds of stone circles in Ireland.'

'No. Dozens maybe. And not all in Limerick. And certainly not that many that are still standing.'

I read on.

According to legend, in early times the area was dominated by a wealthy and powerful tribe whose leaders numbered among the early Irish Kings. Their Druid priests used the circle for their ritual work. A ring of oak trees was said to surround the stones, forming an outer circle. One tree grew particularly strong and tall and outlived its fellow sentries by several hundred years. This oak was said to generate a power of its own and it gradually became identified with the aura surrounding the area.

Apparently their priests made liberal use of blood sacrifices, animals of course -- a practice not unusual in those days. However, when their homes were threatened by invaders, they took more drastic measures to invoke the protection of the local spirits. Human sacrifices were made, not only within the stone circle, but also to the tree spirit. The victims, it is said, went willingly to their deaths, which were arranged so that their blood mingled with the roots of the tree.

That particular oak became the personal protector of the descendants of one of the Irish Kings. It continued to flourish, as did the house of Kranon, until the Middle Ages when, with the arrival of St Patrick, it was struck by lightning. The roots were burnt out by the blast and the tree was apparently dead. (One must acknowledge a not insignificant degree of dramatic licence taken here as, of course, these events did not occur overnight. The fall of the houses of kings and the Christian conversion of Ireland took a great deal longer than this account would indicate.)

But the legend holds that the Kranon priests, determined not to submit to such blasphemy, took the trunk of the tree and carved various artefacts from it -- sword handles, staffs, shields, etc -- creating magical weapons for their own preservation.

Interestingly enough, like early Christian relics, these items turn up from time to time in various

folk tales. And like their Christian counterparts, the
application of these items did seem to be efficacious
to some extent. Their powers undoubtedly lay in the
faith and belief of their handlers.

I sat back from the table, for once lost for words. It was Liam
who spoke.

'Can you see the pattern? The family history in Ireland
repeating itself here. And all that stuff about trees, one tree in
particular. Human sacrifices.'

'Yes, but what does it all mean?'

'I'm not sure yet, it needs thinking about. But the answer's in
there somewhere, I'm certain. However,' he reached over and
turned the computer off, 'it'll have to wait till tomorrow. This
evening we're going out.'

'Are we?'

'Naturally. Have you forgotten it's New Year's Eve? Maggie's
booked us for dinner down at the pub and I promised I'd take the
fiddle and give them a few tunes in exchange for a pint.'

'Oh, is that right? And I'm going with you, am I?'

'Well, of course you are. You don't think for one moment that
I'd leave you in this place on your own, do you? Come on, a quiet
evening with a pint and a song to mark the change of the year.
Where's the harm in that?'

EIGHTEEN

It was well past noon when I woke on New Year's Day. Scenes from the night before floated around inside my head like the debris from a shipwreck. There was something about pigs running all over the road and a contest to see who could round them up first. I recalled slipping into a ditch with a lot of other people. I found my clothes on the floor with my boots, everything covered in mud. I think the pigs won.

I found some clean gear and went out on the deck, trying to shuffle the evening into some sort of order. First we'd said hello to Maggie. She had managed to find plenty of help, and Bev, who had joined her behind the bar for a while, was able to spend the time catching up with the latest gossip. Several people had booked dinner and Maggie's father turned out to be an excellent chef. After that the crowds turned up, everyone in the district apparently. Liam was joined by some guitarists and a whistle player and the tables were pushed back to make way for dancing. Feet were stamped on and beer spilt and come midnight I was kissed by everyone in the place. There was a fight at one point, which would account for the bruises on my arm, but Maggie's father said it was a seasonal tradition. I'm not sure what happened after that; but, as there was no sign of my truck, we must have walked home, which would explain the encounter with the pigs.

I sat on the steps trying to decide if I should report the truck missing. Bramble, sensitive to my fragility, did not bound all over me for once, but lay with her nose on my lap and her big, toffee eyes melting with sympathy. All the local birds were shouting at once and the noise of the cicadas went through my skull like a dentist's drill. Then another sound cut through my ears and set my teeth on edge. There it was again, a sort of high-pitched yelp, but vaguely familiar. Liam burst through the trees pushing Badger in the wheelbarrow. A wicked grin spread over his face when he realised my delicate condition.

'Great party, wasn't it? Do you want to come for a walk?'

'Oh, bugger off!'

'Ah, you're not feeling so good? Perhaps some coffee first, then. I'll put the kettle on.'

'Why don't you put some oil on that bloody wheel?'

'That bad, is it? Well, never mind. A good stroll in the fresh air will put you right.'

Just then a complete stranger drove up in my truck. Liam seemed to know all about it and gave the man coffee, which saved me the effort of talking to either of them. Eventually he left and Liam bullied me into action.

'Bit of exercise — best thing for you. Here, bring your water bottle, the afternoon's going to be a hot one and dehydration's the curse of a hangover.'

He set off through the bush with the dogs as if all that beer he'd swilled hadn't even touched him. I trailed along behind, deciding whether to sulk. I wouldn't have minded so much if my self-appointed chaperon hadn't sounded so damned cheerful. After a good, long trek he halted at a fallen tree and sat down, waiting for me to catch up.

'Are you feeling any better now? Here, take a seat.'

'Thanks. I must be out of practice. You seem none the worse for it.'

'Ah no, where I was brought up the drinking was an essential part of a person's education.'

'I'm all right, you know.'

'Yes, well it usually wears off after a few hours.'

'That's not what I'm talking about. Look, I'm not stupid. We both know it's me, not the dog, who's being taken for a walk. I don't need a bodyguard. I'm a bit stressed, that's all. I'm not being threatened by anything.'

'I wouldn't be so sure of that. After what we found out yesterday I think you could well be taking a risk. I don't want you wandering off on your own.'

'Well, I don't understand it all. Tell me, exactly what is it I'm being protected from?'

He paused for a moment, biting his lip, then took a deep breath.

'Yes, you need to be told, but it's where to start. Now, I'll try to explain, but you're going to have to stretch your imagination. And your credulity.'

'OK. Try me.'

'Well, you know that big tree, the one you introduced me to?' He spoke slowly and carefully, as if he had rehearsed the words. 'You've felt the energy come from it?'

'Yes.'

'And you talk to it, as if it could hear you? You have a sort of relationship with it?'

I nodded.

'So, you'd agree that a tree is a living being, that it could have some form of consciousness? Not like a human, of course, or even an animal, nothing that we'd know of, but, nevertheless, some kind of awareness?'

I thought about the hours I'd spent wandering through the bush and the pines. Those gentle giants with their soft whisperings. The times I had closed my eyes and felt their thoughts stirring, turning towards me. 'Yes, I'll go along with that.'

214

'Now, can you visualise one tree, or even a small group of trees, living for centuries, experiencing the changing seasons, the sun, storms, gales, being touched by generations of other life forms, creatures that dwell in it or alongside it? And, much in the same way that our personalities are formed by experience and interaction, can you conceive that, over a vast passage of time, such events could mould a basic unit of consciousness into something quite distinct and unique?'

'A tree evolving into an individual being? Maybe. But even if a tree had some form of intelligence, what could it do?'

'Well, that intelligence need not be confined to its physical counterpart — in fact over time it would have evolved way beyond its original form. It might be free to move within its environment. It couldn't do anything physically, of course, but it could influence other fields of energy. It might even be able to have some psychological influence over other minds.'

'Like making the crops grow? Or protecting the land from intruders?'

'Precisely. That sounds far-fetched, I know. But that's what people have believed for thousands of years. And they weren't all ignorant, Irish fence-menders like myself. Some of the greatest minds of the ancient world — Roman statesmen, Greek philosophers and the like — have subscribed to this view of nature.'

A tui called from a nearby branch, a call so easily mistaken for something human. I could feel that knot twisting inside my stomach again. I knew where this line of reasoning was going and I wanted to push it back into the pit of superstition it had crawled out of, to heap ridicule on top and stamp the earth flat so I would never have to think about it. But I managed only a weak protest.

'Yes, OK, that's an interesting theory. But where's the proof? If these things—'

'Elemental spirits.'

'— these elemental spirits had been rampaging round the forests of Europe for centuries, surely someone would have noticed them?'

'And indeed they have. Medieval mythology is full of them — the basilisk for instance and the chimera. There's lots of recent versions too, many demanding to be taken seriously. What about the Yeti, and Bigfoot? And there's the Wendigo.'

'Whoa! Back up a bit. I thought a basilisk was a cross between a dragon and a chicken.'

'A rooster, yes, that's right. And a chimera is part lion, goat and serpent.'

'Oh, come on now, you can't be serious.'

'Of course not. Not literally. But, don't you see, that's how we deal with things we can't explain in physical terms. We give them a form we can visualise so we can get a grip on something that otherwise can only be sensed. Isn't that what you do?'

'What do you mean?'

'You invent a form to explain a concept. Like that first piece of sculpture, the one you showed me. Only, not everyone has your creative ability. In order to explain it they had to use ready-made images to tack together a representation of something, describe it in a language of symbols, if you like — symbols that everyone in their social group would understand.'

Around us the trees creaked and stirred, as if they were listening too, and learning. Students at a lecture. Yes, that's how he sounded, as if he'd said all this before.

'I suppose it's like the Jabberwocky,' I said.

'The Jabberwocky?'

'Yes, you know, Lewis Carroll. "Beware the Jabberwock, my son! The jaws that bite, the claws that catch!" Everyone knows what that looks like because every kid has nightmares at some time. But that's fantasy, isn't it? You're talking about something that really existed.'

'Exactly. What was behind the symbol may well have been

something real. Their fear was real enough.'

'But what were they afraid of? Even if there were such things, why would they hurt anyone?'

'They probably wouldn't if left alone. It's only when they come into contact with humans that things go wrong. Why do bears attack forest rangers? Why do tigers raid villages? In the Middle Ages people went into the forest and never came back — too many to be accounted for by natural misfortunes. Whatever the cause, they blamed it on something they thought was lurking there, waiting to kill. Hence the basilisk, a symbol of death.'

'Yes, I can see that. We had one living in the cupboard under the stairs.'

'What, a basilisk?'

'No, a Jabberwocky. At least, that's what my brother told me anyway. Teased me about it for years. I was terrified to go in there. But that was when I was a kid. I did grow out of it. All this other stuff was in the Middle Ages, surely by now . . .'

'As I say, the Wendigo is well documented. It's a creature from the legends of North America. Just an Indian story to frighten the children, they thought. Then white trappers and hunters started reporting encounters with it too. That wouldn't be remarkable if the stories weren't spread over such a vast country and the descriptions, from totally unconnected sightings, remarkably similar. The Indians claim that, like the basilisk, it hunts human flesh. They say it's so thin that, at certain angles, it becomes invisible. Even now hunters report something stalking them, not a bird or a creature, but something invisible. They say it follows them, moving through the treetops and, even though they can't see it, they claim they can feel its thoughts.'

Oh, yes. I knew all about that. The shadow of a shadow, less than a whisper, less than a breath. 'This way,' it said, 'this way . . .' The knot inside me was twisting into a sharp pain; at long last, the first tugs of real fear. 'And you think there's something like that here, something to do with the Sullivan family.'

'Well, I think I can see how it was in Ireland. An embryonic consciousness evolving within the energy field of a stone circle. The gaining of an awareness of itself linked, inherently, to a line of kings and their land, acting as the focus for ritual worship. The giving of sacrificial offerings, food, wine, blood, and, when they became desperate, their own kin. It must have gone on for centuries. And then there was the family — generation after generation, telling the tale, reinforcing the belief, closing in on itself to hide the nightmare.'

'I ought to tell you to stop talking such bloody rubbish. But . . . I'm not sure of anything any more.'

'And if Michael brought it with him, that would explain the fall of the Sullivan dynasty in Ireland and the rise of the family fortunes in New Zealand. But that's the part I don't understand. How the devil did it get here?'

'I don't know. I can't think straight. My head still hurts. Perhaps those early records might tell us — I still think it's worth a visit to the museum.'

'That might well be so, but at this moment I'm more concerned about what's happening to you.' He laid his hand over mine, so gently, as if I were a frightened animal. 'Whatever it is out there, I think you already know all about it. Oh, not what it is or where it came from perhaps. But I believe that you have somehow tuned into it . . .'

I could feel my throat tightening. I had to force the words out. 'That's how it often works when I'm studying a subject. I was trying to express something I felt about the trees, yes. There was something pressing in from a subconscious level, demanding attention, it needed to be given form . . .'

'And if you've become aware of it, then it's become aware of you. Whatever's going on between it and the Sullivan family, you've somehow got yourself caught up in the game.'

'What should I do?'

'You know the answer to that. Get out. Now. Today.'

'Yes, I can see that, but . . .' I felt pulled in a thousand pieces. 'But I have to finish. Just this one sculpture. Just a few more days then I'll go. I will, absolutely.'

His hand tightened over mine. 'For God's sake Regan, there may not be a few days.'

'You really think this thing is that evil?'

'No, not evil in human terms. It's amoral, no more responsible for its actions than a rogue elephant that stampedes a child. It's doing what it's been conditioned to do. It seeks only what it's been taught to expect.'

'You mean it protects the land. In exchange it takes life and blood. Sullivan blood. The three bodies buried up there.'

'And, as you said, there may be a fourth.'

'No there isn't. Sarah's not dead. I'm sorry, I should have told you yesterday. I don't know why I didn't.' So I explained about the visit to that place and what Sarah said about the women. 'She said John tried to kill her and nobody would believe her.'

'If that's the case, then you're in even greater danger than I thought. You must leave.'

'I can't stop now. Just a few more days and it will be finished.'

'Surely you can finish the damned statue somewhere else?' he said.

'It's not a statue and no, I can't. Besides, this is a Sullivan thing. What about all the people who lived on the Limerick estate? All the workers here? They were safe enough.'

'We don't know that.'

'Of course they were. If people had kept dying like that it would have all come out before now. There would be stories about things that lived in the woods. People wouldn't have gone near the place. No, this is a family thing, that's why they've been able to keep it secret all this time. And I'm not family, am I? So why should it concern itself with me? But I promise you, when this piece is finished, then I'll go. A few more sessions, a few hours' work, that's all I need.'

Liam grabbed my shoulder, fingers digging into my skin, jerking me around, forcing me to look into his face.

'You're too involved. It's not your work that's holding you here, is it? It's that thing out there in the trees. Can't you see that?'

But of course I couldn't. I only knew that I was bone tired and that my head still throbbed.

'Oh, come on Liam. Call the dogs. I'm going back to the cottage to lie in a hot bath and chew aspirins.'

We trudged back in silence. He took me to my door and made me promise to stay put until the morning when we'd talk some more. I soaked for ages, and then found something to eat and some red wine. It took the edge of the unease that was now permanently lodged somewhere under my ribs.

Evening came, but there was still a faint glow on the horizon when I fell into bed and waited for the night to carry me away.

I can see the stars. So many stars. Here the sky has depth. It pulls away from the earth, a vast cavern that goes on and on forever. And the stars are not scattered; each hangs poised in its own appointed place. And they move, such a gentle, barely perceptible vibration, expanding through tunnels of past and future. The most distant light has taken centuries to reach my eyes, a journey beyond comprehension. Lying here, the sky is all I see, as if I, too, were a point of light in the universe among my brothers and sisters, and we are all perfectly balanced in this static dance of space and time.

My hand moves at my side and feels for the surface that supports me. It is hard and rough. My fingers discover sharp ridges, and then trace a meandering surface crack. The rock, it must be the rock in the clearing. I do not remember how I got here. Cold. I am dressed, but only lightly. The coldness is not unpleasant; the chill outlines my skin, defining my boundaries, reminding me of who and what I am. Otherwise I may relinquish all sense of self and become lost among the heavens.

There's the Southern Cross. Oh, I wish I had learnt more, learnt the planets and constellations. To call each one by name would make a claim upon its kinship. I know that's the Milky Way, that swath of opalescence, our own galaxy. 'A whirlpool of rampant stars.' I read that somewhere.

How long have I lain here? It could be minutes or hours. My face is wet. I brush my hand over my hair and scatter drops of dew. I am aware of dull pains in my back and shoulders, but the discomfort does not concern me, as if it belongs to someone else.

I reach out to locate the rock's edge but find, instead, something cold and wet. Not dew this time. This is thicker and clings to my skin. There is a pool of it, all down one side, and I realise my leg has lain in it. Now there is something else, something smooth and string-like and when I try to pick it up it is slippery and slides through my fingers.

Sinew.

Fur.

I know what this is and everything inside me convulses. And the smell. I try to pull away and the stench of the butcher's shop rises to choke me. I scramble from the rock and slide through more of the mangled, lifeless things. As I back away my stomach rebels and I stand retching, afraid even to kneel for fear of what I might find on the ground.

Then, weak and shaking, I start to run through the darkness, downhill thank God, grabbing branches for support and even so I trip and fall and stagger to my feet again. Onto the car track and then the lake road. Back towards the cottage which is a black silhouette. But there is a light beyond. And I think I hear music, slow and soulful. I am running and tripping, trying to reach it, and I hear myself sobbing his name.

'Liam, Liam . . .'

221

The light becomes brighter, and I call louder.
'Liam . . .

'. . . Liam!' The last was a shout. The door was flung wide open as I reached it and stumbled through into the yellow glare of an electric bulb.

'What have you done to yourself?'

'It's not me. It's— For God's sake, get it off me.'

'Here sit down. You say you're not hurt?'

I shook my head.

'Then what the hell's all this?'

He grabbed some cleaning rags to wipe my arms and legs, checking for injuries.

'Whose blood is this? Looks like you've been rolling it. Hey, you're shaking. You could do with a wee nip of something.' He poured out half a tumbler of neat whisky. 'Here, get this down you. Do you want to take your shirt off, it's a bit of a mess? I'll find you a clean one.'

He fetched a bowl of hot, soapy water and a facecloth and began to bathe my arms and legs. He was gentle, cautious even, and the water warmed my skin. By then I was shivering violently with cold, or maybe it was shock. A gulp of the whisky nearly choked me but I could feel it burning all the way down, spreading heat from the inside.

'I think it was the rabbits,' I said. 'It was everywhere.'

'That's certainly what it looks like. But how did you manage to get it all over you?'

'They were on that stone slab, the one in the clearing. I told you about it.'

'And I told you to stay put. You promised. Then you go wandering about in the bush at God know what hour—'

'But I didn't, I swear I didn't. I went to bed, just like I said I would, and I woke up there. Must have been sleepwalking or something.'

'Jesus, it gets worse.'

'They were all mangled up on top of the stone and I was lying in the middle of it all — and I don't know how I got there.'

'Shush now, there's nothing to be gained by upsetting yourself. Look, it's all gone. Drink up, it'll do you good. You say they were in bits, laid out on the stone?'

'That's right, as if someone had torn them open.'

'It sounds like some sort of ritual offering. Small animals. Quite typical. Maybe using that stone as a kind of altar.'

'That elemental thing you were talking about, you said it couldn't actually do anything physically.'

'No, but it could influence someone to do something. If these *were* sacrificial they would be offered *to* it. Perhaps some sort of appeasement.'

'It must have been Sullivan, then. He shoots enough of the poor things.'

We were both silent for a moment. I was trying to fit it all together. Then another thought seeped through. 'Badger. What about Badger? It must have been Sullivan after all, then, and it could have been Badger up there. For Christ's sake, what's wrong with the man?'

'He might not have been in control of what was happening. Any more than you wandering off in the middle of the night. Remember how concerned he was about the dog, yet he wouldn't have it anywhere near him. That would make sense now, wouldn't it? Regardless, I think the sooner we're out of here the better.'

'You don't have to stay here, you know. This is my problem. Besides, I'm not sure I believe all this.'

He looked at me long and hard, but said nothing. Then he started collecting up blankets and threw one around my shoulders. 'Come on. Let's get you back to the cottage.'

'What are those for?'

'Well, it's obvious you can't be left alone. I'll sleep on the sofa.'

NINETEEN

A ND a wonderful bodyguard he turned out to be.
I was woken early next morning by an unfamiliar sound
coming from the living area. The bedroom was still gloomy and
through the window I could see banks of dark clouds cloaking
the rising sun. The air wasn't as warm as usual, so I shuffled
into a sweater before creeping out of the bedroom. And there
they were, the pair of them, both snoring their heads off. There
had obviously been some dispute over who owned the sofa and
blankets. Liam was now spread-eagled half on the cushions, legs
trailing on the floor, while Bramble lay across his chest with her
nose in his beard. As I passed en route to the kitchen she opened
one eye, peered at me, then closed it and went back to sleep.

I made myself some tea, retrieved my boots and went outside
to sit on the step. I tried to think about sculpture, but my mind
was filled with what had happened last night. All those mangled
bodies and the blood. Blood sacrifices, that text had said, blood
mingling with the roots of trees. Animal blood, and then
human. But that was hundreds of years ago, another time and
age, another dimension. Nothing to do with here and now and
me. Sullivan's just an old drunk and a bad shot. Not surprising,
with a mother who hung herself and a nutcase for a wife. Who

is this so-called expert of Liam's, anyway? Come to think of it, who is Liam to go bypassing a security system like that? Yes, that's another good question: who is Liam?

I shivered and drained the last of the tea. I didn't want to think about any of that. I was there to work. So I shook the cloth off the wood block and collected some sandpaper and glass. It was moving towards completion — the last, fine details. A couple more days and then I would leave. Liam was right. I ought to get back to some sort of normality, whatever that might be. And then I was touching the wood, stroking the grain and forgetting about everything except line and curve and form.

I must have been working for about an hour before I heard sounds of life from indoors. I quickly threw the cloth over the piece and turned to find Liam in the doorway.

'Ah, there you are.' He looked panic-stricken and half asleep at the same time. 'Thought for a moment you'd gone off again. Are you OK?'

'Yes, everything's fine. You two looked so peaceful I didn't want to disturb you.'

'That's all right then.'

He stood in the doorway dressed only in his T-shirt and underpants. His hair, which for the last week had been so neatly groomed, stuck out again like demented bedsprings. Similarly his bare legs, painfully thin and white, were strewn with curly, black hairs. But it was his feet that fascinated me. The bones were long and thin with each tendon shown in relief, each joint and knuckle exaggerated into angularity, the toes arching and slightly turned. They were the kind of feet the old masters would paint for the crucifixion. They embodied all of human suffering and strength and humility. Those feet would make any artist reach for paper and pencil.

'What are you staring at?'

'Do you know, you have the most beautiful feet I have ever seen?'

'Oh, stop taking the piss, woman. I'm going to put the kettle on.'

Some people you just can't talk to first thing in the morning. I set myself to cleaning and oiling chisels while Mr Grumpy took it out on the coffee beans. After a while he reappeared; he had found his trousers and shirt and had made a point of putting his socks on.

'Here, have some coffee. You've been working already? So, is that what you plan to do this morning?'

'Yes, I thought I could get a few hours in. It's easier while the weather's cooler.'

'I need to do some servicing on the farm vehicles. Do you fancy going into town later, perhaps have a late lunch? We could have a look at that museum.'

This was so obviously a ploy to keep tabs on me. I should have told him to bugger off but . . . Well, after last night I think all those warnings were finally hitting home. Perhaps I didn't want to be left alone. Perhaps I couldn't trust myself to stay in control. Hell, I wasn't in control, was I? I could fall asleep and wake up anywhere. It could be that I wouldn't wake up at all.

'Yeah, OK. Sounds good,' I said

Anyhow, he wasn't bad company.

We sat at a table on the deck, right next to the water where the little boats rocked and heaved against their ropes. The sun had struggled through the clouds so the big umbrella was welcome, as were the ice cubes dancing in our glasses. Liam had hesitated over the menu. I got the impression he would have preferred the steak but, after last night, he was being sensitive to my feelings and we both ordered a mushroom omelette. I thought that was sweet of him. Then we both declined dessert and sat back, watching the water.

'So, what will you do when you leave here?' he asked.

'Go home, I suppose. I've got an apartment in Auckland. The studio's just round the corner and I still need to produce that series for an exhibition: I'll try to develop the theme of the first two pieces. If that doesn't work I'll have to move on to something else. What about you?'

'I've no plans. I might stay on a bit. Keep an eye on things.'

'Look, in case I don't get a chance to say it, I need to thank you. For trying to look after me, I mean. I know I'm not the easiest person to deal with.'

'You don't say?' He looked sideways at me and raised one eyebrow. 'No, you're OK.'

'Perhaps if this other business hadn't happened, all this stuff about trees . . . But you're right, I need to get away and sort my head out. Funny, that's why I came here in the first place, to sort myself out.'

'Young Sir Galahad, was it?'

'Who? Oh, you mean Jason. Yes. But that's history now. '

'Glad to hear it. Come on, let's go and look at those photos.'

The museum was a modern building with high glass walls. The place was quiet and the photographic archive thankfully empty of other visitors. There was a wide, sloping desktop with enough room for several people to sit side by side. Next to it a tall rack held the books. They weren't books actually, but large pieces of hardboard, hinged and strung together like giant notepads. Each was dedicated to a subject, *Earliest Days, Development of Transport*, and so on, and each page filled with photographs and newspaper clippings in chronological order. A typed insert beside each picture gave an explanation.

The photographs were spellbinding — sepia memories of people out of time. They all looked so very serious, solemn even. I know photography was different then: it was portraiture, not fashionable to smile. But it wasn't just that. Their eyes looked sadder. Life was much harder then, I suppose, and they were the settlers in a new world. Deprivation was to be expected, but perhaps anything was better than the life they had fled. Men stiff and defiant in their high collars and waxed moustaches, ready to tame this land and bend it to their will.

But it was the women who broke your heart. You saw the painful attention they gave to the niceties, the polished silver of a three-tiered cake stand, a cameo brooch pinned precisely against the neck of a starched blouse — the things that laid a veneer of elegance over a life of labour. Out of view they waged a daily war against a sea of mud and drew water to scrub shirts for a family of ten. They were the warriors who fought at the front line. Some admitted defeat and went home, but these women in the photographs, they were the ones who had stayed and claimed a victory. Over the page their daughters, in their long white dresses, posed for the annual regatta. Another page and there were their granddaughters, so brave with their bobbed hair, all dressed up for the tennis club ball.

As each board was turned, crinolines changed to bustles, then to flapper dresses, then back to crinolines again as we tried another book. We were there to search for Sullivans but as yet there were none to be found. In 1860 Michael had arrived, and his mother, Katherine, had joined him in 1865. Yes, there were photographs from 1865 but very few. It was a new and untried medium, and even formal portraits of local dignitaries were rare, certainly not for the likes of newcomers such as the Sullivans. But each year, as the magic black box caught on, the pages became more crowded. And suddenly there she was.

1874 Mrs. Katherine Sullivan
Mother of landowner Mr. Michael Sullivan. Taken to commemorate her second year as Chairwoman of the Women's Guild. Mrs. Sullivan was born in Ireland and settled

in New Zealand about ten years before this
portrait was taken.

She looked elderly, though she would have been only sixty-something, and although seated she gave the impression of being short and rather stout. She perched amid flounces of satiny skirt, brown on the photo of course, but the dress would have been some similar, dark colour. A heavy shawl draped her body. A round bonnet, from which frilled streamers hung over her shoulders to frame her face, was the only concession to frivolity. The photo was too small to discern anything beyond a formal expression. Her back, straight as a girder, and the neat folding of hands, gave nothing away.

'I don't think we're going to learn much from this lady,' Liam said. 'Do we know what happened to her?'

'She lived to about eighty, probably died of natural causes. I found her stone in the graveyard, not far from Michael's monument. I know this doesn't help us much but it makes her real. Let's keep looking.'

The next thing we spotted was the house. It was the verandah that gave it away, framed by the familiar carved posts and wreathed with jasmine. But there were people, a family portrait.

1904 The Sullivan family celebrate the arrival of baby Thomas

Mr. David and Mrs. Mary Sullivan are seen here with father, Michael Sullivan. The house, which still stands on the present Sullivan estate, was built by David and Mary at the time of their marriage, two years prior to the birth of their son.

A woman sat on a chair cradling a baby hidden within the

layers of a lace shawl. She wore a high-necked, white blouse and a full-length skirt, her hair piled on top of her head in a concoction of elaborate curls. Two men stood behind her; the hand of the younger one lay on her shoulder. The other stood to one side, an elderly man in a tightly tailored suit, thumb hooked in waistcoat pocket in a parody of nonchalance. They all looked as relaxed and comfortable as French aristocrats on their way to the guillotine.

'So that's him, old Michael himself.'

'Yes,' I whispered. 'And Mary. It couldn't have been long after this was taken that she joined Anne up on the hillside. And which one of them was responsible?'

I looked at the men's faces: perfect masks. One of them was probably her murderer. This woman was the victim in some repeating nightmare and the truth of it slammed into me as though I'd hit a concrete post. Pneumonia, or so the doctor had said, from wandering the hillsides in a rainstorm. I had stood by her grave, walked the same paths she had walked. They say she took to wandering through the hills looking for Anne. Had she felt something watching her as I had? Who, or what, had really killed her?

'As you say, it brings them to life.' Liam drummed his fist on the desk. 'But it tells us nothing.'

'We'll keep looking, though there aren't many books left.' With an effort I kept my voice steady.

'What's this one? *The Worker's Day*. They weren't what you'd call a working-class family, were they? Still, nothing lost by looking.'

These people seemed more relaxed but no happier: road menders still in their waistcoats with their sleeves rolled up, aproned shopkeepers behind counters stacked with lye soap and tins of cocoa. There was a gang of labourers lounging in their break time; one of their women, caught in the relentless brewing of tea, was bending to hook a kettle over an open fire.

We turned a page and found the house again. No trails of jasmine this time.

1902 Moving-in day

Handymen deliver furniture to a newly built house. Although furniture manufacturers had set up business, the most treasured pieces would have been brought over from the old country. The furniture seen here was the property of Mrs. Katherine Sullivan, imported from her husband's estate in Ireland, now to grace the new home of her son and daughter-in-law.

Two workers in flat caps posed by a horse-drawn cart. I don't know much about horses but this one looked uncomfortable, head hung down and ears flattened. The cart was piled high with chairs and tables, hallstands, a brass bedstead . . .

And there it was, the glint of sunlight on the glass, the twisted branches curving round the frame. I grabbed Liam's sleeve so hard I nearly tugged him off the chair.

'That thing in the trees. I know how it came here. It wasn't Michael who brought it. It was his mother.'

Of course it all came out then. It had to. I was too shaken to drive, so Liam took the wheel while I told him about the mirror. I told him about the dreams and the lost hours, of waking up in front of it, or waking up somewhere else. I told him about finding myself in the bush with half the day missing. And I told him about the Watcher and how it could think at me. And it wasn't until I heard myself saying all of this that I realised the enormity of what was happening. Through it all he kept his eyes on the road, chewing his bottom lip and saying nothing, I could see the skin over his knuckles stretched white as he gripped the wheel.

When I'd finished, he said quietly, 'Now, is there anything else you haven't told me? Because if there is I'd better hear it now.'

Back at the cottage Liam examined the mirror. 'Well, I can see that it's old,' he said, 'but you'd know more about that than I would.'

'Yes, very old. But the dressing table isn't. That's oak too, but a very different wood, I'd say not more than two hundred years. But the mirror . . . I've never seen wood like it. I'm sure it's oak, but so finely grained. You can't usually get that depth of detail. And it's hard as iron. I don't understand it.'

'And I can't see how they got the glass into it.' He ran his hands around the frame, feeling with the tips of his fingers. 'There doesn't seem to be any join.'

'The glass is old too, I mean very old. You know glass is a liquid, don't you? Very dense, but even so it does flow downwards over time. See how it's very slightly thicker towards the bottom and it's discoloured with age, tinged with yellow. Yet there's no tarnishing. The backing, quicksilver or whatever they used, it's perfect. Not a mark on it.'

'So, what's it doing here? In the cottage, I mean.'

'Well, it used to be up at the house in Sarah's bedroom. Jason told me how she used to spend hours just looking into it. He brought several things down from the house when he was doing this place up, like the sofa and chairs, so I guess he moved the dressing table as well. I did ask Sullivan about the mirror. He said he hadn't known it had been moved here — in fact he seemed quite upset. Well, not upset exactly, I'm not sure what it was. But he did act a bit odd.'

'Well, I expect he knows a lot more than he's saying. In Sarah's bedroom, was it? Now that would be the master bedroom, wouldn't it? So Jane would have used it before her. And Mary, of course. When she had the old furniture moved into the new house, she probably chose the dressing table for the bridal suite.'

'And Anne must have used it too. Katherine came over shortly before Anne gave birth to David. And it was after that when she started wandering off.'

We both fell silent for a while, me sitting on the edge of the bed feeling miserable while Liam continued to run his fingers over the carved birds and flowers. He peered into it from different angles, as if he were trying to see around corners. It was me who spoke first. 'I still don't understand what it's got to do with that thing out there in the bush. I mean, how did the mirror bring it here?'

He stepped away from the dressing table and came over to sit beside me. 'Well, an elemental isn't a physical being, so distance would mean nothing to it. But it does need a means of access to the physical world, like the tree it developed from. Now, if those stories were true, the original tree was destroyed by lightning.'

'Which would mean that it could no longer get through, right?'

'Right. However, didn't they say that the priests took the wood and made it into various weapons and such things? They could use those to tap into the power of the entity they once worshipped. Can you imagine the shaft of a spear possessed by a force with a craving for blood?'

'Awesome.' I shivered, a coldness creeping over my skin. 'And you reckon this thing's one of them, that it's sort of controlled by something with a taste for sacrificial blood? Of course Anne bled to death, didn't she?'

'But not Mary.'

'No one knows how Mary died,' I said. 'She had pneumonia, yes. But he carried her out of the house wrapped in a sheet. She may not even have been dead. No one saw the body or what he may have done to it.'

'And Jane, she's supposed to have tried to cut her own wrists.'

'No, I don't think she did. Well, think about it. Maggie's mother said she'd lost a lot of blood — there was a pool of it under the tree where they found her. Now, if she'd injured herself that badly how the hell could she go about getting a rope up in a tree. No, it doesn't make any sense.'

'So what do you think happened?' Liam asked.

'Perhaps she did try to hang herself. Then someone came along and slit her wrists.'

'Christ . . . But you're right, that makes more sense.'

'Then Sarah told me her husband tried to kill her but no one would believe her.'

We fell into silence again, silence that was all around us as if the world outside the room had stopped moving. After a while I stood up and moved closer to the dressing table. 'I can understand a spear or a club. But why a mirror?'

'To focus the energy and boost its power. The frame was carved from the wood, of course, then somehow they set the glass into it. Any reflective surface can be used for psychic vision — water, polished metal. It's the depth of the image that's the important factor, being able to see through into another world, a parallel universe. Added to that, certain types of glass contain metallic elements that can retain a charge, like an energy field that can be imprinted with a sort of recorded message. That's how a crystal ball works.'

'So this is like, what, a magic mirror?'

'Yes, I suppose that's what you could call it.'

'As in, "Mirror, mirror on the wall, who is the fairest of them all?"'

'Yes, if you like.'

'But that's a fantasy of course, a fairy tale.'

'Ah, don't forget now, traditional fairy tales are a facet of mythology, which in turn has its origins in the collective beliefs

234

of a culture and is sometimes based on actual events. And if you think about it, in that story the wicked queen was also a victim of the mirror. More so, in fact. If I recall rightly, she allowed it to rule her life and in the end it drove her to murder.'

'Could a mirror do that?'

'Not the mirror itself — that's merely the doorway. It would be some sort of intelligence, some non-physical being that had taken possession of the energy field to gain access to this world.'

'So, are you saying that through the mirror we can call up this elemental spirit?'

'Yes, that's right. But it's far worse than that: through the mirror *it* can summon *us*.'

I shuddered. The whole absurdity of it was edging closer and closer to the line of truth.

'But what can we do? Shouldn't we destroy it? Surely if we break the glass . . . ?'

'No, no it might be harder to break than you imagine. Besides, we've no idea what effect that may have. No, best not to interfere with it.' Liam was lost in thought for a moment. Then he said, 'You say Bramble won't come in here?'

'No. Well, she won't for me. You try her. She was outside a moment ago.'

He went out to the deck and called her. I heard her claws skidding on the floor as she ran to him and I knew she would jump up, paws on shoulders while he patted her back and she licked his face.

'Come on, Bramble, come and say hello to Regan.'

And she trotted behind him as far as the door, but as he stepped into the room she froze. He walked over to the mirror.

'Come on, girl.' He squatted down, arms out ready for a hug or a tumble. But she stood the other side of the doorway, head down and legs rigid, whimpering softly.

'Bramble' — more sharply — 'come here.'

She turned and fled.

'Right, that does it,' he said, 'you're out of here.' And with that he started opening drawers and cupboards, tossing my clothes onto the bed.

'Hey, what do you think you're doing?'

'Saving your life, probably. Now, where's your suitcase?'

'I haven't got one. There's a holdall, and if there's any packing to be done I'll do it, thank you. Don't you think there ought to be some sort of discussion about this?'

'No. I've tried talking to you, and so has Fleur, for all the good it's done.'

He yanked the bag onto the bed and started stuffing my belongings into it. I pulled a pile of T-shirts away from him and tried to fold them properly while he wrenched another drawer open and grabbed a handful of something.

'I said I'd do that and I already told you I'd leave. Tomorrow, perhaps, or the day after. Just a few more hours to finish the piece.'

'Look, you haven't got till tomorrow. As far as your future's concerned there may not be a day after. I don't give a damn what you do with your bloody carving, but you're not spending another night in this room. In fact you're not setting foot in this building again. Is that understood?'

'All right, all right! Just stop waving my knickers about, will you!'

'What?'

Liam looked at his clenched fist and realised what it was he'd been threatening me with. He threw the items into the holdall and I'll swear his face went red behind that beard. Anyway, after that he let me do the packing while he stomped about muttering to himself. Then he snatched up the bag, strode out of the room and onto the deck.

'Hey, what about the rest of my stuff?'

'I'll come back for it in the morning. Will you come away out of there now.'

My head was gyrating. The world had shifted on its axis a dozen times since lunch and I wasn't even sure which way up I was. It was easier to follow the line of least resistance, so I did as I was told. I managed to grab the CD player and my laptop on the way out, and then ran behind him through the trees towards the woolshed. Once he was certain of me following him he strode on in silence.

'Liam?'

'What?'

'Do you think I'm going mad?'

'No, but I think you might do if this were allowed to go on much longer.'

'I'm sorry I got you mixed up in it. I don't know why I didn't tell you everything.'

'It's not your fault. That thing's got inside your head and you don't know what you're doing. It could just as easily have been me.'

'Except you're not a woman.'

'Yes, there is that, of course.'

Once inside the woolshed, Liam dumped my bag on the table. 'Thank God for that,' he said. 'Here, sit down, I'll make us some tea.'

I sat in silence while he filled the kettle, hardly noticing when he placed a mug beside me. Then he slumped into a chair, threw his head back and closed his eyes. He blew an exaggerated sigh into the lock of hair that had fallen over his face, making it flutter.

'So, what now?' I asked.

'Well, I think you're safe here, safer anyway. You'll stay here the night so I can keep an eye on you. Tomorrow we'll make definite arrangements to get you away from here completely.'

'Oh, will we? And what if I have other plans?'

'Well, if they involve spending yet another night in this place you can forget it.'

'God, you're an arrogant sod, aren't you? Don't you ever ask? What happened to "why don't you", or "would you mind"? You know, there are phrases in the English language that allow other people to participate in a conversation.'

Of course it was an accumulation of everything that had happened that day and long before. I could have screamed, I suppose, or burst into tears, but shouting at Liam seemed an equally good way of channelling blocked emotion. And once I'd started the outburst it was impossible to stop.

'You never ask, do you? It's always "do this" or "do that".'

'What are you on about, woman?' He struggled to his feet and stared at me, his jaw hanging.

'You, that's what I'm on about, you and your giving orders, taking over people's lives. Herding me about like I was one of your damned sheep. Well, I've had it up to here. *I'll* decide where I spend the night and *I'll* decide if and when I want to leave—'

'But I only—'

'And if you call me "woman" once more I swear I'll kick—'

And that was as far as I got because his mouth was over mine and he was holding me so tight I couldn't breathe. I suppose it was his way of making me shut up. No doubt it was the same for him: we'd both been living on the edge of a crisis for weeks, and there's a limit to how much tension can be sustained without something going snap. Well, perhaps that's how it started but I know there was much more to it than that.

Oh, and how I wish I could say it was perfect. But it wasn't. All that pent-up emotion might drive you to passion but it does nothing for your co-ordination. I can honestly say it was the worst sex I'd ever had. The earth didn't move for us, but the bedside table got knocked over. Then his hair got tangled up in my buttons and the dogs kept trying to jump up on the bed.

Somehow we managed to get through it.

Afterwards he sat on the edge of the mattress, stroking my hair. He was still wearing his shirt and one sock.

'It'll be better next time,' he said. 'I can do better than that.'

'Me too. Next time.'

'Would you like me to make us some fresh tea? Your last one ended up on the floor when I threw the pillow at Bramble.'

None of that mattered. Not that I felt romantic or elated or any of those things. I just felt as though I'd been way out on the edge for a long, long time and at last I'd found my way home.

TWENTY

My body is bent over, my head bowed. I am looking into a
pool. It is a pool of darkness that cradles the night sky. Stars all
around me now, stars above my head and, below my hands, stars
strewn on a mirror thick as velvet. My fingers quiver towards
the edge where surface tension has moulded a curve. A feather
touch and the tension breaks, tacking to my skin. If I lean over
I can see myself, a silhouette of blackness against the shimmer
of night. I touch the pool again, this time skimming the surface.
Unlike water, the ripples that follow are slow and sluggish. I lift
my hands and it comes away on my fingers, thick and rich. Like
paint it is, like the colours of old that were ground and mixed
with pestle and mortar, ground by hand from natural dyes and
herbs and living things.

Living things.

I scoop the pigment into my palm, holding it like a palette.
My fingers make a brush and sweep lines across the rock. My
name, I am writing my name. It is the same clearing, the same
sky reflected and the same rock on which I had lain, now
emblazoned with my signature. Again I take my fingers to my
palm and carry the stain to my arms and legs, tracing lines
and whorls in imitation of something primitive and savage. I

am a jungle warrior, painting my body for battle; a bride of
the savannah anointing herself with feathers and fur, living
things.

Living things.

Another dip into the pool and I lift my hand to stroke lines
on my face, my brow. The smell rises, catching in my throat,
that unmistakable bite of raw copper. I stagger back from the
rock, gasping and retching, running and falling and snatching
blindly for some way to save myself and my hands reach out
and grasp . . .

. . . the frame of the mirror. I knew it by feel alone, the carved
branches and the little wooden birds. I clung on to it, still
fighting for breath and the smell was still with me. In the
darkness of the bedroom I could barely see my face but I could
feel the sticky path of lines on my naked skin and I knew what
it was and where I had been.

I had thought it was all over. I had thought I was safe and
warm beside Liam. Panic took me to the bathroom where a
blaze of electric light drove the darkness away. I started the
shower and turned it hot and hotter until my skin was red.
And I scrubbed and scrubbed until I was raw and the last trail
of scarlet-stained water swirled away. And then I found lotions
and perfumes to blot out the smell that was gone from my body
but still pervaded the inside of my head.

I hadn't been wearing clothes and there were none left in
the cottage. With a rug from the sofa to cover my shoulders
against the cold, I picked my way through the branches and
back to the woolshed. The door creaked open and floorboards
cracked with each step. Both the dogs stirred in greeting, tails
wagging. But Liam snored, oblivious of my absence and return.
I kicked the borrowed rug under the bed and slipped between
the covers. Liam groaned and shifted, throwing his arm across
my waist and pulling me to him as if nothing had happened.

My heart was beating so hard that my body seemed to rock the bed and would surely wake him. But I needed to be close. I needed the warmth and the sweet sour muskiness of his skin, and I needed the primitive animal comfort of another human body.

Terrified of sleep, I focused on the square of pale light that was the window and waited for dawn. I must have lain awake for hours, trying to see the whole of it, to make a pattern. That was no dream. The blood was real. I had felt it on my skin, saw it thread the water as I fought to rid myself of its stain. So how did I get to the stone? And how could I have found my way back to the cottage? Through the mirror, it had to be. A gateway. Alice through the looking glass. I tried to remember the other dreams and the occasions when I'd lost time or woken in front of the mirror, but each memory came as a realisation that clenched my stomach and sent ripples of ice along my spine. I knew I had to leave.

Eventually sleep overtook me, but this time, thank God, it was the sleep of oblivion.

I was woken by sounds of Liam shuffling around. Although the room was still dim the window was now a watery yellow. He looked as if he were trying to dress without disturbing me, fumbling for buttons and hopping about on one leg. I rolled over and propped myself up on an elbow, wondering if I could persuade him to pose sometime. Sometime when this was all over. Perhaps a head and shoulders cast in bronze to highlight the angularity of that collarbone. Eventually he realised I was watching him and gave me a smile.

'Sorry, I was trying not to wake you.'

'What time is it?'

' 'bout half six.' He came over and sat on the bed, nuzzling my face and stroking my hair. 'There's work needs attending to.

It won't take long. You seem to be sleeping enough for the two of us.'

'Not all night. I spent some time thinking. You're right. I have to get out of here. Today.'

He looked at me, and then closed his eyes, his shoulders dropping as if a weight had fallen from his body. 'Thank the Lord for that. The sooner we're both out of here the better.'

'You're leaving too?'

'This is hardly the sort of place I'd want to call home.'

'But what will you do?'

'Ah, there's always casual work to be found. I quite fancy waiting on tables.'

'You'd have to get a haircut.' I took a deep breath, dredging up courage. 'Look, you wouldn't consider . . . I mean . . . There's plenty of room at my place.'

A broad grin lit up his face. 'I thought you'd never ask,' he said and kissed me on the forehead. 'How soon do you want to go? I might have to follow on later.'

'I thought we'd go together.'

'Well, I can't leave straight away. There's the animals, you see, can't abandon them. And I'll have to talk to Sullivan, not that he can be relied upon to look after the place. I'd better go down to Maggie's, get one of the other hands to keep an eye on the beasts until he can find a replacement. They might even know of someone. No, it's going to be afternoon at least before I can get away. I can always hitch a ride up there.'

Yes, I could see that he couldn't just up and run. But neither could I drive off without him. He might not get a lift, or he might get lost, or change his mind. I might never see him again.

'No. It's all right. I'll wait for you. I'll be all right in here. It's daytime and a few more hours won't make any difference. As long as we don't have to spend another night.'

He thought for a few moments then nodded. 'Right, I'll be as quick as I can. Perhaps you could do with some more sleep.'

And that's what I did, went back to sleep, with the sun pouring through the window like molten honey and cicadas honing the air.

When I woke the day had ripened into a rich, golden noon. I had slept deeply and returned refreshed, as if the very decision to go was enough to restore normality. My arms stretched across the bed to where Liam had lain, trying to catch the last trace of his warmth, but there was only the shape where his head had pressed into the pillow. No matter, he'd be back soon. I rolled over and got up, heading straight for the shower again. Before he returned I intended to demolish the last trace of the waking dream and everything else that went with it. I stood under the jet for ages, the water hot and pounding. In a few hours I would be home; *we* would be home. It felt all right to go back now. All the reasons that brought me here, Jason, the running away, had healed themselves through Liam.

I imagined him in my room, looking through my books, my music albums, telling him who I was by the things that surrounded me. He could get a job in one of the cafés, if that was what he really wanted. I would take breaks from the studio and sit at a pavement table for coffee. He'd pretend I was only a customer and say 'Madam' when he wrote my order. Then he'd wink and sneak me extra marshmallows with my cappuccino. Or perhaps he could play his fiddle, go busking on the street corner. I knew some musicians who met to play regularly at a bar nearby and I could introduce him. Yes, I wanted him to meet my friends, the real friends who had nothing to do with being famous.

I'd been so long under water that my fingers had wrinkled. I looked around for a towel. All that emotional stuff with Jason, it all seemed pathetic now, so trivial. Perhaps, when I got back, I could ring Sally. I'd missed her. And there was just one stupid little towel, barely enough to wrap round me. Damn, I'd left all my bathroom things in the cottage. Surely Liam had more towels than this? And in this heat I'd need some deodorant. I wandered back into the main room, rooting for signs of civilised bathing. There was aftershave on the bedside table and yes, he did possess a comb. That's what I'd do, I'd ring Sally.

There was a holdall under the bed; I could see a towel through the open zip so I hauled it out. I knew it was his private bag and Liam was a private person but I just needed a towel, that's all. I didn't mean to look. But there it was, a small book, thin and covered with dark red fabric. Unmistakable. Embossed with a lion and a unicorn, it was the answer to the riddle.

And I opened it. Of course I opened it.

United Kingdom of Britain and Northern Ireland it said, and the pages were dark red and patterned with a heavy watermark to deter forgers. The information was all on the last page with his photograph. His hair and beard were shorter and more civilised but he still looked like an axe murderer. But then passport photos always do that, don't they? I read the date of birth and worked out that he was ten years older than me. Place of birth — Belfast. Name — Patrick McGovern.

Patrick McGovern looked out at me through Liam Connors' eyes and I flipped through to find a visitor's visa and a temporary work permit that had expired six months before. That's what it was, of course, a quick change of name and disappear into the hills before the authorities could throw him out. He didn't want to go home, that's all. People do it all the time.

I should have left it at that. But no, I had to dig deeper, didn't I? I had to push my hand down through whatever else he had in that bag until my fingers felt the cold metal. I knew what it was straight away. Although I'd never actually seen one for real before, I'd watched enough American TV to recognise the shape by touch alone. I lifted it out of the bag, so carefully, as if it were a thing to be revered. It was grey, not black as I expected, lighter than I would have imagined. It was as if all the weight and the darkness of it had settled in my stomach instead. My limbs felt full of lead and I couldn't move.

For a long time I stared at it, then managed to put it down while I scrabbled into some clothes, my skin and hair still wet. Then what was I to do? Pick it up again, of course, and the passport, one in each hand, and wait for something to happen. And that is how I sat on the edge of the bed until he returned.

I don't know how long I waited: it could have been minutes or hours. Then I heard footsteps outside and the door banged open. Liam bounded in, loud and full of himself.

'Right, it's all settled. Old Roger from over Benson's place will come over for a few days until Sullivan finds a replacement. I said I was getting a lift with you as we were both leaving together. I thought—' Then he saw me and froze.

I stared back at him. The objects in my hands asked all the questions.

'Be very careful with that. It's loaded. Do you know about guns?'

I shook my head.

'Have you touched the safety catch?'

'I don't think so.'

'Then, very gently now, pass it over to me.'

'No, I won't. What do you need the gun for, Patrick? It is Patrick, isn't it? Going rabbit shooting? Or will it be dogs this time?'

'No, wait, you don't understand.'

He looked as if I had struck him. His hands were shaking.

'Is this the gun you used to shoot Badger? Who was your next sacrifice going to be? Was it Bramble you had in mind? Or me perhaps?'

'God, why would I hurt you? I've been trying to protect you.'

246

'Protecting me, were you? Or were you guarding me? Keeping me close to you?'

'Is that what you think last night was about?'

'I don't know. I don't know anything any more. But you seem to know everything, don't you? Why is that, Patrick McGovern? That thing out there in the trees that watches me, how come you know all about it? I'm being preyed on by some . . . some medieval ghoul and the hired hand just happens to be the world's leading expert on these things. Bit of a coincidence, isn't it?'

'Yes . . . No, well . . . This has been happening for hundreds of years. Sooner or later someone who realised what was going on was bound to turn up. There may well have been others before. Heaven knows who's been involved with this in the past.'

'And that's supposed to explain everything, is it? Who you are and why you're here and why you've got a gun? And why you lied to me, Patrick McGovern? Or *is* it Connors? Or perhaps it's Sullivan? The Irish branch of the family, are you, come to claim your land? At what cost? My blood as a condition of ownership?'

'Ah, no. Look, there you are again, running off half-cocked when you know nothing.'

'Well, tell me then. Oh, there's a reasonable explanation, I'm sure. I'm surprised you haven't rehearsed it all beforehand.'

'How can I think straight when you're waving that gun at me?'

He turned and walked over to the window, hands covering his face. After a while he shook his head, then turned back to me and said quietly, 'It's nothing like that. I just want to get you away from here. I want us to be together, yes, but most of all I want you safe. Isn't that what I've been saying all along? Can't you see that?'

What he said was true, and that's what was so confusing.

'I don't know any more.' I felt sobs choking my throat, tears swimming behind my eyes till I couldn't think straight. 'I don't know what to do.'

'Leave, Regan. Leave now. If you won't go with me then go on your own. I won't stop you and I won't follow you. I swear you'll never see me again, if that's what you really want. But go now, while you can.'

Nothing made sense any longer. I was trying to remember why I was here and why I hadn't left when all this first started.

'I can't go without my work. I need to finish.'

'Oh, not that again! Sod the bloody work. Your life's more important.'

'But it *is* my life. I thought you understood that. Those carvings are part of me.'

'Leave them here. Forget them. Go now and forget everything.'

'That's what you want, is it? For me to forget it all. Forget what you were trying to do to me. Well, I'm not going without my work.'

'They're bits of wood, Regan, they're not worth dying for. Now give me that bloody gun!'

He seemed to rush at me and slammed into my hand. The gun was sent flying as he caught my wrists, but it didn't go off. We both watched it slide under the table and come to rest. He held me hard, the muscles of his arms taut as wire. There was no way I could pull free.

'OK,' he gasped, 'let's see what this is all about.'

'What do you mean?'

'What is this mind-blowing artwork that you can't bear to abandon? Come on. I want to know exactly what's been going on between you and that thing.'

He dragged me to my feet and out the door. I yelled and swore at him. Branches whipped my bare legs and tangled my feet but he strode on without relenting. I wrestled and kicked every inch of the way and eventually hauled myself up to him, sinking my teeth into his arm. He let go with one hand, holding the palm flat above me.

'Now, you listen to me,' he growled, 'I've never hit a woman in my life and thought I never would. But if that's what it takes to make you see reason, I swear I'm willing to give it a try.'

He was far stronger than me; in a hands-on fight I wouldn't stand a chance. After that I allowed myself to be towed through the trees and onto the cottage deck.

'Now, perhaps we'll see what this is all about.'

He grabbed me by the back of my neck, as if I were a puppy, and forced me to look at the workbench. With his free hand he threw the cover from the wood block and we both gazed at the figure.

Silence pierced the air and a sickening chill seeped through my body.

When he spoke, it was in a whisper. 'Jesus, Regan, what have you done? What *is* that?'

It was the most beautiful face I'd ever seen. Not a man, not quite, but close enough to be judged and found perfect. The face of an angel, that's what it was. But how could anything so exquisite bear such an expression? The curl of the lip, the flare of the nose? And the eyes, ah yes, the eyes! It was evil in its very essence, the way a fallen angel would be — a being conceived in heaven and nurtured on corruption. Its body was of some other creature, something more akin to the tree from which it had evolved. At its feet was something torn and broken that may once have been human and was now beyond recognition.

'It's . . . I think . . . It . . .' I struggled. My throat had closed and my tongue cleaved to the roof of my mouth. It was a form that I'd created, that I'd lived and breathed for weeks, and yet I was seeing it for the first time. 'I didn't know,' I whispered, 'I swear I didn't know.'

'No, you probably didn't. And I wonder if you know now? This is what you should be afraid of. It's been using you and it's not finished yet, not by a long way.'

He flung the cloth over the object, as if it did not deserve the light of day, and we were no longer forced to look at it.

'But why me? I'm not a Sullivan, I'm not part of it.' I walked down from the deck and he sat on the steps.

'I'm not so sure. Perhaps we're assuming too much. Because the women were all married into the family we knew about them. But there may have been others with different sorts of connections. What else do they have in common? They were all mature, late twenties, early thirties.'

'Like me. But they had all had children.'

'Yes, but not necessarily the heir. Old Michael's mother lived into old age. It was the first wife who died. But they'd all proved that they could bear children. Maybe that was it.'

'I thought sacrificial victims were supposed to be young virgins.'

'No, that's only in fiction. All the Sullivan women were ripe and fertile. Land is always hungry — what would be the use of a barren offering?'

'But I'm . . .' I started to say, and then fell silent.

There was that memory of the waiting room. Of the polished desk and, behind it, the secretary with the polished nails. It was my second year at university. He was very kind, the surgeon, no reproaches, no judgement. It was his secretary who took the cheque. Not my cheque, of course — as if I would have that sort of money. It was my tutor who'd paid. He could afford the private clinic. What he couldn't afford was the scandal.

I expect my face told everything and for a moment Liam looked hurt.

'It's all right, I won't ask. I expect you'll tell me if and when you want to. But that does make a difference. Mature and proven fertile. And there was a physical relationship with a Sullivan. Is that so?'

I nodded.

'That may well be enough. And on top of that you were able to connect with that thing in a way none of the others could. No wonder it's holding you here. You've got to get away. Come with me now, Regan. Please.'

I looked at him. Liam and yet not Liam. A stranger. Patrick McGovern was someone who had lied to me. And he had a gun. Why the gun?

'Regan, please! Trust me, will you?'

'Trust you? *Why* should I trust you? You've never trusted me, have you?' I started to back away from him. 'You know everything about me and I don't even know who you are. Leave me alone, will you. Just leave me alone.'

And I turned and fled, with him calling after me. It was late afternoon and, as I ducked between the branches, lengthening shadows were gathering beneath the trees.

TWENTY-ONE

I ran fuelled on anger, hands clenched into fists and punching the air in rhythm with my pounding feet. All the fear and confusion I'd been stockpiling for weeks exploded inside my head and fused into one tight ball of seething, red rage. I threw it all at Patrick McGovern.

Everything he'd said to me was a lie. He'd done it so well he actually had me convinced that he cared about what was happening. All the time he was messing with my mind. All his talk of pagans and blood and human sacrifice. He'd filled me with delusions and driven me to the brink of psychosis. He'd taken my art, the thing that gave me life, and warped it into part of his mind-fuck. But the worst thing was he'd taken Liam away from me.

Yeah, OK, so I wasn't being rational. By this time rational had abdicated in favour of mental anarchy. I suppose I thought if I ran far enough I might get back to where everything was all right between us. So I ran away to put distance between me and Patrick McGovern and the gun and that vile thing I had created out of wood.

I didn't stop to think that I might be running straight towards it.

Eventually I was forced to slow down and then stop. I was a mess, a physical and emotional wreck, sobbing and panting. Fire throbbed in my leg muscles and deep gasps scoured my lungs. I found myself on the lake path, heading in the direction of the house. The sun had gone down and shadows were gathering around the edge of the water. I forced myself to stumble on and there was just enough left of the evening light to see where I was going. And where was I heading? I couldn't go back for the truck, *he* would be there. Perhaps the house? Sullivan would be at the house and it was Sullivan I should be afraid of. Or maybe that wasn't right any more. Maybe I should be afraid of whatever was lurking in the trees? The Watcher? Or was it a basilisk or the Jabberwocky, or just something Patrick McGovern had invented?

As soon as the thought came, I was aware of movement among the pines. I could feel it, a point of coldness crawling over my skin like the slimy path of a snail. I was being watched. I shivered and moved on, concentrating on the road to the house, all the time aware of the something that skulked among the shadows. There was a sharp crack, and my whole body jolted and my heart rate leapt. It was a branch snapping, that was all, some small animal. That's what I had to believe.

I walked on, more quickly now, trying not to look behind me. I had to reach the house. No guaranteeing that would be safe, but I might find some answers there. I couldn't trust Patrick McGovern any more, but I might get the truth out of that old drunk.

The house looked dark, but Sullivan's ancient Jeep was parked at the side and, as I stepped into the hall, light was spilling from one of the side doors. Shuffling sounds came from the room, then a crash followed by incoherent muttering. I crept closer, pushing the door open, and found Sullivan kneeling on the floor.

The room was lit by a lamp hanging low over a central table, leaving the corners in shadow. It must, at one time, have been an elegant dining room, but even in that dim light it looked dull and dusty. It was unlikely anyone had eaten here for years and the big table had been taken over by heaps of paperwork. I guessed Sullivan used this as a makeshift office, though his attempts at administration looked pretty chaotic. He appeared unaware of my arrival as he grovelled on the floor collecting pieces of smashed china.

'Mr Sullivan? I hope you don't mind, the door was open.'

His body jolted as he swung round. His hair hung over his face in greasy strings and his eyes were wide and fearful.

'Ah, Regan, it's you.' There seemed to be some measure of relief in his voice. He swept an open hand over the shards and shook his head.

'Here, let me help.'

I bent down beside him and gathered up the pieces. It looked as though it had been a vase, white with a design painted in shades of blue, fine porcelain and probably quite old and precious. I placed the pieces on the table.

'It belonged to Sarah,' he said as if this were some sort of explanation. 'She liked Dresden. Bought this in a junk shop.' He scrambled to his feet.

'I came to tell you I've decided it's time I moved on,' I said. 'I'll be leaving very soon.'

'Yes. Perhaps that's just as well. This isn't a good place for outsiders.'

'Especially women,' I whispered.

'Yes, especially women.'

He reached for a whisky bottle from the sideboard, and two glasses. 'You'll join me?'

I was about to refuse, then realised I could do with a shot of something. We both sat at the table and he poured two stiff measures, downing half of his in one gulp. He put down his glass and started to sort through the remains of the vase. I took a mouthful of my whisky and forced it down while looking around the room There was a carved sideboard and a dresser filled with what must have been Sarah's collection of china. The walls were papered in something reminiscent of William Morris and hung with landscapes in gilt frames.

'This must have been a beautiful house once,' I said.

'Yes, it was. I'm afraid I've let things go. There didn't seem to be much point without Sarah. Then the lad grew up and left. After that things seemed to run away from me.'

Under the focused light his face looked drawn, the skin tinged with yellow. I guessed his liver had taken some punishment over the years and now his blood was flooded with poisons. God knows what it had done to his brain cells. His hands shook as he fingered the pieces, trying to fit them together.

'She loved pretty things like this, did my Sarah.' He turned over a chunk of the vase on which was painted a blue flower. 'Her eyes were just this colour. I doubt it can be mended now, it's beyond repair.'

'You loved her, didn't you? You still do. Then why?'

Sullivan didn't answer. He looked down at his hands and the hopeless shards.

'I've seen her, Mr Sullivan. I went to visit Sarah.'

He looked at me as if he didn't understand the words.

'I went to see her at that place, Harston House. Maggie told me where she was.'

'You've seen Sarah? My Sarah?'

'Yes.'

There was a long silence while he took this in. I thought he might be angry. Then, 'How is she? Is she . . . well?'

'Yes, she seems well. I don't know if she's well enough to come home, though.'

'That's not possible. She's safer where she is.'

'Like Badger, you mean? He's safer in the woolshed, isn't he, safer away from this house?'

He hung his head and said nothing. I waited. He glanced briefly in my direction then took another long swig from his glass.

'Sarah's taken up painting,' I said. 'Did you know she was an artist? She has some talent.'

'Is that right?'

'Trees, Mr Sullivan. She paints trees. Nothing *but* trees. Now why would that be?'

'I wouldn't know.' He drained his glass.

'I think you do. She told me you tried to kill her.'

'No!' He slammed his fist down onto the table. Then quietly, almost a whisper, 'No. I couldn't hurt Sarah. That's the irony of it, you see, I tried *not* to kill her.'

He lowered his head onto his hands and murmured softly. I could barely hear the words, as if they were intended more for himself than for me.

'I thought I could fight it. For a long while I did. Oh yes, I could see what was happening to her. At first I thought it was — you know, the way she was, on top of the world one moment then locked up inside herself the next. The doctors had explained how she was unwell, but that only made it easier for me to lie to myself. So when she started wandering off I reasoned that it was all part of her sickness. Then she began to isolate herself, locking herself in her room, taking herself off to the cottage. It was the mirror, you see, the one that's in the cottage now. I didn't understand about the mirror at first. By the time I realised what was going on it was too late.

'Perhaps I should have taken her away from here, but somehow I couldn't make myself leave. That's a kind of sickness too, the way the Sullivans are bound to this land as surely as if our souls were rooted like the trees. I think that was all part of it. So we stayed and it got worse, until in the end I almost lost the fight.

'It was Sarah who tried to kill herself and me that stopped her. She didn't know what she was doing, you see. And she saw me with the knife in my hand. I'd taken it away from her. Even then it was all I could do to stop myself from turning the blade into her.

'But no, I didn't try to kill Sarah. But seeing how she's ended up, maybe it would have been better if I had.'

'What do you know about the mirror, Mr Sullivan? Sarah had it in her room, didn't she? Did you know it came from Ireland?'

'I don't know where it came from. It was my mother's before Sarah had it.'

'And your mother died when you were a baby.'

'They said it was suicide but I know better now. Her things were still here, in the house. There were some old photographs, so I knew what she looked like. I'd stand in front of that mirror sometimes and picture her smiling back at me. My father never spoke about her, only the land. That's what he cared about. To him the land was everything. It was like an obsession with him. "It's a living thing," he'd say. "It demands your devotion. You must feed it with work and sweat and time. You must give it your best beloved and then it will serve you well." Over and over he'd tell me, and then, when I refused to listen any more, he started on young Jason.'

He fell silent and I stared into my drink, trying to think what it was that sounded so familiar. Then I remembered. 'That's what Sarah said. She said you called her your best beloved, then you tried to kill her. What does that mean, Sullivan?'

'It means it's time for you to move on. Get away from this place. There is nothing for you here.'

'Yes, that's what Liam Connors tells me I should do. What do you know about him? What has he got to do with all this?'

He looked confused. 'Connors? Nothing as far as I know. He's a work hand. He's leaving anyway.'

Perhaps that was true. I hesitated for a moment, not knowing how hard to push this. What the hell, I'd come this far.

'It's not just the land that has to be fed, is it? What about the Watcher?'

'The what?'

'You know, the tree spirit, the thing that lives out on the hillside? What did your father tell you about that?'

Sullivan stumbled to his feet, knocking the chair over behind him. 'There are things here that are none of your concern. Connors is right to tell you to leave. If you've got any sense you'll go now.'

He reached for the bottle and refilled his glass, hitting the rim and spilling whisky over the table. I decided I'd gone far enough and started to back towards the door before he became really violent. But no, when he looked at me it was with such sadness and his voice was suddenly gentle.

'I'm sorry. I don't want any harm to come to you, that's all it is. That's all.'

A full moon had risen and the clearing surrounding the house was washed with blue light. My truck stood at the edge of the path with Liam leaning against it. A shout of sheer joy rose in me then sank again when I remembered he was Patrick McGovern. I was caught between the two of them, McGovern and Sullivan. I could run away for a second time, but there was nowhere left, only the trees and whatever it was that haunted them. So I sauntered over to the truck in an attempt to brazen it out. As I approached he lifted his hand and dangled the keys in front of me. But as I tried to take them he snatched his hand away, hiding them behind his back.

'No, you don't get away so easily this time. How's Sullivan?'

'Mad as a March hare. Give me my keys.'

'No, not yet. Before I came to look for you I did some thinking.'

'Oh, really? And what conclusion did you come to?'

'Well, for a start, I'm not prepared to let you go without putting up a fight. And for another, you're absolutely right. You don't know who I am and why the hell should you trust me? And if there's to be any future there has to be trust between us.'

'So?'

'So, here's the deal. We both get in the truck. You sit behind the wheel and I keep the keys. Then I'll tell you what I swore I would never tell anyone. And when I've finished I'll give your keys back and you can go anywhere you want, with or without me. OK?'

There was no choice really. And, like him, I knew I couldn't give up that easily. He unlocked the door for me to climb into the driver's seat. I gripped the wheel as if I were going somewhere while he went round to the other side and swung up beside me.

'How did you know I was in there?' I asked.

'Not too hard to figure out. I went round the house and saw you and Sullivan through the window. You were having a drink together and you seemed OK. I didn't know what he was up to and I thought if I blundered in it might make things worse. So I waited outside and kept an eye on things. Oh, by the way, I found something while I was sneaking round the back. It's something you ought to see, but it can wait a little while.'

'So what was it you wanted to tell me?'

He looked through the windscreen, as if studying the passage of moonlight across the grass. Then he took a deep breath and held it for a moment before he spoke.

'My name is Patrick McGovern and for the past three years I've been running for my life. I came halfway round the world to hide. Australia first, and then New Zealand. It's a small country, but easy to get lost in. I couldn't hide the accent, but Liam Connors is a good name and I think I've covered my trail well enough. They probably won't even bother looking now — they've plenty of other traitors to hunt down. It's myself I'm still running from.'

'Who are *they*? What did you do?'

'I'd better start at the beginning. I was born in Belfast, and so I grew up in the seventies during the worst of it. The McGoverns were a good Catholic family so they bred like the proverbial rabbits. There were seven of us, all boys: our family favoured males. I was somewhere in the middle, all of us crammed into one small terraced house in the working-class side of the city. Then there was the army of cousins and half-cousins and uncles. All devout Catholics and all staunch members of the Cause.'

'What, the IRA you mean?'

'Members of Sinn Fein, we called ourselves, the political party. But yes, it was the IRA. There's not much hope for the poor in Northern Ireland, except for false promises pledged by those two mighty institutions that rule their lives, the Church and the Sinn Fein. Between them they've managed to put a stranglehold on the whole nation.

'So, it was Mass every morning with my mother, then the secret knock on the back door at night and my father and uncles would be away. They never said where they went but there were always headlines in the papers the next morning. It was no time before my brothers started going with them. Sean, he was the eldest, he went out one night and never came back. Men in black balaclavas fired guns over his grave — a salute to a dead hero, they said. His death only served to fuel the hatred, and the Church, as usual, stood back and looked the other way.'

'And you joined them? You were part of it?'

'No, I wasn't. Of course I was swept along with the ideology, the fanaticism. I knew nothing else. But when they discovered I had a brain, the only one in the family it seems, they had other plans for me and I was exempt. I was put to schoolwork, then entry for university. So while my brothers built road blocks and hijacked cars, I studied maths and history.'

'And you went to Dublin?'

'No, it was Cambridge, England. A special scholarship they persuaded me to go in for. Some daft notion about Cambridge's connections with the British government. I was to be a hero, too, an infiltrator. Only it didn't work out like that.'

'Why, what happened?'

'When you live all your life in a cesspit you grow up thinking the whole world smells of shit. I'm not saying the dreaming spires don't generate their own academic crap, but at least the odour was sweeter. And I was reading history, Irish history in particular, and the Famine. What I learned was not what I'd been taught. Yes, the British had a lot to answer for, but there was plenty to lay at our own doorstep. It was really about the rich bleeding the poor. There was many a wealthy Irish landowner filling ships with corn and beef to line his pockets with English gold, while his neighbours died in a ditch. And many an English child kept body and soul together by slaving in a factory built with money extorted by Irish landowners for their English overlords. I also learned that hatred breeds hatred and religious brainwashing isn't limited to minor cults.'

'So what about your family?'

'Each time I went home I felt more alienated from them. In the end I stopped going and they wrote me off. All except my brother, Devlin. Two years younger than me so we were close as kids. He came to visit me once in Cambridge and then, when I moved to Dublin, we saw a lot of each other. He'd doss down at my place for weekends and we'd do the pubs.'

'So you did go back to Ireland?'

'Southern Ireland, yes. After I'd graduated I got a teaching post at the University College of Dublin, specialist in Ireland and Britain in the Middle Ages, twelfth-century religious and intellectual life, and the mythology of the Celts.'

'So, you really are an expert in this stuff?'

'Yes, but it sounds more impressive than it is. Anyway, I lived in Dublin, I was even married for a while but it didn't work out. Then, three years ago my mother died and I went home for the funeral. Devlin was there, of course, with his wife and three kids. Next day he took me for a drink and introduced me to some of his mates. Oh, I was aware he was still involved with the Cause, but I hadn't realised how deep it went.'

'I thought it was all over by then. Wasn't there a ceasefire?'

'It's never over. It's in the bone and the blood. There were those who wanted the treaty destroyed because violence was the only way they knew how to live. When Devlin was eight years old he was patrolling the Falls Road with a brick in his hand looking for an English car window to lob it through. Our father, who taught him that little trick, said there was no way soldiers were going to open fire on the kids. It's handed down, generations upon generation. You can't stamp out that sort of indoctrination with the wipe of a pen.

'Anyway his mates got talking and through the drink things were said that I wasn't supposed to hear. In Gordon Street there's a bar called the Retreat — late-night licence, disco, ecstasy supplied by the bouncers, you know the sort of place. Saturday night and it'd be full of kids out for a good time, no different from the kids I'd be tutoring on Monday morning. A car bomb, that's what they'd planned. Not very original but security levels had relaxed by then and, in all probability, they'd have got away with it. The carnage would have broken the ceasefire beyond redemption and the whole merry-go-round would have started up again. I had to make the phone call.

'Come Saturday night Gordon Street was crawling with army and police and the bomb was defused. Then they went after those responsible. Shots were fired and some were taken prisoner. Devlin was the only casualty. Dead on arrival.'

Liam fell silent. Moonlight caught the wet streaks running into his beard. Those were private tears and I didn't intrude, but my hand slid across to his and he grasped it as if it were the only thing holding him together. I waited and an owl swooped from a nearby tree, preying on some small creature. Its life was taken swiftly and without a sound.

Eventually Liam spoke again.

'Oh, they knew it was me all right. Do you know what they

do to traitors? No, and you wouldn't want to. I had a friend in Dublin, a good friend, he's another historian. He helped me to get away, got things from my flat, passport and stuff. I had to take money from him as my credit cards would be too easy to trace.'

'Was he the friend you emailed? The one who sent you that stuff on Ireland?'

'Yes. I've never phoned him, they could tap into it. But we keep in touch through emails because they're easier to disguise. So it was the ferry to Liverpool then the Channel tunnel to France. Germany, and from there a plane to Australia. Then here. Casual jobs, labouring, busking for the fair.'

'And you happened to stumble on this place.'

'No, not quite. I'd picked up rumours about the Sullivans and their family history. Couldn't resist a bit of hands-on research — old habits die hard. I hadn't reckoned on you being here.' He wiped his face with his hand. 'That's all of it, I think.'

'And the gun? What about the gun?'

'Bought it from one of the travellers. No I don't have a licence, and yes I do know how to use it.'

'All that stuff about stone circles on the website, did you write that?'

'God no, that was one of my students, part of his research. But I remembered reading it.'

'And the PIN, the one to access the university records? Is that traceable?'

'If anyone from the organisation is monitoring the university computer, and they may be for several reasons, it would alert them to the fact that I'd been there. I doubt they could trace the exact origin of the contact, though they might be able to identify the country and know where to start looking.'

'But you took that risk? For me?'

'I doubt they'd even bother now. Especially not this far away. More to do with me being paranoid.'

We both fell silent, each caught in our own thoughts.

Then there was a sound from the house. Sullivan came down the deck steps. He hesitated a moment and looked around, as if trying to get his bearings, but I don't think he noticed my truck. He lurched off towards his Jeep. A moment later we heard the engine fire and the vehicle drove off along the lake path.

'I wonder where he's off to,' I murmured.

'Oh, he'll be heading for Maggie's place. You've been keeping the man from his drinking — usually he'd be there by now. We won't see him again for a couple of hours.'

'I was just thinking about you and old Michael Sullivan. How you both came from Ireland, both running away from something secret and violent, something evil, passed down through family generations.'

' "The sins of the father . . . " That sort of thing?'

'It's true for the Sullivans. It followed them here and it's still happening. And you're still looking over your shoulder, aren't you? Does it ever end?'

He sighed. 'Here, you'd better have your keys back. What do you want to do now? Shall I stay in the truck or go?'

Another silence. Every pulse of my body wanted to reach out to him, and yet . . .

I was trapped between the two of them, Liam and Sullivan. No, there were three; there was also the Watcher, the thing that walked among the pines, that crawled inside my head and made me dream. I didn't doubt it was real, but it wasn't *physical*. It needed someone physical to work through. It took someone human to shoot Badger, someone human to put those mangled carcasses on the stone.

Sullivan was the hunter. But Liam was the one with the gun.

'For Christ's sake, Regan, say something, if it's only to tell me to bugger off.'

'You said you had something to show me?'

'Oh, yes. It may mean nothing but . . . Well, come and see for yourself.'

TWENTY-TWO

Well, what am I supposed to be looking at?'

Liam nodded towards a clump of bushes. I didn't get it. So I moved closer, walking round to see what I'd missed.

'No, sorry. Just some branches.'

But then, as I took another step, moonlight caught something behind the leaves. It was shiny, metallic. I pulled a branch back and it came away in my hand. It wasn't a bush but a pile of cut limbs laid over something. Liam pulled more leaves away and exposed what they must have been put there to conceal.

'It's the young lad's bike, isn't it?' he asked.

'Yes, Jason's. I rode on it a few times — I'm certain it's the same one. But what's it doing here?'

'Didn't he take it back to Auckland with him at Christmas?'

'Well, I thought he did. He certainly arrived on it.'

'And before that, when it was stored here, he left it in one of the barns where the tractors are kept. You haven't seen him at all?'

'No, not since Christmas,' I said. 'He could have arrived without me knowing, of course, though I'm surprised he didn't come to the cottage.'

'If he'd been driving about the place we would have heard the engine. So, why hide his bike like this? And where the hell is he now?'

A dark thought gathered over me like a storm cloud.

'Liam, you know I was in there with Sullivan a while ago?'

'Did he say anything about this?'

'No, but what he did say . . . Well, I told him I'd been to see Sarah and what she had said about him trying to murder her. And he didn't actually deny it. What he said was . . . now let me get this right. He said, "No, I couldn't hurt Sarah. That's the irony of it, you see, I tried *not* to kill her."'

'As if something else was trying to make him do it?'

'It could have been. Oh, God, you don't think the . . . the whatever it is . . . might hurt Jason, do you?'

'There's no telling what it might do. Sullivan may have managed to fight it with Sarah, but that was before he took to the drinking. What was he like when you left him?'

'Upset, angry. He'd been talking about his father, how he was obsessed with the land. "You must give it your best beloved then it will serve you well" — that's what his father drummed into him. And that's what Sarah said he called her, his best beloved. Then he said he didn't want *me* to be harmed. Do you think he could have turned on Jason?'

'What, sacrifice his son? Like Abraham and Isaac, you mean? It's possible, I suppose.'

'It could be that Jason's in the house. We ought to take a look round while Sullivan's out of the way.'

'Jason could be anywhere. I'm not sure I give a damn about either of them, to be honest.'

'We've got to do something, Liam, we just can't leave him.'

'Yeah, I suppose you're right. Come on, just a quick look, then we're out of here.'

The house was thick with darkness. Floorboards cracked with every footstep and the doors squeaked on their hinges.

'Where's the damned light switch?' I'd no idea why I was whispering.

'No, don't turn on the lights. If Sullivan comes back he'll spot it a mile away. I think he keeps a torch in the cupboard under the sink. Wait here.'

Liam fumbled his way down the hall, returning after a few moments with a circle of light that he kept trained close to the floor. The place looked no less intimidating but at least we didn't bump into the furniture. We searched the ground floor: two large living rooms and the big kitchen as well as Sullivan's dining-room-cum-office. All were equally dusty and neglected. Huge sofas and dressers crouched in the darkness like sleeping dragons. But no sign of life. And no sign of Jason.

'The place is empty,' Liam said, 'we're wasting time.'

'He must be upstairs,' I hissed.

'You realise we're trespassing?'

'Oh, big deal. Here, give me the torch.'

'Wait, all right, let me go first.'

Every stair groaned in warning of our arrival. At the top there was a long hallway with five doors leading off it, two each side and one at the far end. The first turned out to be Sullivan's bedroom. Apart from the smell of stale booze there was nothing remarkable about it. The room next to it was a spare bedroom, the mattress stripped down and the furniture bare. Opposite Sullivan's room we found a bathroom with a dripping tap and rusted tub, and a washbasin encrusted with generations of old soap. I could understand why Jason didn't come home very often. Liam opened the door beside the bathroom, scanned the room with the torch beam, then stepped in and switched on the light. That was no problem: the windows were blacked out.

'Jason's darkroom. Sullivan told me about this. Fixed it up for his son when he was younger.'

'Well, it's obviously still in use. Look here, these trays are full of chemicals. Someone's been working in here recently.'

There were scraps of paper lying about, trimmings from a guillotine, but no prints hanging up to dry. The cupboards held the usual photographic supplies and equipment but told us nothing. I ran my hand round the edge of the sink. It came away wet. The room had been used within the last couple of hours.

There was one door left to try. I turned the handle but nothing moved.

'I bet this is Sarah's room. Sullivan told me he keeps it locked because Jason used to go in there. That's where the mirror was kept. Apparently Sarah spent hours sitting in front of it, just staring. After she left, Jason took to hiding in there, probably trying to get close to his mother. I'll bet that's where he is.'

'Try calling him.'

I laid my ear to the door and tapped gently.

'Jason? Are you in there?' No answer. I tried again only much louder. 'Jason, it's me, Regan. Please open up.'

Still no sound from inside.

'It's no good. You'll have to break it down.'

'What do you mean, I'll have to break it down? How am I supposed to do that?'

'Just throw yourself at it, for God's sake. Look, he could be hurt in there or worse.'

'Or he could be down the pub with Sullivan.'

'Then why hide his bike? No, there's something wrong, I can feel it. We've got to do something. Try the door, please Liam.'

He looked at me with that 'there you go again' expression, then rolled his eyes in defeat and said, 'OK, stand back. I'll take a run at it.'

From the other end of the hall he hurled himself full pelt at the door, bounced like a rubber ball off a brick wall, then stood doubled over, clutching his shoulder and cursing.

'Oh, God, I'm sorry. It always works on TV.'

'This is not a frigging film set.'

'Could you try once more?'

'No, I bloody couldn't. Wait a minute, let's think about this. We're assuming Sullivan locked it from the outside. Which means Jason must be at least alive and probably conscious. So why isn't he answering? But if Jason uses the room he would have a key of his own. That means he either has it with him, in which case he could let himself out, unless . . . Wait a moment.'

Liam dived back into the darkroom. I heard him slamming cupboard doors. He came back brandishing a key.

'Logical place. Old Man Sullivan's unlikely to go looking for it in a developing tank. Here, you hold the torch beam on the lock.'

'But you reckon he's not in there?'

'I very much doubt it. However,' he said inserting the key, 'I never could resist the mystery of a locked room.' He gave me a sly wink and twisted his hand. 'There.'

Levers clicked and Liam pushed the door open. I stepped through, sweeping the beam around the walls. Jason wasn't there. But I was.

I was everywhere.

Photographs.

On the walls, doors, over the bed, anywhere there was an inch of space. And they were all of me. Every photograph Jason had ever taken. Me working, lazing on a deck, drinking wine, me dancing, leaning on the rail of a boat. Small candles, night-lights, flickered around the room, making the pictures dance as if they were alive.

We both stood in silence, turning slowly, the images revolving around us. It was like being in a hall of mirrors in some crazy fairground, seeing myself reflected a thousand times, grinning and waving. There I was at the Christmas lunch table, spooning ice cream. But how come there was a picture of me working in the early morning? And there I was walking through the bush with Bramble.

'Jesus, what the hell's all this?' That was Liam. 'My God, it looks like some sort of shrine.' He snatched down a picture of the two of us sitting under the huge tree. 'I thought Jason went home on Christmas Day?'

I nodded.

'But this was taken on Boxing Day. You remember we went for that walk? Look, there's Badger's wheelbarrow. And this one's been taken at night. Did you know he was here then?'

'No,' I whispered.

I felt as if I were sinking through cold water and I began to tremble. I felt violated and degraded in a way that was beyond any physical assault. I could understand why some tribesmen are afraid of cameras, think they can steal your soul away. It was as if my essence were being sucked out of me.

'And what's this?'

Liam picked up a large print that was propped up on the dresser. Me, of course, at night, in the clearing by the stone. I was naked and smearing my body with something dark.

'Oh, no. That was last night.' I could barely form the words. 'You were asleep. At first I thought I was dreaming. Then I woke up at the cottage again, in front of the mirror.'

'You didn't tell me. Why didn't you wake me?'

'It was awful. I felt ashamed. Unclean.'

Liam rubbed his hand over my shoulder.

In most of the pictures I was laughing or smiling. I didn't know I smiled so much. Another time I might have been glad of that insight but right then it seemed as if I were mocking myself, as if it were all some, weird, schizophrenic joke.

'Liam, this isn't right.'

'No, it's warped, sick. What the fuck's going on in his head?'

'No, I mean *this* isn't right. Look. The exhibition where Jason and I met. But we met at the opening. This was taken while it was being set up, at least three days before. And look at this.'

I pointed to a street scene, a pavement café where Sally and I were drinking coffee. Although the sun was shining we both wore coats.

'I remember this. It was still winter. At least a month before Jason and I met. And this one. My hair is long but I had it cut ages ago. What does it mean?'

'It means, my girl, that you've been set up. Young lover boy has stitched you up good and proper.' He held me very tightly and pressed his face into my hair. 'I think it's time to go.'

This time there was no debate. We were down the stairs and into the truck, Liam throwing me into the driver's seat. I fired the engine and released the brake while he was still climbing into the passenger side.

The wheel spun as I took us onto the lake path.

'We'll need to get our stuff. Lucky it's all at the woolshed.'

'No, I need my tools.'

'We're not going inside the cottage.'

'No. They're on the deck. What's left inside can stay. But I can't go without my tools.'

'OK, but we stick together.'

I thanked God I was disciplined and kept my gear stored properly in its bag. Liam snatched it up while I grabbed one or two other things. Then I hesitated, looking at the two carvings under their cloths. Liam looked straight at me, his eyes like stone.

'Leave it. Just leave it.'

'The workbench.'

'Is it replaceable?'

I nodded.

'Then replace it.'

I didn't argue. We were back in the truck and I circled it round the trees to the woolshed. Again we both jumped out and ran inside, leaving the engine running. I hadn't unpacked my clothes and Liam threw his into the holdall and a backpack. With my computer and CD player and Liam's fiddle it took a couple of runs to get everything stowed. On the second trip Bramble came bounding up, hoping for a ride. I froze.

'Liam, the dogs. We can't leave the dogs.'

'But they're not ours.'

'You saw what happened to the rabbits. God knows what he'll do to them.'

A moment's thought, and then, 'You're right. You keep Bramble in the truck. I'll carry Badger, it'll be quicker.'

I got back behind the wheel ready to go, with Bramble behind me, stuffing her wet nose down the back of my shirt. I turned round in my seat and leaned against the driver's door so I could watch Liam through the passenger window. He crossed to the building, a dark silhouette against the light from the headlamps, and disappeared inside. A few moments and he would reappear, staggering with the weight of Badger in his arms.

A few seconds more.

If I counted to ten he'd be back.

One, two . . . I got as far as four.

The driver's door was wrenched open and I tumbled out backward, gasping. A strong arm clamped my shoulders. Before I could scream something wet was slapped over my nose and mouth. The smell! Hospitals. Dentists. I tried to claw it away but my hands had lost all their strength.

There was a glimpse of moonlight then everything went black and the world fell away . . .

TWENTY-THREE

. . . down, down into darkness. Down through the dew, the grass, the black soil, soft as the night.

I am drifting on a tide of earth, as vast and flowing as a sea. Crumbling loam surges against my skin, its dank muskiness flooding my mouth and nose. Roots, ivory coloured and slippery smooth, twist around me like the tentacled arms of creatures risen from the deep. I flounder, then steady, then find a way to be borne on the current.

She is ahead, walking as I had seen her before, her long cloak trailing behind. I follow the tracery of crimson threads that marks her passing. Then I am walking too, a path forming beneath my feet. White roots thrash around me; they snatch at my hands, my legs, and I struggle against their hold. I must reach Anne, I must warn her.

Or maybe the warning is for me?

I see her, there, up ahead, her face silhouetted against a distant glowing greenness. She is close now, her mouth full and strong, eyes wide. She has been beautiful. But, as she turns, I see the other side of her face, the bruised cheek, crushed forehead, jagged splinters of bone matted with hair. I stagger back, repulsed. She raises an arm, pointing the way towards the light.

I move on, I'm not sure how; I could be walking, or floating or gliding. But I am following the path. It is there, the Watcher, its feather touch on the edge on my mind.

This way, *it says*, this way . . .

I nearly don't see her. She is standing to one side, half hidden in a bower of deformed tendrils. Of course I know her from the photograph, the neat button shoes, the long straight skirt and high-necked blouse. As I come nearer, Mary raises a delicate hand and touches the buttons at her throat. The white silk ruffle is pulled to one side and there, above her collarbone, where the skin should be creamy and smooth, is a jagged black hole. She smiles at me softly, wistfully and I want to cry for her.

I stumble on.

This way, *it says*, this way . . .

And I am drawing nearer to . . . to the place I have to be. Roots crowd in over the path, barring my way. They snare in my clothes and whip at my ankles. I push and tear at them, snapping and kicking, fighting so frantically that at first I do not feel it.

The steady drip, drip, drip . . .

On my arm, on my shoulder, a spot of red. And then another.

I look up and there she is. I know her. And she knows I am there, despite her closed eyes, despite her head drooped, unnaturally, onto her shoulder. Her body hangs limply above me, legs and feet bare, arms loose at her sides. Blood oozes from her wrists, pooling in the palms of her hands, then it falls, drip by drip, from the tips of her fingers. I watch each droplet, entranced by the slowness of its falling, by the pearl formed when it touches my skin.

But I must not stop.

This way, this way . . .

I struggle on until the roots part and I am in a clearing, my eyes flooded with the acid light of a subterranean moon.

Then a silhouette — a shadow — a form. I know the face, I shaped it myself as if it were my own child, cut and carved it from the wood. The face of an angel with dark, hollowed eyes.

TWENTY-FOUR

THE night was everything.

Then a sound, a repetitive ringing. It grew louder and harsher, pulsating, as if a chainsaw were cutting my head open. I forced my eyelids apart. Lights, faint. They swam and separated, then merged into pinpoints. Stars. I was lying on my back, looking up at the night sky. The noise also lost its sharp edge and centred itself. It was my own blood pumping through my ears. A deep moaning came from the back of my throat, but when I tried to speak my mouth wouldn't open. I struggled to move and found my arms were trapped.

'Hush. Everything's fine. You've been asleep, that's all.'

I knew the voice. If I could remember . . .

Someone was doing something to my hands.

'Keep still now. Don't fight, you'll only make it harder for us both.'

Jason? What was happening? I was on the ground. There was that awful smell. Did I fall from the truck? Yes, that's right, because I was still lying next to it, my head against the wheel. But we were at the woolshed then and this was a different place. Trees all around, closing in, small patches of sky between the branches. The grass I was lying in was cold and wet.

Again I fought to move and managed to lift my arms. I saw my hands and wrists were bound together with a cord, as if I were praying. I tried to kick out and yell but my voice still wouldn't work and there was something heavy on my legs.

'Now don't struggle, you'll hurt yourself.'

Yes, it was Jason. I knew his touch, his smell. He was lying next to me, the weight of his leg across mine, his hand beneath my neck.

'It's all right. I'm just lifting you to put this on.' Something was slipped over my head. 'There, all done. Now, I don't want you to feel uncomfortable, so if you promise to be really quiet, I'll take the tape off your mouth. But you must promise not to make a sound. Will you do that?'

I nodded in compliance. The gag was ripped from my face. Of course I gasped for air then yelled, 'Liam! Li—'

His fist came from nowhere and struck my jaw like a hammer. Pain shot through my head and down my neck as the world slewed sideways. I thought I was going to pass out again, but Jason's hand clamped down over my mouth and wrenched my face towards him.

'Now, that wasn't very nice of you, Regan.'

He was so close his hair fell into my eyes and I could feel his breath on my skin.

'I'm sorry I had to do that but it was your own fault, you know. You did promise. It's absolutely pointless making a fuss. Your bodyguard is way back there — nothing he can do now even if he did know where to find you. Do you understand? OK, we'll try again.'

He took his hand away. I could taste salt where my lip had split from the blow.

'Oh, now look, you've hurt yourself. That won't do.' He took a handkerchief from his pocket and gently dabbed the blood from my chin.

'That's better. Are you ready now? I've done my best to make it easy, brought you as far as possible, but you're going to have to walk the rest of the way by yourself. I'll have to trust you not to make a sound. And you won't try to run off, will you? Because if you do, I'll have to give a little tug on this.'

Something yanked at my throat. I gagged and realised that what he had put round my neck was a rope with a slipknot that would choke me if I pulled against it.

'But I'm warning you, if you don't co-operate, well, I'll simply have to put you back to sleep and next time you may not wake up. Do I make myself clear? It's very important that we do it like this, that you make your own way there. So, you won't let me down, will you? Good. Do you think you can stand? Here, let me help you up.'

He grabbed my arm, dragging me to my feet. My vision still swam and my head was pounding.

'Come on now, you know the way.'

He tugged at the rope and I had no option but to stumble after him, trying to work out how I'd got into this. I knew I had reason to be afraid, more afraid than I'd ever been before, but my confusion took the edge off it. There were the photographs, I remembered, and I knew I'd been waiting for Liam. It was Jason we were running from, and yet Jason was here. The remnant effects of the anaesthetic, combined with the blow from his fist, had left me disorientated. Had I been fully aware of what was going on, I would have been too terrified to move.

The path began to look familiar. Yes, I knew where we were. He must have driven around the lake and up through the old vehicle track. It was only a short walk through the bush to the clearing and the big stone.

The Watcher was there. I could feel it all around us, everywhere and nowhere. It was a separate thing from Jason and yet I sensed them feeding off of each other, a symbiosis of nurture and wanting. At the same time I could feel it probing into my own mind. I didn't know how to fight it and I knew Jason had no wish to. Trees pressed in around us like an expectant crowd lining the route of a pageant. Branches swayed and sighed as our small procession passed between them and the full moon leered down at us through the branches.

Whenever I tripped or halted to gain a breath he coaxed me on, his voice patient and encouraging, all the while tugging viciously at the rope until the skin at my throat burned with red weals. Then my foot caught in a tree root and I went sprawling. Jason yanked the rope until I choked and retched.

'Now, that's really not good enough, Regan. I know you can do better than this.'

I scrambled to my feet, coughing, my eyes streaming. 'Why, Jason? Why are you doing this?'

'But you know why, of course you do. You and your Irish wolfhound have figured it all out between you. You found the press records and the photographs. All those visits to the churchyard and Maggie's place, to say nothing of your little walks in the moonlight. And my mother, you talked to my dear mother. I know you, Regan, you're not stupid.'

'You set me up, didn't you? Right from the beginning, before I even met you?'

'Why, of course. This isn't the sort of choice one makes lightly. I'd been studying you for a long while. And then I needed time to get ready for your arrival.'

'That's what you were doing all those times you disappeared?'

'Yes, the cottage is perfect for you, isn't it? But then, you see, I know you so very well.'

'And you moved the mirror down from the house so I'd get trapped in it.'

The trees whispered among themselves as if they had heard and approved.

'But how did you know I would come here? Oh, my God, of course. Sally! You used Sally. That night I found you with her.

That was all about making me go away, wasn't it?'

'I'm surprised it took you so long to work that out. You're usually very perceptive. I certainly wouldn't have touched the silly bitch for any other reason.'

'And you knew about . . . about . . .'

'Oh, that nasty little business at the abortion clinic. Well, of course. Your medical records were easy enough to tap into. You and the professor, eh? That made everything perfect.'

'And why Badger? It *was* you who shot him, wasn't it?'

'Ah, yes, poor Badger. It would have been a small gift, a promise of something greater yet to come. A clean shot would have been quick and painless, but I misfired. I didn't mean to hurt him. I'd never hurt an animal. Come on, we're nearly there.'

The Watcher was there, moving with us, invisible, palpable. A sudden gust of wind rattled the branches like a thrill of excitement passing through the waiting crowd and I began to realise that I might not get out of this alive.

We reached the clearing. The trees made way, leaving an arena open to the night sky, the central stone awash with blue-white light. There were dark marks on its surface, no doubt the residue from previous offerings. Jason backed towards it, coaxing me along with gentle tugs on the rope.

'You see, you came willingly. That's how it should be. Now, this is the altar stone. But you know that, of course, you've lain on it before.'

'Jason, please no. I can't.'

He stepped towards me and placed a hand on my shoulder. 'I can see you need help. Don't worry. That's why I'm here.'

Quick as a whip his leg locked around mine, pulling my feet from under me. I went crashing to the ground with his weight on top. With the free end of the rope he bound my ankles tight so that any movement of my legs would choke me. Then he lifted me up and placed me on the stone.

Moonlight touched his hair, his face and the wetness of his

mouth. His hand traced the soft light on my shoulders, and ran down my calf.

'Perfect,' he whispered, 'you're the perfect gift. A carver of wood. What could be more fitting? A fertile woman who communes with the spirit that guards this land, who can form an image of its likeness. A woman who knows and understands trees, who can recreate their creator.'

'Isn't that enough, Jason? You have the carvings. Let me go. Your father let your mother live.'

'My father's a loser. Look what he's done to the land. Let it run to ruin while he drinks himself to death for a crazy wife he'll never see again. She was flawed, you know that? That's why she wasn't taken and why the land lies fallow. Father said it was a curse on our family. But my grandfather, he knew better. He taught me how to tame it. "You must feed it with work and sweat and time," he'd say. "You must give it your best beloved and then it will serve you well."'

He stood back and looked around him, surveying the tree tops and the distant hills.

'All this is my inheritance,' he bent down and laid a kiss, very gently, on my forehead, 'and you, my best beloved, are its salvation.'

I was crying silently, partly from fear of what he would do to me, but there were also tears of shame; it was my own blind stupidity that had led me into this.

'Jason, you said you loved me once. Don't do this.'

'Love you? Of course I love you. You *are* my best beloved. That's why we must be together. I'm not like my father, not weak and sentimental. I am stronger than that, strong enough to make you part of my land. You'll live with me here, forever. In the earth.'

There was a sound, a metallic click, soft but in the night air it echoed clear and sharp. As we both turned towards it my eyes were dazzled by a light blazing across the clearing.

'Get away from her, Jason. Leave her be.'

Hope surged through me like a fire.

'Ah, your Irish friend, come to join us, has he? Well, an unexpected pleasure.' Jason stepped back from the stone. 'No doubt you have some notion of rescuing the lady. Well, let me assure you, she came here of her own free will and your assistance isn't required.'

The torch beam moved over Jason, allowing my eyes to refocus. At first Liam was an outline against the sky. Then, as my vision cleared, I saw he held the gun.

'I'm not here to listen to your bloody nonsense. I didn't want to hurt anyone but I'll use this if I have to.'

'Shoot me? I don't think so. It takes a certain refinement to be a hero.'

'For pity's sake, man, let her go.'

'Get away from here, Connors, this is a Sullivan matter.'

Another shadow was moving through the undergrowth. She must have followed him and got delayed by one of her constant diversions. Jason was intent on enjoying this moment and didn't notice the dog as she sighted Liam and bounded across the open grass towards him. The tension between the two men was electric and neither turned as I called out to her.

'Bramble! No! This way!'

Too late.

All my senses were at full pitch and I could see exactly what was going to happen. Everything went into slow motion as she lunged at Liam's back. He staggered under the impact and the light from the torch wavered, allowing Jason to dart forward. He gave a flying kick, spinning the gun from Liam's hand. Liam went down and I heard the crack as his skull hit the rocks. The torch rolled back and forth on the ground and, in its strobe-like beam, a thin streak of red spread across the earth. My mouth formed his name like a prayer.

'Hush now, he won't bother us any more.'

'No, please, Jason. I've got to help him. He's hurt badly. He might die if we leave him.'

'Now is as good a time as any. You realise, of course, there was never any question of him leaving here.'

'This won't do you any good, Jason. Someone's bound to come looking for us.'

'Oh really? Who's going to come looking for the likes of him? As for you, well you left town suddenly, told no one where you were going. But they all knew about the bust-up with Sally. And then, weeks later, you rang your friends and told them you were OK and needed some time out. Of course, if the police do ask I'll have to tell them you stayed here. I'll say you made me promise to keep it secret. Then you ran off with the hired help.'

'What about the people here? The men at the bar.'

'Oh, Maggie's crowd? Yes, but they all know you left this afternoon. Connors told them you were giving him a lift to God knows where. Even arranged for one of the other hands to come by in the morning to do his chores. By then, of course, you'll have joined my ancestors on the hillside. Liam Connors will be inside your truck, along with all your other worldly goods, at the bottom of the lake.'

Bramble had wandered off on another foray and I was alone. I think at that moment I gave up.

The trees were whispering and waiting in the darkness and the Watcher was all around us. I could feel its intensity and hunger like a thick miasma. Yet I sensed that its awareness was now centred fully on Jason. More than that, it was saturating him as if it were seeping in through the pores of his skin.

Jason smiled and looked towards Liam, who lay motionless.

'Look at your friend there, see how easy it is to die when you accept it.'

He tugged at my waistband and drew the chain from my pocket with the folding knife, his Christmas gift. 'Ah, you brought it with you. I knew you would. I had it made especially for this occasion.

See, it has your name on it. You even sharpened it yourself on this very stone.'

He prised the blade open and ran his thumb over the edge.

'This is all it takes, you know. I'm told it's a very gentle death, almost painless. I'll make a little cut to start with, just to prove how easy it is, then you won't be afraid.'

He wiped the blade over the side of my throat. It was cold, a slight sting, that was all. Perhaps he was right and it would be easy. Easy not to fight. Easy to accept. I looked up at the sky. I really should have taken the time to learn the constellations. The stars would be the last thing I would see and I didn't even know their names.

A warm thread ran down my neck.

'There, that doesn't hurt, does it? All I have to do is make another cut, a little further, a little deeper, and your own heart will do the rest.'

Maybe it was the moonlight, but as he spoke his eyes and his skin seemed faintly luminescent. And there was something in his expression. I thought I saw another face in his, the hollow eyes, the traced grain of the wood on the face that I had carved.

'It doesn't take long. You'll start to feel weak, then sleepy. A few minutes, that's all, and you'll simply drift away.'

As he bent over me the blade glinted in the cold light and a fallen angel looked out through his blue eyes. I turned away and looked towards Liam. He hadn't moved.

Then I turned my face to the sky and waited.

The world exploded in a flash of yellow fire.

I thought my head had burst. Jason fell against me then rolled away, a large stain spreading across his chest. He looked up at the stars now, but his eyes saw nothing. The ringing in my ears was so loud I barely heard the clatter of the knife as it bounced off the stones.

It was Sullivan.

He stood not far from where Liam lay. Liam's gun was in his

hand and his face was whiter than the moon. A sudden gust of wind caught the branches of the trees. They gasped and swayed and turned away in despair. We were a tableau, the four of us, against the backdrop of the night.

I don't know how long we would have remained like that if Bramble hadn't returned. She snuffled up to Liam, tail wagging, and slapped his face with her tongue. He turned his head and moaned softly. It was the sweetest sound I'd ever heard.

Sullivan heard him too and shifted his gaze away from his son.

'Connors? Connors, can you hear me? Are you OK?'

'No, I'm bloody not. What happened? Where's Regan?'

'I'm all right. I will be.'

'Connors, can you get to your feet?'

'I think so. Give me a minute.'

Liam rolled over and sat up, shaking his head and wiping his face with his hands. Bramble wandered over to Sullivan who stroked her head, scratching behind her ears. He still held the gun.

'Connors, get her down from there.'

Liam struggled to his feet and staggered over to the stone, held me for a moment, then looked in confusion at the ropes.

'There's a knife,' I said. 'It's on the ground somewhere.'

He managed to retrieve it and sliced through the strands. We both retreated and checked each other's injuries. The bleeding from the split on Liam's head had slowed to a sticky oozing. The cut on my neck was only a scratch but the rope burns hurt like hell.

When we looked back to the stone, Sullivan was bent over his son, touching his face, his hands, as if he might wake.

'I'm sorry lad,' he whispered, 'I should have done something sooner. It wasn't your fault. It was never your fault.'

He looked up at us.

'I wanted everything to be right, you see. I thought that after

284

Sarah . . . I hoped for more than this. But there'll be no more Sullivans now. It ends here.'

The two men faced each other and it was the way they looked, as if something passed between them from which I was excluded.

'Come on, we're going now.' Liam grasped my wrist and pulled me towards the path.

'Wait, don't you think—'

'No, I don't. Bramble, here girl, come on, quickly, back to the truck.'

For the second time I was being dragged along that path and, though I was grateful for my life, I wasn't going to be ordered about like that.

'What the hell do you think you're doing?'

'Leaving. I've got the keys, found them in the ignition on the way up. Get in the truck before—'

A second shot split the night.

Heartbeats passed by while birds scattered from their roosts in a shrieking cloud and Liam and I turned to stone. I knew what had happened, what Jason's father had meant when he said there'd be no more Sullivans.

'Liam, quickly, *do* something!'

I turned to run back up to the stone but Liam caught my wrist and pulled me back to him.

'Leave it! It has to end somewhere.' He wrapped his arms round me, very tightly. 'Just leave it now. Let's get back to the truck.'

TWENTY-FIVE

Poor Badger had been abandoned back at the woolshed, so we had to go there first. Liam was still concussed from his encounter with the rock, so I drove. This time we went in together. Under the electric light we were able to get a better look at the damage.

'That cut looks worse than I thought.' I reached up and rummaged among his hair. 'I think it needs a stitch. We should get you to a hospital.'

'While we're there we'd better get someone to look at your chin. You should see the colour of it.'

'Yes, I think I might have a tooth loose. And my neck feels really bad. How are we going to explain this to the medical staff?'

'Lovers' tiff?'

We were both able to smile for the first time, and we leaned against each other for comfort. Then Liam said, 'I wasn't much help up there, was I? How did he put it, it takes a certain refinement to be a hero?'

'I've never been so scared. I really thought he'd killed you. Strange, that's exactly what Fleur said would happen. She said there was one who would come to my aid but he might not prevail. She saw it in the cards.'

'Really? What else did she say?'

'Well, she said there was a sacrifice. And one of the cards was a tower with bodies falling from it, the end of a dynasty. None of it made sense at the time.'

'These things often don't.'

'She said it would end in death and fire.'

I felt Liam's arms tense. He pulled away from me.

'Now that's a thought, isn't it? Wait here.'

He went through the connecting door that led to the main part of the building, returning within a moment and carrying a can of petrol.

'Come on, let's get Badger shifted.'

Minutes later we were pulling up outside the cottage. Liam uncapped the can and went inside. I could hear petrol splashing the floorboards. The smell was overwhelming. He called out something.

'What's that?'

'Matches? Do you have any?'

'In the kitchen drawer.'

Then he reappeared, backing towards me and spilling fuel across the deck as he went. When he came to my workbench he stopped and looked at me, the question in his face. I looked up at the covered figure. For all its horror, it was the most remarkable work I'd ever produced, but there was no hesitation. I nodded and Liam soaked the cloth in fuel.

We both stood well back from the steps as he tossed the match. The material blossomed with fire, quickly disintegrating to reveal the face beneath. The features seemed to writhe beneath the flames. Then a section of burning cover fell to the floor and a yellow and red serpent sped across the deck and into the building. There was a soft whoosh of air and all the windows turned to gold.

We dived for the truck, the dogs already safe inside. I slammed my foot to the floor and sped along the lake and up into the pines, not stopping until we reached the crest of the hill. Only then did we turn to witness what we had done.

The cottage was a crimson and gold flower dancing on the edge of the lake. Already flames were beginning to spread to the trees around it.

'Oh, Christ, I think we've started a bush fire.'

'That's no bad thing,' muttered Liam, 'this land is soured. Fire is a great cleanser.'

'What about the animals?'

'No, they're way over in the paddocks, safe enough for now. Look at the colour of that sky, it'll be seen for miles around. Help will be here soon enough. We'd better make ourselves scarce.'

So that's what we did.

And that was the last I saw of the place before we turned down towards the gate and the road home. By morning there would be nothing left of the cottage.

And the mirror? Would it burn? I'm not sure. For all I know it is still there.

But then, that's the strange thing about wood. In a way it never dies.

Not completely.

One

MIRIAM WAS dead.

I tried saying it over to myself: Miriam's dead — she
died — her death occurred at . . . It made a flat, jagged sound
that lost more of its meaning each time I said it.

I stood alone on the city street where the morning split
the air in shafts of sharp, lemon light. The crowds parted
and moved around me. Nearby a man sat on a wall eating a
sandwich and reading his newspaper, just as if nothing had
happened. The glare of the sun stung my eyes, already red
and gritty from lack of sleep. I don't think I had been crying;
I didn't believe it enough to cry. I can remember feeling a
sort of detachment, as if an invisible mantle separated me
from the rest of the world. Everything seemed distant and
subdued: the voices of passers-by were muffled, students
cycled past on silent wheels, cars droned and purred. A bus
rasped a sigh of air brakes as it swished along the kerb,
causing the few, early-fallen leaves to skitter across the
pavement. I stood, hovering on the edge of the city, holding
onto a deep emptiness for fear that something more dreadful
would take its place.

So what was I supposed to do next? There were things I ought to do, but I was too exhausted even to think about then. Then suddenly I was aware of the day. She always loved this time of year, the thinning of the summer sun into a paler light, the subtle pungency of decay in the cooling air. But this time she would not be sharing it with me. This was my first day without Miriam, and the first time I saw *him*.

I'm making this sound as if it all happened a long time ago and it feels almost like another lifetime, but in reality it's only been a few weeks. Early September it was, and the leaves had started to turn from gold to flame. Even now the last of their kind, the most determined, are still clinging to the trees. I'm trying hard to keep the image of that day in my mind. I must take all the memories, polish them clean like pebbles, collect them safely in a secret place. But already the picture is fading. I suppose that must be part of it, some sort of enchantment that steals away every memory that would lead me to him.

And I wonder how much, if anything, he'll remember of me.

Just a few steps away there was a small, French-style caf and a rich miasma of freshly ground coffee thickened the air. Miniature orange trees in wooden tubs stood on either side of the swinging doors. The fruit must be plastic. Oranges wouldn't grow on an English street, would they? This piece of trivia took on such heightened significance that I found myself walking towards the doorway to investigate. Yes, they were plastic, but the menu in the window was handwritten. At that moment I doubted I could ever eat or drink again, yet I walked inside and sat down, studying the grey and white swirls of the marble tabletop. Coffee was placed in front of me, even though I could not recall ordering anything. I lifted the spoon and traced lines in the creamy foam.

The three of us, that is how it had always been. Miriam

is — was — my grandmother, Hannah her daughter and my mother, and then there was me, Chloe. Mother, daughter, child. Three slivers of brittle glass, edging and grinding away at each other. And then there was him, although up until that moment I didn't know he existed. He must have known some of it. And Miriam? Of course Miriam knew everything. What about Hannah? I'm still not sure how much she was aware of.

I, of course, knew nothing. They'd all made sure of that.

My hand was hurting. I found it grasping the pendant, holding onto it so tightly that red and purple marks were scored across my palm like stigmata. My eyes were hot and sore and I could feel tears pricking the corners, but I was determined not to cry. Grief is a private matter, Hannah would say. My mother never approved of public displays of emotion, would never be seen to lose control. Miriam pitied her for that and many other things. A strange thing to feel for one's own daughter — not love or pride, but pity.

There was flurry near the door, a swirl of brown and black, a long dark coat, ebony hair slicked back and caught into a smooth tail, the scraping of a metal chair against a tiled floor.

'You won't mind if I join you.' It was a statement, not a request for permission. I wished he would go away. Instead he sat down opposite me, the hem of his coat sweeping the floor, and leaned his head down sideways to peer up into my face.

'It is, indeed, a beautiful morning. You are Cliohna, aren't you? Though of course you prefer to be called Chloe.'

I swallowed back the tears. My voice came out in a broken whisper. 'Yes. Do I know you?'

'Miriam, I know . . . I knew your grandmother, Miriam.' I looked up into eyes that were more gold than brown, a sweep of black lashes, and black brows arched like wings on a pale forehead. He could have been my age, early twenties, but it was difficult to tell: his age seemed to change from moment to moment. He lowered his eyelids, his mouth pulled taut. Like me, he seemed to be bearing the sorrow of a loss and struggling to maintain a public face.

'I don't know you, do I? I don't think we've ever met.' I knew we hadn't. He wasn't someone to be overlooked. 'You say you knew Miriam?'

He looked directly into my eyes and nodded. 'Yes, I have known her a long time. A long time.' Then his gaze drifted to the window and he was silent for so long that I thought he'd forgotten about me.

Suddenly, without looking back but in a voice so clear that I was startled, he said, 'You could say that through her I have known you, also.'

'Oh,' I scratched around for something to say. 'Perhaps she spoke about you. I'm afraid I don't remember. I'm sorry, this is embarrassing. You seem to know who I am, but I don't know anything about you.' To be honest, I didn't care who he was; I just hoped he would go away and leave me alone to nurture my misery. I thought that if I maintained a cool politeness it would somehow sustain the distance between us, but this strategy failed.

'My name is . . . It's difficult to pronounce. It would be easier if you called me Iolair. That's what she called me.'

'Iolair? That's easier, is it? What sort of name is that?'

'It's Celtic, like your own Cliohna, from the Gaelic. I know you prefer Chloe, but didn't Miriam sometimes call you Little Wren?'

This was too much, too intimate, this closeness from a total stranger. Who was he to know my name? What else did he know about me? I felt exposed, undefended, a small animal trapped by the intensity of those golden brown eyes. As if he sensed my unease he straightened, pushing backwards in his chair to break the spell.

'I'll have some coffee. Dark and sweet and very strong. That's what's needed at moments like this.' He smiled at me, and before I could help it I had smiled back. He raised a long, slender hand in the slightest of gestures and a waiter, busy at a far table, his back towards us, turned from his task and walked over to our corner. At the time my thoughts were too jumbled to register the significance of this. Nor was I concerned when, having brought a second cup to place next to mine, the waiter failed to place with it the slip of paper for the till. It's only now, knowing what I know, that all the tiny shards of abnormality begin to fall into place.

'You managed to get some sleep.' Again it was a statement.

'Yes, a little.'

I had slept, but fitfully. Paul had pressed some tablets into my hand, insisting that I go home and try to get some rest. I had drifted in and out of dreams filled with images of my grandmother weaving her magical stories, and Hannah, tight-faced and weeping. And there was a bird, a large, brown bird with a vicious beak and talons and the saddest of sad eyes. Its outstretched wings beat against the rushing of wind. Images of Miriam were pierced by its sharp eyes and its strange cry, a scream of pain and despair so real that it woke me several times.

'I didn't think I would sleep,' I said, 'but I managed to catch a few hours. I woke early. There seems to be so much to do and I don't really know where to start. It's all very confusing. I've just come from the undertakers. What an odd word that is. When I was little I thought they were the people who took you under when you died. You know, under the ground. I'm still not sure why they're called that.' Oh, God, I thought, why am I blathering on like this? I sound like an idiot.

The doors continued to open and close. The room was

made hot and humid by the polished chrome machines constantly exhaling gasps of aromatic steam. Iolair sipped his coffee, watching me, unblinking, unerring, forcing me to prattle on.

'The man there was very solemn and respectful. He talked in whispers, and minced around me as if I were an invalid. He reminded me of an old-fashioned butler, the sort you see in a Noel Coward play. He kept asking me all sorts of questions about what sort of funeral it was to be, where it would be held, and how many cars did I want. And I kept saying that I didn't know. At one point I said that I'd have to ask Miriam. I felt so stupid. He kept referring to her as "the deceased" and talking about "the arrangements". I wanted to shout at him, tell him that her name is Miriam and that she's dead and I just have to bury her. He was a kind man and he was only trying to be helpful, and I felt like punching him in the face.'

'There will be a lot of that, I'm afraid — people using the correct words, making the proper gestures. It's all part of the ritual, the process of grieving. You will have to make allowances.'

I picked up the spoon and stirred my unwanted coffee while he took a sip of his, then another, his eyes closing and the tip of his tongue circling his lips.

'You know, this is an excellent blend. Strong on flavour but gentle on the palate. A slightly nutty taste. It's got quite a zing to it. You should drink yours — it will kick some life back into you.'

'I gather you're not one of those people, are you?'

'One of who? Or is it whom? I'm never quite sure.'

'People who go through the ritual, say all the correct words. Try to give comfort.'

'Would you like me to? I'm willing to give it a try, although I've not had much practice.'

'No, I couldn't bear that.'

For something to do, I picked up my cup and took a few sips. He was right: the coffee was good. Then I felt guilty about enjoying it.

'You know, I'm not sure what I'm supposed to be feeling.' The line of his eyebrows flicked up in question at my words. 'I mean, I'm all hollow and empty. Waiting for it to start hurting. They say that at first you forget that it's happened, especially first thing in the morning. I had a friend lost her boyfriend in a car accident. She'd wake up looking forward to meeting John for lunch, or thinking she'd get him to look at a faulty plug on her kettle. Silly things like that. Then she would remember that he was dead and it would all come flooding in again. It was like she lost him over and over again each day. I wonder how long it will be before I understand that Miriam has gone.'

'She loved you very much, you know. In a way she could not love Hannah.'

'How would you know? Oh, sorry, I didn't mean to be . . . But you're right. I think it's because I can enter her world, you know, the stuff she writes, the stories and folk tales. Hannah always hated all that. Besides they've hardly spoken for years.'

'That made things difficult for you.'

'Well, it's not easy. It's like I'm trying to be two different people. There, see. I'm doing it already. Talking as if Miriam were still here. I'll have to get used to saying *was*. It *was* difficult. She *did* love me.'

The stranger said nothing. He leaned across the table and covered my hand with his. A sudden rush of salt-hot tears gushed down my face. I rummaged in my pocket for some tissues, trying to disown the helpless sobs and gulps that shook my body. A few people fidgeted, embarrassed, and politely turned away. It was easier to study the pattern of fine blue veins that traced his wrist bone and the delicate curve of the thumb. He waited, still and silent, until the storm had subsided. I began to apologise and search for more tissues.

It was as I bent down to retrieve my bag that my jacket fell open and the pendant swung forward, clinking against the rim of my cup. Iolair jolted violently, as if a surge of energy had coursed through him. He stared at the silver ornament and for a moment stopped breathing, his body held rigid.

'It suits you well, the talisman.'

'Talisman? Is that what it is? I'm not sure what that means. It was Miriam's.'

'Yes, I know. She always wore it. And now you seem to be in possession of it.' His fingers gripped the rim of the marble table. 'An intriguing design. Celtic obviously. Do you know anything about it?'

'No, only that she wore it constantly. She gave it to me last night.'

'Did she, indeed?' His voice fell to a whisper. 'Did she?' His arm reached out. 'May I?' Slim fingertips took hold of the silver shape, tracing the interwoven lines and knots of the pattern. His hands were shaking. How pale they were, almost silvery blue, long and tapered with a delicate webbing of skin between each finger. 'I would like to see it more closely. Would you mind just slipping it off for a moment?'

It was a reasonable request, a harmless curiosity, and I responded accordingly. Or was it the habit of obedience? 'Do as you're told, there's a good girl.' I took the chain in both hands, about to lift it over my head. Then something held me back, something Miriam had said as she gave it to me. I thought at the time she must be delirious and I should humour her, but I had given my word. It was a promise, the last one I ever made her. I hesitated, then let go of the chain, allowing it to fall back into place.

'No. No, I'm sorry, but I'd rather not if you don't mind.

It's very special. I don't want to take it off, well not yet anyway.'

He sighed heavily. 'Of course not. How insensitive. I should never have asked, I apologise. I know how very precious it must be to you.'

'She told me never to part with it. As you say, she always wore it. Perhaps I will too.'

'Perhaps.' He looked suddenly weary and defeated, slumping back into the chair, his head thrown back.

I thought of the bird I had seen in my dreams, its cry of despair. I watched the angular line of his throat rise and fall as he struggled to hold down his own distress. Why should Miriam have meant so much to him? We had become very close, my grandmother and I, over the last few years. It was strange that she had not spoken to me of this man.

He looked at me again and his expression softened into a gentle smile. 'I have intruded upon you long enough.' His departure was as abrupt as his arrival, and for a moment I almost asked him to stay. But then didn't. 'We shall meet again soon, Little Wren.' He stood and turned from his chair, and his long black coat swirled around him like a cloak. At the door he turned and looked back to me. 'Try talking to Greg Uson. I'm sure he can help.' Then he was gone.

The caf subsided back into normality, and all the mundane noises of dampened conversation and clinking china sank in to fill the spaces where he had been. The only evidence of his presence was a half-finished cup of coffee.

After a few moments, I began to wonder if he had ever been there at all.

Kitty

When 18-year-old Kitty Carlisle's father dies in 1838, her mother is left with little more than the possibility of her beautiful daughter making a good marriage. But when Kitty is compromised by an unscrupulous adventurer, her reputation is destroyed. In disgrace, she is banished to the colonies with her dour missionary uncle and his long-suffering wife.

In the untamed Bay of Islands, missionaries struggle to establish Victorian England across the harbour from the infamous whaling port of Kororareka, Hell-Hole of the Pacific. There Kitty falls in love with Rian Farrell, an aloof and irreverent sea captain, but discovers he has secrets of his own. When shocking events force her to flee the Bay of Islands, she takes refuge in Sydney, but her independent heart leads her into a web of illicit sexual liaison, betrayal and death.

෨෨෨

Deborah Challinor is a writer and historian living in the Waikato. Author of the bestselling Children of War historical romance series: *Tamar*, *White Feathers* and *Blue Smoke*, her most recent novel, *Union Belle*, was an instant bestseller.

HarperCollinsPublishers

Union Belle

When the first effects of the 1951 waterfront workers' strike ripple through the country, Ellen McCabe — wife, mother, union supporter — is happy with her life in Pukemiro, a small Waikato coal-mining town. Even when her husband's union lays down tools in support and the strain of making ends meet begins to wear her down, she's ready to play her part in the lean months ahead.

But when Jack Vaughan comes to town, something inside her shifts. Jack is handsome, a charismatic war veteran — and a friend of her husband's. Suddenly everything changes, with irrevocable consequences, as the turmoil and divided loyalties swirling through the town threaten to tear Ellen apart.

Union Belle is a story of love, duty and passion played out against the backdrop of the infamous strike that turned friends into enemies, shattered communities and almost brought New Zealand to its knees.

▓ HarperCollins*Publishers*

Tamar

When Tamar Deane is orphaned at seventeen in a small Cornish village, she seizes the chance for a new life and emigrates to New Zealand. In March 1879, alone and frightened on the Plymouth quay, she is befriended by an extraordinary woman. Myrna McTaggert is travelling to Auckland with plans to establish the finest brothel in the southern hemisphere, and her unconventional friendship proves invaluable when Tamar makes disastrous choices in the new colony. Tragedy and scandal befall her, until unexpected good fortune brings vast changes to Tamar's life. As the century draws to a close, uncertainty looms when a distant war lures her loved ones to South Africa. This dramatic story — the first in a sweeping three-volume family sags — has a vivacious and compelling heroine who will live with the reader long after the final page has been turned.

HarperCollinsPublishers

White Feathers

In 1914, Tamar Murdoch's brothelkeeping days are behind her. Her life is one of ease and contentment at Kenmore, a prosperous estate in the Hawke's Bay, as storm clouds over Europe begin casting long shadows.

In this gripping second instalment of Deborah Challinor's sweeping family saga, Tamar's love for her children is sorely tested as one by one they are called, or driven, into the living hell of World War One.

During the Boer War, Joseph, her illegitimate eldest son, fought as a European, but this time he is determined to enlist in the Maori Battalion, despite his growing attraction for his childhood friend, Erin. As loyalties within the Murdoch clan are divided, and the war takes Tamar and Andrew's only daughter far from her sheltered upbringing, the people and experiences their children encounter will shape the destiny of the Murdoch clan for generations to come.

HarperCollinsPublishers

Blue Smoke

On 3 February 1931, Napier is devastated by a powerful earthquake — and Tamar Murdoch, beloved matriarch of Kenmore, is seriously injured. As she recovers, Tamar is preoccupied with the ongoing effects of the Great Depression. When her grandson threatens to leave for Spain to join the International Brigade, she feels a familiar dread — once again her family is threatened by war and heartbreak, as Hitler's armies march.

In the final volume of the Tamar trilogy, the story of the feisty Cornish seamstress who became a brothelkeeper and landowner is brought to a stirring and memorable conclusion.

HarperCollins*Publishers*

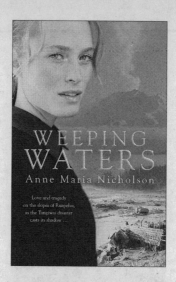

Weeping Waters

On Christmas Eve 1953 a lahar gushed out of Mount Ruapehu's crater lake and swept down a darkened valley, fatally weakening a railway bridge at Tangiwai. Minutes later a packed overnight express train nose-dived into the river. Most of the 285 passengers were asleep and 151 perished in one of the world's worst train disasters.

For Maori the tragedy was inevitable. Tangiwai means weeping waters and was known as the place of torrential flows and death.

When a young vulcanologist comes to research early warning systems on the mountain, she finds herself in the middle of a raging debate between local landowners, iwi and government agencies. She also finds herself torn between two men, each on opposing sides . . . And another deadly lahar is building.

In a taut, atmospheric action romance, Anne Maria Nicholson introduces Frances Nelson, a scientist who walks a fine line between life and death, in a haunting contemporary love story set against a fiery and potentially deadly volcano.

HarperCollinsPublishers